Readers love
Z. ALLORA

The Great Wall

"I am very excited to check out the next books when they come out and definitely recommend this book and author."

—Rainbow Gold Reviews

"The growing love is sweet and strong despite all the difficulties."

—Diverse Reader

The Librarian's Rake

"If you are looking for a quick, relaxing read I would recommend picking this up."

—Just Love: Queer Book Reviews

"*The Librarian's Rake* by Z. Allora was an extremely sweet and cute book."

—Love Bytes

Secured and Free

"This is a great story full of well-rounded characters who are full of emotions. I loved each and every character in it."

—Long and Short Reviews

By Z. Allora

The Craving
Illusions & Dreams
The Librarian's Rake
Rocking Thin Ice

ENTWINED DREAMS
Lock and Key
Secured and Free

MADE IN CHINA
The Great Wall
The Temple of Heaven

Published by Dreamspinner Press
www.dreamspinnerpress.com

ROCKING THIN ICE

Z. ALLORA

Published by
DREAMSPINNER PRESS

5032 Capital Circle SW, Suite 2, PMB# 279, Tallahassee, FL 32305-7886 USA
www.dreamspinnerpress.com

Rocking Thin Ice
© 2019 Z. Allora

Cover Art
© 2019 Tiferet Design
http://www.tiferetdesign.com/
Cover content is for illustrative purposes only and any person depicted on the cover is a model.

Trade Paperback ISBN: 978-1-64405-426-0
Digital ISBN: 978-1-64405-425-3
Library of Congress Control Number: 2019932236
Trade Paperback published July 2019
v. 1.0

Printed in the United States of America
∞
This paper meets the requirements of
ANSI/NISO Z39.48-1992 (Permanence of Paper).

To my sister dragon, Danny Bruggeman, & the wonderful Val Wolfe.
Thank you for my skating plot bunny and not letting me give him up.
I adore you both.

Acknowledgments

JENNIFER BROWN Blevins: Drake thanks you for *his* badass pose. Leaning against the wall, thumb in belt loop, his index finger in pocket, with one foot crossed over, in black boots and jeans....

Thank you to Tracy Hanson and Meredith King for assistance on Connecticut information, because beyond *Mystic Pizza*, I was at a loss.

Kyle Christian, you rocked as my lip ring consultant.

Cherie Noel, I appreciate you taking the time to assist me.

Thank you to my aunt Barbara and my father for putting me on skates when I was two years old, giving me a love of flying over the ice.

Sending hugs to Amy P. for living in Breckenridge and sharing your wonderful town with me. If Colorado had air, I'd move there. Gorgeous state!

Hugs to my incredible editor Desi and her amazing team.

Many thanks to Eden Winters, Andrew Marks, and MT for going through my tangled words to help me find the story.

As always, thank you to my love for skating beside me and picking me up when I fall.

Prologue

LIKE EVERY typical weekday afternoon, Drake Keys hung out at Taylor Johnson's house, playing guitar while pretending to do homework. They were both almost eighteen, but they'd done this after school since they met and became best friends in third grade.

"Drake! He's on," Jasmine, Taylor's sister, bellowed from the dining room.

Squinting at Taylor didn't offer a clue, so he hollered from his spot in the living room, across the space to where Jazzy sat at the dining room table, "Who's on, Jazzy?"

"That skater... Blaze Parker is finally back on the ice after two years." Jasmine waved him over to her laptop.

"Who?" Drake pretended he didn't know, but he jumped to his feet and set down his guitar. So what if he followed Blaze Parker's Instagram and Twitterfeeds? She didn't know that. He meandered over with the best uninterested swagger he could muster. "Who are you screaming about?"

"Please! You know, that white boy who moves like he's having sex." Even though she was only fifteen years old, Jazzy never fell for Drake's line of bullshit.

Taylor growled, "And how exactly would you know, Jasmine?"

She flipped her braids and laughed in a way meant to provoke her older brother. "He's a complete badass like Surya Bonaly, but wow. And like her, he gives the judges what for...."

Jazzy had been taking skating lessons since she was seven and planned to follow in the footsteps of Surya Bonaly. On ice, Jazzy was like a mini-Surya, just as strong and beautiful. The French skater fought racism and gender expectations by not giving in to them. According to Jasmine, Surya was herself unapologetic, even if it cost her points. She even did an illegal backflip at the Olympics when she had no chance of medaling—because she could.

And Blaze Parker would definitely do something like that to thumb his nose at the judges.

Drake peered over Jazzy's shoulder and silently concurred with her sex-on-skates assessment as the skating program began. *Wow.*

"How old is he?" Taylor asked.

"He's twenty," Jazzy answered.

God! He was so beautiful gliding across the rink like a defiant ice prince. The way his body transitioned from liquid to pure strength as the music rose to a crescendo set Drake's heart racing. Drake was glad Blaze hadn't let that YouTube video stop him from making a comeback.

"This is the first time he's back competing after two years," Jasmine said, her voice low.

"Huh? Was he injured?" Taylor had remained clueless about the drama that had unfolded in the skating world.

"No, it was because he's openly gay," Jasmine growled.

Drake needed to set the record straight. "It wasn't because he's gay. He got caught on tape—and he took time off."

Jasmine huffed out an irritated breath. "He was robbed every single time he was on the ice because he doesn't conform to who they think he should be. Exactly like Surya."

"Caught on tape?" Taylor stared at Drake with narrowed eyes.

Drake motioned with fist to his mouth, making his cheek protrude in the universal mime for blowjob, silently explaining the basics.

"Oh." Taylor grimaced.

"People acted like he killed someone. It was only a bj—watch him." Jasmine gasped.

Since Drake couldn't take his eyes off Sex On Blades, that wasn't a problem. Damn, that ass. Blaze landed an incredible triple axel. "Looks like he put his time off to good use."

When Blaze built up speed for his next jump, the way his muscles worked—

"Hey, Drake." Taylor elbowed Drake in the gut.

"What, Tay?" Drake couldn't unglue his gaze—which was locked on to that butt—to look at Taylor. The way Blaze gave the judges a sneer, daring them to mark him down for the perfectly executed jump, was all kinds of hot.

Taylor smacked him. "Come on, I got something to show you."

"In a minute." Drake didn't want to tear his gaze away.

Taylor manhandled Drake into his bedroom.

Drake released the breath he hadn't realized he'd been holding and bit back a sigh. He'd stream the competition later. Truth be told, there were a couple of skaters, both male and female, who piqued his… interest.

"What?" He looked around Taylor's room for the object he'd been dragged in to see.

"Man, wipe the drool off your face," Taylor stated, the cut without humor.

"What?" Drake touched his chin.

Tay gestured at Drake's jeans. "You got a boner watching that dude skate."

"What?" He didn't need a quick look down to know he couldn't get away with a lie. "It's not a big deal. A stiff wind can do that."

"Are you or are you not attracted to that skater?" Taylor persisted.

Actually, Blaze Parker starred in way too many of Drake's daily jerk-off sessions to deny that. The way Blaze's ass undulated when he skated backward was a sight to behold. Excitement rippled through Drake at the thought of having new images. "So what? I might have a thing for skaters. Some of the girls on the Russian team—"

"Do you find other guys hot?" Detective Taylor was on the case and wouldn't be swayed.

If he could be honest with anyone, Taylor would be the one. As images of rock stars, football players, and a few guys in their year at school flashed through his brain, Drake shrugged and admitted, "I don't know—I guess some."

"You're bi." Taylor pasted the label on Drake like he had the right to do so.

"Just 'cause you're trans doesn't mean you get to label people." Granted, Taylor had researched gender identity, orientation, and all parts of the rainbow as if it were his future career. And he'd been seeing a therapist for years, so he was all in tune with the identity stuff.

"Oh my God! Nope. I will not have my best friend deny who he is. I don't want you to wind up like those men who go to bookstores because they can't admit their orientation."

Say what, now? "Bookstores? Why would they go—"

"I won't let you be a heteroflexible creeper who uses men for blowjobs but can't admit who they are." Taylor pulled on a plaid flannel shirt over his T-shirt.

"Full stop. Blowjobs in bookstores? Wow, Barnes and Noble, here I come… *literally*," he joked, but maybe that bore looking into.

Taylor punched his arm.

"Ouch. Fuck! Since you've started on testosterone, you're a bully." Not really, but saying that sounded good. Drake hauled off and punched Tay back.

"Ow!" Taylor grinned. "You're lucky my dark skin won't show your abuse, 'cause that's going to bruise."

"Ha, abuse. You deserved it." Ever since Taylor came out to him, Drake treated him like he would any other guy. And if any guy asked for a punch, he gave one. "Now back to those bookstore blowjobs…."

Taylor growled, "No, back to you accepting you're attracted to both women and men."

"So what if I am?" His mind played a clip of Blaze. God, Blaze was the perfect name 'cause he sure smoked up the ice with all his heat.

"That makes you bisexual. I'm not saying you have to come out, but you should know where you fall on the spectrum. Otherwise you might make poor life choices."

Taylor's time with therapists had matured him, and Drake needed to play counterbalance. "Like getting one of those bookstore blowjobs?"

Taylor waved his balled fist.

"Fine. I'm bisexual. Now what?" Admitting his truth out loud wasn't as scary as he'd expected, especially since Taylor was supportive, and maybe now Taylor would stop punching him.

"Thank you for sharing that." Taylor's overcompensatingly adult tone annoyed Drake just a little.

"I didn't have a choice. I didn't want you to punch me again." Drake smirked. "And admitting I'm bi isn't a big deal."

"It can be, though. Some people can be jackasses about it. Visibility is great, but only when you're safe to do so. You got me?" Taylor grabbed his shoulder, conveying with a squeeze that he'd always have Drake's back.

Drake felt a tightness in his chest at Taylor's concern, but he had to play the ass. "Aw, are we going to bro-hug now? Or should I wax poetic about your gorgeous brown unbruised skin or how smart and sexy you are?"

Taylor smirked. "Well, it is a fact all the ladies find me sexy."

"What ladies?" It was true Taylor had quite the following at school, but Drake's snort turned into a full-belly laugh as Taylor got more riled by his laughter.

Rolling his eyes, Taylor slammed his shoulder into Drake.

A COUPLE of months later, dinner began like any other in the Keyses' household. Drake sat with his mom and dad around their dining room table. His dad taught kindergarten and got home at three thirty in the afternoon, so he showed off his would-be chef skills by cooking for them. The meals were usually delicious. On occasion there had been some misses—like last week when Dad made the flaming… well, Drake and his mom never figured out what exactly that charred dinner was meant to be, and neither had asked. Mom simply rescued the family by ordering Chinese food.

"Homework done?" his dad asked.

"Almost. I did most of my math and English at Taylor's. I've got a bit of science to read." In between working on his songs, he had forced himself to do some schoolwork.

"How are Taylor and Jasmine?" his mom asked.

"Fine." Drake popped one of the tangy orange-sauced shrimp into his mouth.

His mom and Taylor's mom had been best friends since first grade and still were. "Next time try to remember to take back their casserole dish. I still have it from our game night."

"Sure." Drake doubted he would succeed in actually remembering, but he'd try.

"Anything new and exciting happening?" Mom looked at him, then to Dad.

Dad shrugged. "Same old, same old. If I said it once today, I said it ten times—'Paste is not a snack. You don't eat paste.'"

Drake snorted. "Maybe they were hungry."

"No, nap time means you lie down. It's not time to break open a jar of paste for a gluey treat." His father took a gulp of his favorite microbrewed beer.

Mom gave Dad a consoling hand squeeze. "They're a handful at that age."

Dad nodded. "Drake, how about you?"

"Nah, no one ate paste in any of my classes."

Dad and Mom both gave him the expected laugh.

Tay had gotten Drake all geared up at the Gay-Straight Alliance meeting at their school. He talked about the importance of being visible, and Drake had been thinking about how much shit some of the openly gay kids—like that smart kid, Steward—had to put up with at school. Though Drake didn't think coming out as bi would help anyone, he also didn't want to be someone who didn't live his truth. But he needed to tell his parents before the rest of his friends.

He cleared his throat and made sure both of his parents were looking at him. "I've got to tell you something."

In the space of a heartbeat, the playful dinner atmosphere morphed into something serious. His mom nodded and pressed her lips together like she was bracing for something major. Dad leaned toward him.

The pressure built.

Then Mom jumped out of her chair and hurried to Drake's side of the table. Grabbing him into a big hug, she combed her fingers through his hair, like he had just turned five. "It's okay to be gay, Drake. You know we love you, and—"

"Honey, it's his coming out. Let him do it his way," Dad interjected, waving Mom down.

Wait! What were they expecting? "How do you know I'm coming out? Why do you think I'm gay? Maybe it's something else."

His dad gripped the table. "Wait…? Did you get a girl pregnant? I'll support any decision you and she—"

"I didn't know you were even seeing anyone!" Mom covered her mouth, muffling her gasp. "Why didn't you use protection?"

For the love of—

"I'm not seeing anyone, Mom. And, Dad, no one is pregnant." *Oh, dear God!*

Dad sagged in his chair like someone had let the air out of him. "Whew. Okay."

Mom kissed Drake's cheek and returned to her chair. "So you're gay."

"Mom, I'm not gay." He raised his voice in exasperation.

His mother froze in picking up her fork. "You don't have to deny your orientation. You know your father and I support the rainbow community."

Drake wiped the beads of sweat from his forehead. This shouldn't be so difficult with open-minded parents. "I know, Mom. We've gone to enough Pride marches and festivals to know you support the LGBTQ community."

"IA," his mom added.

His father put a finger out in front of him. "Wait, isn't it LGBTQIAPK?"

She tilted her head and asked, "What's the PK for?"

"Polyamorous and kink." His father used his teaching voice.

His mom squinted her eyes. "Oh, I thought it was—"

"I'm bi," he blurted out over both their voices, hoping to redirect the discussion back to him.

"What do you want to buy, sweetheart? Have you saved your allowance, or do you need to borrow some money?" his mom asked.

Oh my God! Did she forget they were having an LGBTQIA whatever discussion? This was about his coming out. "No, I'm—"

"Congratulations!" his father exclaimed. "He means bisexual, honey. Our son is bi."

His mother nodded. "Yes. I know the term; I just didn't hear him. Though I don't think we're supposed to shout our congratulations at him. We should say, 'thank you for sharing your orientation with us. We love you very much.'"

Drake almost wished for Taylor's punches. Sighing, he knew they were trying their very best. He had hoped to spit it out in one go and hadn't expected to be caught in the chaos of their conclusion-jumping acceptance.

Drake nodded and tried to bring this Hallmark movie to a conclusion. "I love you too. I thought I should let you know."

"Well, thank you and good for you." His mom beamed.

"If you discover more you'd like to share about this or anything else, let us know," his dad added.

Drake nodded, knowing he'd email since it would be quicker.

DRAKE'S PARENTS went to their room to watch movies, and once they retired for the night, they never came back out, so he had privacy. Still, he locked his bedroom door, not wanting to become the punch line of a masturbation joke. He put on a playlist, loud enough to block noise but low enough not to raise suspicion.

He grabbed his phone and crashed onto his bed. An unlimited data plan meant he could stream anything, anytime he wanted, and right now he wanted to watch skaters.

Skipping through most of the women's competition, he did slow down for Tanya Maya's boobs 'cause they were lovely. *She is stacked.*

When he finished ogling Tanya, he fast-forwarded to the men's competition. *Where is he?*

Drake skimmed through the first four male skaters. They were too overly alpha. None fit the bill. He definitely had a type when it came to guys, and Blaze Parker embodied it. He liked guys who were pretty but strong, with long, toned limbs and rounded asses. Blaze's light brown hair was chin-length and long enough to grab on to. But it was the air of defiance—that Blaze could put anyone in their place—that really turned Drake's crank.

A close-up on Blaze's face let Drake catch the glint of determination in Blaze's hazel eyes and made Drake shiver with anticipation.

On Drake's phone, Blaze Parker skated to the rink's center. He wore sexy emo eyeliner and dark shadow on his lids, making his eyes look huge. When he lowered his head, his hair fell over his face like a curtain. His sparkly dark purple outfit clung to his body like a second skin.

Good God. Drake's heart raced. Seeing Blaze's Instagram pictures of his dog and drawings of dragons were cool, but nothing beat seeing him on the ice.

The music started. Blaze went into his first spin, and tails of pink and lavender unfurled from his costume's waist as he twirled. Why purple and pink silk fabric equated to sexy didn't matter in Drake's head—they just were.

Drake drank in each twist and turn as Blaze nailed every jump. God, the determined way his muscles worked so he could take flight enthralled Drake.

Damn, they were only two years apart, but the way Blaze moved suggested he had centuries more experience.

Last year Drake had a girlfriend for about three weeks. They had done some stuff but not much. Two months ago, he hooked up with a girl at a party, but she went to a different school, and he hadn't seen her since. Maybe he should have texted her?

Look at Blaze Parker's ass! He rubbed the front of his jeans with impatience. Pausing the video, he kicked off his pants and climbed back onto the bed to utilize the video.

THE NEXT day in the school cafeteria, Drake decided to come out to his friends at lunch. "Hey, it's no big deal or anything, but I'm bi. I just wanted you to know."

"You're like Steward—I mean, you know, that weirdo in physics?" Dixon Fox, one of the guys Drake had known since grade school, could be all right, but sometimes *idiot* was the best word to describe him.

"Steward Fudson, who is probably going to be our class valedictorian?" Drake asked.

"Yeah, I guess. Whatever, man. You're gay like him?" Yet again, Dixon spoke before he thought.

"Don't out people, asshole," Taylor growled.

"What? Everyone knows." Dixon looked at those sitting around the table.

"Whatever. May karma pay you a visit." Taylor waved him off and took some deep breaths.

"Nothing wrong with being gay, but I'm bisexual," Drake clarified.

"So gay," Dixon insisted like a dumbass.

"The word *bi* is key to his statement," Taylor bit out. He glanced around, daring anyone to challenge him.

Dixon backed away from Taylor. "Okay, down, boy. Down."

"Did you just call me *boy*?" Taylor geared up to kick his ass.

Fuck, Dixon must be a moron. Did the idiot not know that was a racial slur? Drake wrapped an arm around Taylor to keep him in his seat. "No need, man. Not worth it."

"Fine." Taylor shrugged off Drake's restraining grip.

Dixon shook his head. "Bi is fine and all, but if you're planning to be a guitar player in an *actual* band, you should really only be seen with the girls."

Was Dixon suggesting Drake stay in the damned closet?

"What a stupid fu—" Taylor growled.

Drake grabbed Taylor in another restraining embrace. "Don't trouble yourself, Tay. Besides, Piper's looking your way."

Would Piper's smile be enough to disengage Taylor's attack mode?

Taylor immediately stopped trying to pound on Dixon and grinned back across the lunchroom at the girl with the lovely smile.

Piper was hot.

Yeah, Drake was definitely bi.

Chapter 1

Five years later…

BLAZE SLIPPED in his earbuds and listened to "Nobody but You" by Midnight Shadow as he went through his precompetition stretches. The lyrics weaved their way into his heart, and the driving guitar fed his soul.

Ha! That was ridiculous, but the words kept getting embedded in him, making him wonder what he was missing. *Whatever.* He had started following Drake Keys on social media, and the guy was all kinds of hot—a real rock-star pinup, with his guitar strung low at his hips.

When the song drew to a close, Blaze pushed down the emotions that tried to surface, and tuned into the skating competition's broadcast. His coach would kill him, but he wanted to hear what the announcers were saying as he continued his warm-up. He extended his arms as he listened.

"The bitter rivalry between twenty-seven-year-old Trent Richards and twenty-five-year-old Blaze Parker might be settled here tonight on this very ice. Seven years ago, they were rink mates, and even shared a coach. I've heard it said they now care more about beating each other than securing a spot on the men's Olympic team." The ex-Olympic ice dance champion turned announcer didn't bother to keep the titillation out of his voice.

His ice dancing partner, and now co-announcer, *tsk*ed. "Though that's just hearsay. We'd understand if it were true, after everything that happened between them. Very sad."

Blaze rolled his eyes as he jogged in place. *Yeah*, sad…. Rub salt in the open gashes caused by Trent's betrayal.

It happened seven years ago, but every sharp and painful detail had etched itself into his brain like the drama went down yesterday. He had been such an idiot.

He couldn't believe he'd gotten his first invitation to a party thrown by the other skaters. Maybe they were finally accepting him. But even better, Trent would be there.

During the party, Blaze had sat mostly by himself in a chair off to one corner as the others talked in little groups scattered around the room.

He felt like an outsider, observing them, until Trent approached him. *"You want to go someplace and... talk?"*

Trent's invitation had Blaze tripping up the stairs after him like an eager puppy.

There wasn't much talking. Trent unzipped his pants and asked, "So, Blaze, do you spit or swallow?"

"I gargle. Want to see?" Blaze tried to be bold yet graceful as he dropped to his knees. He was thrilled to have the guy he was half in love with offer him exactly what he wanted to do.

Even now, mortification swamped him. He hadn't had much experience, but he'd idolized Trent since he was ten, so he never even considered Trent didn't feel the same way.

Rooted in his brain was how calmly his older brother, Luke, took the fact that Blaze had become infamous at eighteen. Trent and his friends had posted the G-rated parts of the hidden video they had taken, ensuring Trent remained anonymous but Blaze's stupid comment could be heard, and the bobbing of his head clearly implied everything that happened. As much as Blaze missed his parents, he was grateful they hadn't been alive to see him humiliated in such a way.

His coach had already been on him about being *too gay*. Blaze had tried being more masculine. He wanted to please his coach and the judges, he really did, but that simply wasn't him. His scores suffered for his inability to pretend to be someone he wasn't.

The announcer broke into Blaze's trip down Bullshit Lane.

"For the audience not in the know... a compromising video resulted in Blaze Parker losing his coach and forced him to take a hiatus from skating competition." No one could miss the smirk in the guy's voice or the fact he didn't place any of the blame on the poster of the video. Somehow when people figured out it was Trent, he had been cast as the injured party by having slutty Blaze in his sphere.

Maybe Blaze should have been over the mortifying event by now, but he had lost everything. His coach dropped him, his friends wouldn't talk to him, and the cruelty at school had become so intolerable that he left before graduation. He took the GED. His brother, who had taken care of Blaze since their parents died, made yet another sacrifice for him and took a promotion he hadn't wanted so they could move away from the situation Blaze's stupidity had created.

Basically, Blaze had been forced to start from scratch in Safe Haven, Colorado, while Trent got sympathy and understanding.

Granted, the new town had scored high on being LGBTQIA friendly, had a skating rink and several Olympic-level coaches, but to be victimized and then have to suffer all the consequences ate at him.

The female announcer lowered her voice and said, "Though Anna Orlov took him on, and over the last seven years, he has remade himself."

"I wonder how much she has to do with Blaze's image."

"All of it," Blaze muttered to himself.

His coach had stopped him from feeding the social media trolls and living down to expectations. She taught him how to respect and develop Blaze Parker as a brand. After a couple of years, people associated him with skating, his tiny dog, silly happy memes, and dragons—not blowing a bastard—but still the injustice ate at him.

"Ladies and gentleman, Trent Richards is taking the ice."

It wasn't lost on Blaze that much of his success with skating had been partially due to the move and getting Anna on his team. Maybe some people could have gotten over what happened, but he couldn't seem to get past it. His fury coated his exposed weaknesses with vengeance.

Anna stepped in front of him and yanked the earbuds out of his ears. He paused only for a moment, then went back to his warm-up routine. "Why are you listening to this nonsense?"

Several of the other skaters stopped and glanced in his direction.

Foiled again, though he gave her his wide-eyed "I'm innocent" look. Apparently the expression didn't work on her as well as it did on his brother.

"Just keeping you on your toes," he said, then sighed.

Anna pointed to his costume. "I thought we decided you'd wear the red."

He smiled and dusted off his all-black costume—even his fingerless gloves were a mesh black. It had taken him forever to crochet them, but one of the kindly seamstresses in town had taken him under her wing and given him some assistance. "*You* decided you wanted me to wear red. I decided since I was the one wearing it, I'd go with my choice."

She shook her head and groaned. "Why do you always wear black? Is it to mourn the death of my patience?"

Blaze needed to stop relieving his competition stress by trying to bug her. But habits die hard. Giving her a suitable glare, he snarked, "No, the demise of mine."

Anna chuckled and yanked him into a hug.

He kissed both of her cheeks and slid on his skates. "I found new music."

"Did you?"

Blaze cued the song on his phone and handed her the earbuds. "Here, listen."

He tied on his skates and did some bends while he studied her reaction. Well, she didn't hate the music; she listened to the entire song.

She gave him a nod. "Decent. What is this music?"

After shrugging into the new rainbow-colored sequined crop jacket he'd worked on for weeks, he did a slow spin. "See, my costume's not all black."

She fussed with his asymmetric chin-length hair like the strands had done her wrong. "There. You are stunning. Now tell me about the song?"

"It's 'Nobody but You' by Midnight Shadow."

"Never heard of them. Good sound. They're different, like you," she mused, more to herself than to him.

"They're a band that has been touring with my brother's favorite band, Velvet Touch." Luke had dragged him to the concert when they played in Denver a couple of months ago.

She guided him to the hallway. "You're almost up. I'll see if you can use the music in the *future*."

Future... aka the Olympics. She refused to name the games for fear of jinxing him.

He grinned. "Thanks. I'll gladly let you deal with all the nonsense of musical rights and usage, as usual."

When he stood at the ice and looked around the stands filled with people, he found several waving signs and plushie dragons. The show of support never failed to make him feel wanted.

Anna pocketed his phone and tugged on her gloves. "I'll see you on the other side."

He gave her a nod and pulled off his skate guards.

During practice, he could feel the coldness of the rink, but during a competition, he burned with energy. The tension he chose to name as excitement kept his body close to boiling.

As Blaze stood to the side of the entrance, Trent stopped at the boards near him, the crowd still going wild for the ass clown.

Why come over to this side of the rink? "Trent, shouldn't you be on the other side at the kiss and cry? Or in your case, the crying place?"

Trent continued to blow kisses at his fans but took the time to lean toward Blaze with a smirk. "Looks like I'm going to fuck your ass tonight, Blaze. I hope you brought lube." Then he skated off.

Blaze swallowed his rage.

Why had he made that stupid bet? How could he possibly think winning this bet would allow him to move on? The whole thing was insane, but his mouth got in front of him, and before he could call back the words, the asshole had accepted. Though Blaze had no plans of losing and he fully expected Trent to back out.

"We'll see," Blaze muttered, waiting for the idiot to clear the ice.

He stepped onto the ice and felt everything start to change.

Gliding across the rink, Blaze felt emboldened by his fury, which funneled into determination, and he inhaled the brisk air laced with popcorn, soda, and the smell of possibility. This was destiny.

He stretched his arms out and did a slow circle on the ice. Luke and Anna always teased him that he marked his territory the same way his puppy did. In a way, he did. He swayed his hips to skate to the middle of the ice, giving the crowd languid movements to refocus all their attention onto him.

Once in the center, he spun to a stop and went into a stance with hands behind his back. The audience hushed.

Every second he was on the ice had been a fight, and everything boiled down to these moments of battle. Like all athletes, he fought his body to push past limitations, and he usually won the daily battle. The fight against expectations wasn't always an easy win.

Not even "butching it up," as his first coach recommended, had worked, because his delicate, more feminine features weren't something he could change. The fact misogyny is one of the factors that contribute to homophobia hadn't been lost on him, but instead of addressing it head-on, he fought the ugliness by not giving people the opportunity to invalidate him.

The throbbing guitar of "Hit Me With Your Best Shot" blared over the ice, filling him. Pat Benatar's song had become his theme song through the years, and a dare to the Skating Federation. However, when you issued this kind of invitation, you had to back that with skill and perfection.

He might look breakable, but he'd show the audience his core had been forged of titanium from the hell he'd gone through. The song got everyone clapping while he danced into his first quad and then his second. The driving '80s backbeat fit his jump-heavy program.

The lyrics of the song fed his intentions. He'd dealt with feeling like a loser for too long, and he was done. The time had come to retrieve what Trent had taken from him.

Hard-rocking lyrics demanded he take back his power as he soared over the ice and into a triple. So unless Trent had left every bit of himself on the ice… this competition would be Blaze's. No one and nothing would take this away from him.

He lost himself in the music, moving his body and allowing muscle memory to take over. The culmination of years filled with hurt and anger morphed into triple axels and lutzes that would ensure his victory.

Winning this competition and dealing with Trent would finally allow him to break free of the chains that had kept him bound to his past mortification and feelings of unworthiness. He'd be able to move beyond Trent and stupid decisions—although Anna would point out, not if Blaze kept making dumbass decisions.

What was I thinking with this bet?

Focus!

At the halfway point, Benatar's fighting words transmuted into the slower "We Are the Champions" by Queen. Blaze needed to live the music. The transition worked and allowed him a few seconds to breathe. He skated by the judges mentally, singing how he had paid his dues.…

Fuck. He gave more than his fair share. The judges, in turn, lowered his score whenever they could get away with the travesty, even the ones not from openly homophobic countries. It was the reason he'd worked incredibly hard to seek perfection, because anything else wouldn't count.

The pinging keys of the piano echoed through the rink, paving the way for some intricate footwork. Queen's music allowed him to use his more feminine movements as a foil, making his next set of jumps seem that much more unexpected and powerful. He'd fuck expectations of the feminine being weak as often as he could.

Freddie Mercury sang how he'd committed no crime. Blaze gained speed, thinking about his biggest mistake. How many times would he be punished for simply giving head to someone he'd liked?

Fury at needing to prove he wasn't the hurt kid they'd tried to shame out of competition attempted to invade him. He crushed the emotions and accessed the control that drove him forward.

The music ramped to a climax, and all the way, Blaze did lutzes, salchows, toe loops, triple axels, and ended in a motherfucking quad. All in the second half of the program… because he could.

The crowd lost their minds and screamed for him. When Freddie sang about taking bows, Blaze glided past the judges, showing them more respect than most of them ever showed him.

If the closed-circuit TV got a close-up of his face, surely the irony at the lyrics he skated to could easily be read in his expression. But like the song, he would keep fighting well past the end.

Exhaustion caught him, but he nailed the last two jumps 'cause he was a goddamned fucking champion and no one would take that from him.

Final spin, ending in Freddie Mercury's victorious pose with fist raised, and done.

A sea of dragons rained down on the ice around him as he desperately sought air. Familiar tears slipped down his face as the plushies made the loss of his parents surface. His mom and dad hadn't been there when he'd claimed his silver medal at the Olympics, and they wouldn't be there in physical body this time either when he hopefully took home the gold. He scooped up one of the plush dragons closest to him and hugged the little plushie. Once again, he was reminded that death didn't end a relationship… death only changed it.

He took a lap to blow kisses to the audience and clapped for their appreciation and support of him. Gratitude for them being there for him—even if the skating community wasn't always in his corner—never failed to close his throat with emotion.

As soon as he glided off the ice, Anna enveloped him in a warm hug. "Your footwork in the second half could be called good, but we need to sharpen every step before the games."

Blaze laughed at Anna's confidence, as well as her accurate critique, as he hugged his brother and then used him to balance while sliding on the skate guards. They trudged over to the kiss and cry. Hopefully, he wouldn't be the one crying.

One of the reporters stepped in front of him. "You gave the performance of a lifetime. How do you feel, Blaze?"

"Filled with fire, fury, and a desire to go back to the Olympics. How about you?" He sat down with Luke on one side and Anna on the other, leaving the reporter struggling for a response.

During the next few minutes, chaos ensued as his numbers meant he was bound for the Olympics… and he'd won the bet.

IN THE morning he texted Anna, *Any response from Midnight Shadow? Can I use that song?*

Of course their manager agreed, as long as you work in the band's name at the Olympics during an interview.

He fist-pumped to the ceiling. His mind was already moving to where to place the jumps. *Great!*

I saw Trent Richards going into your room last night.

And? Somehow that she knew made his skin crawl, but the deed was done. The debt was paid. They were even.

Why did Blaze feel like such an asshole?

You're better than that.

From now on, he'd try to be. *I don't disagree.*

So, you revenge fucked him. Congratulations.

Trent made a fool of me. Why did he feel the need to justify his behavior? Maybe now skating could be about him and not beating Trent.

I'm sorry, my little Ice Dragon. I know that bastard hurt you, but he gave you an unhealthy twisted view of relationships and life.

He tried to smile, but it felt more like a grimace. *I've done a 25 yr study & the results are in—people SUCK!*

Plane is in 5 hours. I'll meet you downstairs for lunch in 2.

K.

Blaze checked his Instagram. Pictures of last night's competition got a little under ten thousand hits. Not bad. He checked his Twitter.

A shiver of excitement ran through him when his notification said Drake Keys liked three of his posts. No big deal. He had several actors, actresses, and singers following him. But every time the guitar player hearted his entry, it felt like the ultimate approval.

He loved that he'd be skating to music Drake Keys helped create.

Scrolling through the pictures Drake posted, Blaze caught his breath on one—Drake onstage, playing the guitar, his head thrown back like the picture captured him in the middle of ecstasy. Each frozen pose held poetry from his body language that spoke to Blaze.

Blaze caught himself. Stupid, but he couldn't stop from liking a couple of Drake's pictures, but not all, because he didn't want to look like he rode the like train to Stalkerville.

He saved the one of Drake onstage. *Was that his orgasm face?*

Drake orgasming… the thought got lodged in Blaze's brain, so he jerked off to the delicious vision.

Chapter 2

AFTER THE third song, Midnight Shadow's lead singer, Summer Simpson, glanced over at Drake with that gleam in her eyes. That sparkle always spelled trouble for someone in the band. "Drake darling, come on over here."

Aw, shit! He ignored Dixon and glanced over at Artano and Jessie. No hope of rescue, because his bastard bandmates were laughing their asses off at him. His last hope was Amanda, but all she gave him was a sexy drumbeat and a smirk instead of assistance.

Glaring at them, Drake took the long way across the stage. He strolled along the front of the screaming fans. Most were fans of the main act, Velvet Touch, but he believed Midnight Shadow won some over.

He showed off with some riffs as he strutted over to Summer. When he got there, his eyes said, *Please stop the shit,* while her expression answered, *Not in this life.*

"It's Drake's twenty-third birthday. Everyone, please help us celebrate." Summer grabbed his hand, refusing to let him retreat back to his comfort zone, then started singing "Happy Birthday."

Oh, good Lord, why did Summer and the rest of the band make such a big deal? So what if it was his birthday?

The rest of the arena joined in.

Drake sniffed. *Fuck! There's something about fifty thousand people singing to you that's… special.*

Midnight Shadow went right into the next song of the set. Artano took lead, which allowed Drake to get his shit together. After a nod, he caught up to Artano's guitar work and recaptured the lead.

He poured everything into the rest of the show.

Now that was a twenty-third birthday! Drake threw his final guitar pick into the crowd and glided off the stage. The guitar players headlining the tour slapped him on the back.

He followed the rest of Midnight Shadow into their dressing room and didn't quite know what to do with his euphoria.

Summer sipped a beer and allowed a group of men to chat her up. It wasn't public knowledge that she had a fiancé.

Out of the corner of his eye, Drake saw Amanda and Artano were trapped by the band's manager, Frank Lewis. The brother-and-sister duo kept backing away, but the sleazeball continued his advance. Maybe Drake should—

Jessie bounced over.

"We did it!" Jessie Barker played bass and was the heart of the band. Her enthusiasm got Drake through the constant dive bars they had played through the years on their way here.

Trailing after her had been proof the world was too damned small. Dixon Fox, Drake's nemesis from high school, played keyboards. Dix handed an empty bottle to a roadie and grabbed another beer. "Back in high school, did you ever think we'd make it this far?"

"No, but I'm fucking stoked to be here." Savoring the dream come true of being the opening act for his favorite band filled Drake with awe. Being here now made all the holes-in-the-wall they'd played in worth the trouble.

Swinging an arm around Drake's neck, Dixon slurred, "See, I'm always right. You can have all the pussy you want… but stay away from the *D*."

Stay away from dick. The shitastic warning threw cold water on Drake. He'd never had a boyfriend, a few quick hookups, but not because of Dix's homophobic advice. He never found the right guy. There had been several great girlfriends since graduation, but they eventually broke up with Drake. Gigs that interfered with birthdays, practices that ran long, traveling to a show every weekend, made trying to maintain a relationship next to impossible.

Things were changing… though not many musicians in the business were openly in same-sex relationships. However true the advice appeared to be, Dix pointing the fact out made Drake seethe.

But then again, Dixon always complicated his life. When they first joined the band, Drake wished he'd had the foresight to tape Dixon's mouth shut. Why Dix decided to share Drake's orientation was anyone's guess, but he made sure everyone knew Drake identified as bisexual.

Immediately, their manager weighed in with "That's fine. Bisexuality is trendy." As if someone would take an orientation label for branding purposes! Frank *requested* Drake downplay any attraction toward men, or at least do *that* quietly, in consideration of the band's rapid success.

Since Drake hadn't seen many men in the past, appearing to comply hadn't been a problem, but Frank's implied ultimatum irked him. And to think Dixon had been involved—

No, he couldn't go there. He rolled his shoulders and tried to shake it off.

Drake pushed Dixon's arm off him. He wasn't going to let a drunken ass steal his pleasure and ruin his birthday. He remained flying high.

Jessie shoulder-bumped him and pointed to the two groupies in the corner. "I think they're interested in *meeting* you."

Drake glanced over, hoping to appear nonchalant. Damn, but those were some gorgeous women. If they were of age and game, he would have a very happy birthday. He unstrapped his guitar.

Frank edged over to him. "Looks like you've got some attention of the female variety."

One grimacing glance at Frank and Jessie made herself scarce under the guise of putting away her bass.

Drake shrugged. He didn't like talking to Frank all that much. It always made him want a shower after.

Frank checked his gaudy gold-plated knockoff Rolex and leered at the girls. "Well, you've got time before the bus leaves. Why not make good use of it and have at them?"

"Maybe," Drake hedged.

"Doing two girls… would be great for your rep."

Could Frank be any sleazier? What the fuck was wrong with him? Somehow doing anything that appeared Drake took the asshole's input made Drake nauseated. "I'm not going to have sex for promotional reasons."

"I didn't say you should." Frank tried to play innocent.

Dixon chimed in, "Even if he did, so what? You get your dick wet and look cool for our fans doing the deed. Total win-win."

Glaring at Dixon, Drake sighed. He never liked to be told what to do.

The expression on Jessie's face said she heard the idiots. She walked over to him and whispered, "Don't let these two assholes cockblock you. If you want them, go for it. Don't spite your cock 'cause these two are dicks."

Jessie always had a way with words. Drake smirked as she meandered away toward another group. He fussed with putting his guitar away, and when he glanced up, Jessie was leaving with one of the guys in tow. *Good for her.*

Snapping his guitar case closed, Drake was happy there were roadies to load their equipment now. He wearily set his baby with the shit belonging to Midnight Shadow and sent a prayer to the God and Goddess of Music, asking that no harm come to his favorite six-string.

The two ladies beckoned him with a wave of their long purple nails.

Why the fuck not? He grabbed a beer out of the ice chest, unscrewed the top, and strutted over. "Did you like the show?"

Blondie stepped closer, smelling of flowers. "I loved it. You were great on the guitar."

The redhead nodded. "You're so talented."

Somehow those compliments rang hollow, but he gave them a small smile of appreciation and sipped some beer. "Thanks."

"We'd like to thank you for a wonderful performance if you're *up* for it." The blonde dragged her extremely long nails down the zipper of his jeans.

He usually liked to work a little, but he wouldn't say no to the benefits of being a guitar player. "Sounds good. Where?"

The blonde purred, "There's an empty stairwell near the back entrance."

Huh… okay. Why not? Good thing he wasn't a prude. Living with a band on a tour bus meant very little privacy, so you learned to get off wherever you could. He swallowed the rest of the beer and set the bottle down. "Shall we?"

Both girls giggled, throwing their arms around him as they headed out the door.

Frank shouted, "Drake!"

Drake turned and a flash went off.

The redhead exclaimed, "How fun! Captured. When you upload it, tag me at GroupiesSuck405."

Disgust fought annoyance, battling for top spot in Drake's brain.

DRAKE WAVED bye to the lovely but one-track-minded groupies, then climbed into the tour bus. The vehicle was a bit worse for wear. It smelled like whiskey, body odor, and cum, but there were seats and even berths to sleep in. Though chances all horizontal places were filled with bandmates getting lucky while in transit had skyrocketed with their success.

"About time you got here," Dixon sniped.

Drake flipped him the bird as he stumbled past. After collapsing into the somewhat stained seat, he checked his messages. He scrolled past all the well-wishes for his birthday.

Taylor had texted thirty minutes ago. *Happy birthday! Heard you rocked your show.*

Drake grinned and texted back, *Thanks & I did.*

I see you actually got the lip piercing.

How do you know that? He touched his tongue to the new lip piercing. He'd gotten the decoration as a present to himself to symbolize all he'd accomplished by refusing to be anyone but himself. He looked forward to changing out the ball to a ring as soon as it healed enough.

Little dots danced on his screen, and then a text popped. *Looks like those girls were happy to celebrate with you.*

What girls? How did Tay know any of this?

Taylor sent a picture that had been taken in the dressing room… from Frank's angle. Jesus, the quick bastard uploaded the shot already.

Where did you get that? The sex had been less than satisfying. None of them had a condom, so he'd gotten them off with his fingers, or at least, they sounded like he'd been successful.

Internet, baby! You're a big star! The pic was on Midnight Shadow's Instagram feed.

Argh! Before Drake could rant, another text came in from Taylor. *How were they?*

Should Drake front as expected? Nah, not with his best friend. *Exactly how you'd expect a hookup with strangers would go.*

Awesome?

Ha-ha. Try awkward and weird. Enjoying the moment had never been his thing. He did better with someone steady.

Sorry. Sucks.

Drake wished they had. Maybe then he wouldn't have had to finish himself off in the men's room. But he wasn't famous enough for them to ruin their lipstick for…. *Live and learn.*

Get some sleep—T

Night—D

Sleep wouldn't come, so Drake checked Twitter. The band got some retweets and a number of likes. Then he put in his earbuds and clicked over to YouTube. Of course, they recommended horror outtakes, science tricks, a couple new rock bands, and some ice skating competition clips.

He watched science tricks until he got bored, smoked a little weed, then switched to the skating videos from the World Championships he'd missed when it aired weeks ago.

Several of the women upped the difficulty of their programs to impressive levels. He had been glad to see them all do well, especially one of Jasmine's favorites. The men's skating came on. He snorted when the announcer called Blaze Parker "the bad boy of figure skating." Catching the groans and moans coming out of the back of the bus, Drake decided the announcer didn't know many guys… or women.

Though he couldn't deny Blaze's routines were drenched in sex and innuendo. Blaze constantly pushed and bent the rules… and God, that ass.

That Drake was thrilled Blaze Parker would be using a Midnight Shadow song at the Olympics for the free skate was the understatement of all time. Frank also had let it slip Blaze might want to use more of their music in the future. *Incredible.*

He watched Blaze's routine three times and fell asleep with a smile on his face. His dream skater's score meant Blaze was headed to the Olympics. Future song lyrics danced in his head just out of reach.

A couple months later…

DRAKE'S CELL shook in his pocket with another text, probably from Taylor.

So your 1st big tour is done. How does it feel?

Drake wasn't sure. He couldn't believe the tour was over, but he texted, *Great.*

Tay sent an applause emoji. *Have you parted ways with Ms. Thing yet?*

She's not that bad. No clue why he defended Brenda; she was kind of terrible. Not like the sweet women he'd dated before. He didn't appreciate Brenda's snarky comments and her jealous and mean-spirited nature.

I take that as a no.

I will. He would. Why should he feel so guilty? He glanced over at Brenda, who was flirting with Dixon.

I've told you to follow the rocker rule: fuck a groupie through two cities, no issue. Any longer, you're the one who's screwed.

In his head, somehow fucking meant *together.* He really needed to adjust his head to match everyone else's reality.

Brenda playfully slapped Dixon's thigh.

Drake texted, *It just happened.*

Make it unhappen. Screw a chick that's crazy in bed, not crazy in the head. I know you like steady, but going by what you have said, she's not for you, man.

Maybe.

Several of your other groupies on the road were cool. This one not so much.

I know, man. I know. And Drake did.

Jazzy said your skater liked your last post and even commented on a couple. She's losing her damned mind.

He sent a shrug emoji, like it didn't give him a secret thrill that his adolescent crush followed him on social media and occasionally liked or commented on his tweets. Granted, the rush of excitement of seeing anything Blaze Parker–related never left him.

"Fuck me with a two-by-four!" Frank growled at the phone he held out in front of him. "How long?"

Trouble in paradise. Frank's on a tear. Later, Tay.

Good luck.

"What do you mean, can't be repaired tonight?" Not exactly what you wanted to hear after the last show of the tour, especially when you were hungover from last night's party and just wanted to get on the bus and crash.

Drake went on high alert and stepped over to Frank. Artano and Dixon joined him.

Amanda twirled her drumsticks between her fingers. "What's up?"

Jessie finished putting her bass away and joined the semicircle.

"The goddamned bus broke down." Frank's anger had coiled in on itself and appeared ready to be unleashed. Drake had learned to steer clear of him when he got into this kind of a mood.

Everyone groaned at the dismal news.

A couple of minutes later, Summer gathered them into a band huddle with interlocking arms and all. "I'm going to miss my babies," she purred, sounding like she really meant the words.

Artano and Amanda *aww*ed.

"I'm not going to miss any of you, since I'm going to sleep for the entire two and a half months in a king-sized bed," Jessie snarked.

Drake bumped her with his hip.

"Remember, due to the remote places I'll be traveling to, I won't have internet or cell service during parts of the break, so if I don't respond to a message, I will as soon as I can," Summer added.

Frank broke into the circle right between Artano and his sister, something no one else would dare do. "Make sure you practice during the break. Usually you don't get a break during concert season, but I want you all ready to start laying down some tracks the first day we're all back."

"Killjoy," Amanda called out.

Frank shook his head. "Hey, recording time is expensive. We're lucky to have found a studio so close to our first show."

Their family atmosphere shattered yet again by Frank, Summer started clicking on her phone. "I'm heading to the nearest airport via Lyft if anyone's going my way."

A chorus of *no* morphed into another round of byes.

"Might as well go back to the dressing room and wait there." Dixon headed in that direction, probably hoping for more alcohol.

Brenda trailed after the group, moving to the dressing room.

Drake did need to talk to Brenda. Where did groupies go during the hiatus? Why had he gotten himself into this entanglement? He followed and plopped onto the sofa.

She nabbed the space next to him after giving a predatory glare to Jessie, then started watching a sitcom on her phone.

Jessie, not one to get into unnecessary tussles, rolled her eyes and slid down a wall to the floor. She strummed her bass.

After waving to everyone, Amanda grabbed the hand of a guy who'd been hanging around since they hit the East Coast. "Artie and I are going to catch a ride with Joe. Have fun."

Artano fist-bumped Drake on the way out the door.

That left Dixon, Frank, Brenda, and Jessie, along with a few hangers-on milling around. Velvet Touch rocked a roaring crowd above them.

Drake put in his earbuds and watched a few YouTube videos. The clips that were recommended looked good, but first he watched Blaze Parker skate to Midnight Shadow's song in the men's free skate.

Damn, it was crazy hearing his lyrics echoing off Olympic ice. He must have watched the video every day since the Olympics, and yet he somehow scrolled past the most recent post-Olympic interview with Blaze Parker.

Drake had a full battery, so he hit Play.

An attractive brunette waved to the YouTube watchers. "Hi, I'm Lauren Bewell, and I'm here with Blaze Parker. Tell us about what it's like to be an openly gay skater."

The only indication Blaze gave that suggested he didn't appreciate the question was the muscle near his eye jumped, but he gave the interviewer a sinful smile. "Well, being gay doesn't mean I trip over the rainbows my blades reflect on the ice."

"I'll say, you sure didn't trip over anything at the Olympics." Pictures of Blaze doing a quad and then on the podium kissing his gold medal flashed on the screen.

"Thank you. It was an honor to represent my country." Blaze gave a full smile to Lauren and her viewers, but it felt like he was speaking directly to Drake.

"Back to my question, I mean, have you ever been harassed or given a lower score because of your orientation? You know that before you, there's only been one other openly gay skater who made the Olympic team."

"Of course, anything less than a perfect score and there must be a nefarious reason." His bubbly laugh chased away some of the harsh tone his words held. "Seriously, I'd like to believe the skating world is beyond judging people for who they are attracted to."

Ha, right. Drake was surprised Blaze could make that carefully crafted claim with a straight face. Drake had watched a number of competitions where points and medals were robbed from Blaze for something other than his near-perfect performance. And unless you looked for the homophobia, you could easily miss it.

Lauren Bewell's mouth dropped open, but she got back to the questions. "Blaze, there's been a dramatic shift in your attitude since World's. Has something changed?"

She made a good point. Blaze might still be the "bad boy," at least in Iceskatinglandia, but his skating held more happiness and less defiance. Maybe finally leaving Trent Richards in the dust brightened his spirits.

"I've been working hard, and all my focus has been on the Olympics."

"Your evolution is nothing short of stunning—what caused it?" Lauren asked.

Blaze shrugged. "I realized this is my life, and I'm the only one who can live it. I need to do what fulfills me."

Lauren leaned closer to him. "How do you feel about being a role model for the gay community?"

He batted his eyelashes and fluffed his hair. "Am I? I know I'm pretty, but model… no."

Drake cracked up right along with Lauren. She giggled. "You're very silly."

Blaze licked his lush mouth. Why was Drake hyperaware of Blaze's mouth? Blaze had such nice full lips, good shape and a pretty color—

"Tell us about your exhibition skate. That's coming up," Lauren asked.

Blaze raked his fingers through his hair. "Everyone at my home rink wants to celebrate the Olympics, so we decided on an exhibition skate. It'll have some very talented young—"

Brenda snatched his earbuds out. "What are you watching?"

"Just some stuff." Drake turned his phone over.

"What *stuff*?"

"Stuff." He didn't want to share this with her, and that spoke volumes. They didn't know each other, and as sad as it was, he had to admit he didn't really want to get to know her better.

Brenda sighed and rolled her eyes. "I bet you're watching that *guy* again."

"What guy?" His lame attempt at diversion failed as he turned his silver thumb ring.

Pointing to his phone, she sniped, "That guy. Geez, it's the same shit just a different day."

"Huh?" *Why the bitchiness?*

Folding her arms over her ample chest, Brenda stared him down. "You are way more into that skater guy than you are me."

"Blaze Parker? I don't even know—" Following someone on Twitter, Instagram, and Facebook really didn't count. Ignoring the quiver of pleasure he got when Blaze recently commented directly to him couldn't be considered either.

She exhaled hard. "This reminds me of how you were a couple nights ago."

"What?" What was she talking about?

"The guy after the last concert in New Orleans, he looked like the skater. Same light brown hair and twinkie look—you wanted him more than me."

He had thought they'd had a good time back at the hotel room.

"I'll be backstage if anyone needs me." Jessie grabbed her bass case and rushed out the door to avoid the scene Brenda geared up to make.

Drake almost wished he could flee with her, but he needed to deal with Brenda. "We usually go with who you want, and they're usually girls. I thought we could mix it up. Your issue is, for once you weren't the center of the attention."

"You two were making out nonstop."

The guy liked to kiss; why did she see that as a crime? Drake got off on making out. He could brush lips for decades, but Brenda couldn't be bothered. Why hadn't he seen how selfish she acted in and out of bed?

His exhaustion let fury take control of his mouth. "How many times have I been on the sidelines while you and another woman went at it?"

She stood and put her hands on her hips. "You've never complained before. I thought you liked to watch."

Dixon and Frank chuckled, reminding Drake he and Brenda weren't alone; though, fuck it. He was done with Brenda and everyone else telling him what he should and shouldn't do. "No. *You're* the one who wants threesomes."

Brenda shook her head, causing the riot of auburn curls to shimmer in the light. "We're polyamorous."

"No, you are." Drake felt childish, but he needed to stop letting other people label him. "I'm bisexual."

"What? You've been pretending?" Her horrified expression spoke volumes.

"I didn't say that." Was he? Not really, but he wanted a relationship with someone, one someone, and that someone wasn't Brenda.

"Yeah, well, I think you were all over that guy because he looks like the skater."

"Brenda, you were the one who insisted on opening our—whatever this is between us." Exasperation didn't even begin to cover the frustration threatening to swallow him. How could she be so clueless?

She glanced over at their audience. Drake could have sworn there was a calculated glint in her eyes before the waterworks turned on. "I didn't want to lose you. We're bi, we don't have to choose, so we shouldn't limit ourselves."

However fake her tears might be, they still made him feel like shit. "Being bi doesn't mean you can't be monogamous. Poly works for a lot of people, just not for me."

"It worked for you with *that* guy. Hell, it *worked* for you twice!"

Tired of arguing, he certainly wasn't going to justify what he'd done in bed. "Brenda, I'm sorry, but we're done."

Drake hurried to the cooler and pulled out a beer. The craft brew felt good going down as he tried to ignore her dramatic slamming-the-door-swearing exit.

Relief that they were finally over swamped him.

"Dude?" Dixon studied him with wide eyes.

"Not your business." Why did he have to point that out?

Dixon tightened his hands into fists. "The band is my business as much as it is yours. Bisexuality is easier to sell than gay. I told you that years ago."

"Who the hell are you to tell me anything?"

Frank squinted and struck like a cobra. "Well, I'm the manager, and I'm telling you you're out."

Drake must have misunderstood. "What?"

"You're done with Midnight Shadow. I told you when I first found out—bi was fine, just keep your dick to women."

Did he not understand what bi meant? Wait… Frank kicked him out of the band?

Dixon shook his head and grimaced. "I told you, man. I told you."

"You're kicking me out of the band?" His level of disbelief elevated past the roof.

"I warned you. You can label yourself whatever the fuck you want, but fans need to see you with women. Sure, there's some gays floating about the music business, but they've established themselves first, or they have enough of a fanbase who eats that rainbow shit with a spoon."

Drake focused on the words, but only bullshit came out of Frank's mouth.

Frank shoved his hands into his pants pockets. "You'll be paid for your songs *if* the band still uses them for the album. But we now have an irate scorned groupie, who is probably dragging the band's good name through the mud as we speak. Thanks to you."

"I'm on it." Dixon rushed out of the dressing room.

Drake stood there. He should move, but he couldn't. "So I'm out?"

"Yes. You're a no-name guitar player. Who's going to miss you?"

And that was it. He'd been with the goddamned band for years, since the original band, Shadows in the Night, first got together.

"Remember, Drake, per your contract, we'll announce your departure, not you." Frank had his hands on his hips, smirking.

Storming out of the room, Drake clicked for an Uber, because if he stayed, he would hurt his strumming hand on Frank's face.

Thankfully the roadies hadn't packed his favorite guitar. Grabbing his guitar and messenger bag out of Midnight Shadow's pile, he saw Dixon and Brenda.

Her leg was tucked around Dixon's waist, her head thrown back as she took his cock with noisy grunts, but she paid enough attention to give Drake the middle finger as he stumbled past.

The car idled in place when he got outside. He and his guitar got in.

"Where are you going?"

"I've no clue." Drake's Twitter account notified him that Blaze Parker liked the pictures Drake posted of tonight's show. "Take me to a rental car company."

Chapter 3

THE LIGHTS dimmed.

Blaze stood on a platform perched high above the arena. *Fuck, that's a long way down.* He took a deep breath and stepped off. Clutching two red strips of fabric, he swung over the ice in head-to-toe crimson with sparkly fingerless gloves and matching skates.

Though he executed only some very basic somersaults and turn poses, he flew through the air over the rink. The crowd went wild. A soft spotlight guided his air ballet. He eased down until his blades touched the ice.

The lights went out, and he unhooked the safety harness his brother and coach had demanded, then pressed a button hidden in his sleeve. He turned on a light that hit tiny bits of silk at the bottom of his skates, making it appear like fire sparked off his blades when he strutted more than glided across the ice.

The applause was deafening as the lights came up.

When Blaze had turned twelve he tried this stunt with actual flares and spent the next two days chipping out the blackened ash that speckled the ice.

Damn, Blaze loved the song he skated to. Summer Simpson's voice wrapped around him, and the words burrowed into his soul. He'd gotten gold with this Midnight Shadow song in the free skate. Using it for this exhibition had been a no-brainer.

When folks found out Blaze was going to use "Nobody but You" for his Olympic free skate program, the band secured a record deal.

Other than the aerial work and some silliness he'd ad lib later for the exhibition, Blaze had done this program hundreds of times, each move etched into his muscles. A lush spin flowed into a jump combination. It didn't matter that the rink was packed to celebrate his victory at the Olympics. He simply let the song ease him into that gorgeous place where ice, music, and movement merged into something special.

Competition was about fury, and it exhausted him, but exhibitions were about sharing his passion and joy for the sport. He got to reclaim his love of skating.

Aching and needing but always left wanting…
My heart longs with desire….

The lyrics highlighted a hunger within him that he barely understood and chose not to analyze. As the lights brightened, he shifted his body into position for his second salchow.

The meaning of the song was unquestionably sexual. Simpson's sinful voice sang about cravings and lust, and the words echoed Blaze's emptiness, emphasizing that physical satisfaction was incomplete.

Perfect landing. Why couldn't he have owned the ice with ease and confidence at the Olympics? The difference between competition and exhibition was that one was play and the other was a death match. The Olympics were over, he got the gold, but it was best left in the past—with everything else he'd gotten closure on this past year.

But where was his place? What did he do now? Why did he feel so lost? The lyrics plucked his pain, mocking him.

Then I looked into your eyes
You knew my dreams, you read my thoughts

Apart from his brother somewhat—and Anna to a lesser extent—no one really knew his innermost self. They did well at guessing some things based on his actions and by making logical deductions, but had he ever shared his feelings? No, best not to reveal a weakness to anyone.

Taunting me with things I cannot have
You say you want to love me
And you light my soul on fire….

Here came the first triple axel of the program. Blaze threw his hands up, making the jump more difficult simply because he could. Showing off and performance was separated by a fine line that too often became blurred.

Anna's voice sounded in Blaze's head as he skated into his quad. "Don't overthink. Jump. Let muscle memory allow you to fly."

Yes! Another flawless landing on his quad. He let the musical notes invade his body so the words bled out in every subtle move.

Trusting you makes life worthwhile
You're my everything
You make me smile

Right! Yeah, seeing someone made everything better. What a load of—
He'd never have that. But fuck, he couldn't crush the longing for
that kind of connection. Yes, he could. Only an idiot leaves himself open
to such nonsense.

The screaming guitar fed him the energy he required for the quad
combo with a triple, and he nailed it, the stop timed to the music.

*Being someone's everything—what would that feel like? Probably
incredible. Ha!* He didn't fancy giving anyone the ability to hurt him ever
again. *Trust, right!* Blocking out the lyrics that kept revealing his deep
scars on his psyche, he concentrated on the sensuality of the melody.

Give me more than just one night
Let me love you and hold you tight....

He executed a slow hip roll, then footwork, and he'd lock this
competition down. *Wait, no, this is an exhibition.* Playfully he rushed to
the kickboard and did a handstand, mimicking a skateboarder. Then he
ski-skated to the center, twitching his ass in the way judges had always
hated, and then spun. He grabbed a blade, pulled out of the spin, and
unwound down to two skates.

Take a chance and put aside your misplaced ire
Time to live and laugh a while

Had he ever lived? He skated, competed, and practiced. When was
the last time he laughed with anyone other than Luke or his dog?

Blaze twirled to the wall, held on, and scissor kicked his legs out in
back of him, smiling blindly into the crowd. He chuckled at the roar the
unexpected move forced the crowd to give.

Love me like you did back then
Don't lock me up
And waste our chance again.

The guitar amped Blaze in a major way. He used the energy and added a one-handed cartwheel at the start of his step sequence, because this was his victory lap and the quirky move seemed to be the thing to do.

You've got the key to release us from our broken dreams
And break us out of our handmade hell.

He'd promised Anna and Luke he wouldn't attempt the next move unless his ankles felt good and they were good enough. The crowd loved him, and he wanted to give this to them.

Aching and needing but always left wanting….
My heart longing with desire….
Until there was you.

Blaze strutted and then executed a Bonaly. He did the backflip and landed on one foot, which allowed him to skate two strides, and then he jumped into an air split. The backflip had been deemed too dangerous and illegal in competition, but in exhibitions, he had to pay homage to his role model, Surya Bonaly.

He took a lap around the ice, enjoying the love, before he spun, snapped to a stop, and dropped to a split on the ice on the last note of the song.

Air, air, need air. Keep smiling. Fuck, my ankle! He was used to smiling through the pain.

Applause echoed through the arena. He drank in the appreciation, then gracefully popped out of the split.

As he glided around the ice, stuffed dragons rained down around him. The younger skaters rushed to herd the beasts into a pile, where they would be donated to Safe Haven's police station and the children's hospital.

Bowing and waving to the crowd, he meandered around the ice, and then skated to the exit. He had fulfilled his purpose and given the audience something to enjoy.

Blaze smiled at the trembling young kid who presented a silver tray with Blaze's skate guards on it. "Thanks."

"Mr. Parker, you're the best. I mean… you're welcome…. *Eeeeeee!*" Then the kid ran off.

Slipping on the blade protectors, Blaze morphed into his brand's persona and swaggered over to the kiss and cry.

No scores to worry about, just reporters who lay in wait for him. Predators lingering for him to misspeak so they could get a good sound bite that would follow him to the next round of competition. If there would be a next round.

"This was your only scheduled exhibition. What's next for Blaze Parker?" asked the reporter from *Skating Times*.

Damn good question! For years, he hadn't thought past taking revenge on Trent. Then he poured all his angst and energy into training for the Olympics. Once he performed at the games and got the gold, he had fucked his way through the Olympic Village, as if he had been trying to nab the gold in casual sex.

But now what?

Nothing came to mind. Well, he needed an answer that would work for his "bad boy with a heart of gold" brand. What could his body handle? And more to the point, what did he want?

He gave the reporters what his brother called Blaze Parker's million-dollar smile. "What's next? Well, I've got a few endorsement spots to do, and I'm going to take a break before choreographing my routines for next season. I'll probably teach some classes here."

In truth, he'd done all his spots, even filmed his YouTube channel's influencer clips, and his possible future routines had already been mapped out except for the music. He'd hang out with his brother, skate, help the rink with teaching a class or two, and sleep. Exactly what he'd done for the last bit of forever.

"What do you have planned for next season?"

That was the question he didn't know the answer to... not really. So he was vague. "More."

"You just brought home the gold. What does *more* mean?"

The consistency of their questions should have provided stability, but it had started to feel stifling and deadened him. *Not this time.* "I'm going to write a list of things I've never done before and start checking things off my list."

"Sounds good." The reporter smiled.

It did. Maybe he would do that.

Another reporter asked, "What is the first thing on your list?"

Hmmm, when in doubt tell the truth. "Don't know yet. I have to start the list first."

"What's it like to be an openly gay skater?" The reporter's recording device was poised as if Blaze would reveal some major secret.

There's a question he hadn't been asked… in at least a week. Apparently where he put his dick was of great interest to the skating sphere and the world at large. Should he pretend homophobia was stamped out in a sport where international judges came from places like Russia where they had gay purges and consistently marked him lower? Or how skaters weren't gay until they were done competing? How coaches told him to butch it up?

No, they wanted to pretend how fixed the world was, now that LGBTQIA people had a few rights that others took for granted. And he should definitely ignore how the rights they earned were constantly under attack.

Blaze longed to blurt out "I credit anal sex for making me a better jumper." Or "Cum is actually a super skating potion," but he didn't.

He batted his eyelashes and softened his voice. "I've been asked that question a lot. Officially I didn't come out, though I guess I never needed to. People made assumptions…." Between the video and, honestly, he'd never tried to act *straight*, so in truth he had never been in the closet.

That was why most of the male skaters gave him a wide berth, especially those tucked away in their own closets behind all their sparkles and sequins. "I believe we all need to be ourselves because we're the only ones who can be. I used to be afraid of being too gay."

"Too gay?" a different reporter from a skating blog gasped.

"Yes, but my expression and presentation of who Blaze Parker is… is just that. I need to be me."

"Some consider you a danger to skating norms." The older reporter's tone held anger that implied Blaze had damaged the sport.

Blaze ignored the sting the reporter's stab gave him, and scoffed, "You use your ice skates as nunchucks one time, and suddenly you're a danger to society. Ha, well, I guess that's why they say I shouldn't be left unsupervised."

Funny to watch the expressions to see who got the joke and who happened to be a dipshit.

The reporter shook his head. "That's not what I meant. I—"

"I know. But visibility is important." Blaze refused to let the asshole spew hate. "Besides, God only lets the strong be as gay as me."

Lots of smiles and several giggles washed through the reporters.

"Well, I think you're great and an asset to the sport. Is there anyone special?" A vlogger asked the most dreaded question.

No matter how he answered, people got upset. Yes, and he angered those who didn't think gay people have the right to be happily partnered. If he said no, the ones who believed everyone should be coupled up like they were boarding the ark would be sad.

Blaze impressed himself yet again by not laughing. He wanted to say, "Well no, though I do believe in the benefits of a satisfying fifteen- or twenty-minute relationship a few times a month." Instead, he went with "Not yet."

Who the fuck is that?

Leaning against the wall, one long, black-denim-encased leg crossed over the other, was a man who brought to mind every filthy fantasy Blaze ever had. The black leather jacket that hugged his muscles remained opened, but thumbs hooked into belt loops kept most of the light blue T-shirt hidden. His dark brown hair tangled past his shoulders, accenting high cheekbones, and those perfect lips—with a sexy lip ring that seemed made to be glided along Blaze's cock—twisted into a grin.

"Um, what?" Blaze shook himself out of his lust and tried to focus on the reporters, who were still asking him questions.

"Do you consider this your home rink?" someone asked.

His gaze kept returning to the man, who was staring—eye fucking would have been a more appropriate description. Blaze attempted to stay aloof, though he'd settle for appearing calm. Now was not the time to throw wood.

After a few more moments, he said, "Yes, I do. Thank you. Have a great day and enjoy watching the finale. The kids all worked really hard on the routine."

The reporters dispersed, leaving a gaping expanse of empty space between him and... *oh my fucking God!* He rushed across the carpet. "You're Drake Keys."

Dropping his arms, the guy pushed off the wall. He tilted his head but didn't pause in the eye sex. "You know me?"

Screaming "I love your music and follow you on social media" followed by "Holy shit, Drake Keys saw me skate" would be the opposite of playing it cool. Blaze went with "You're the guitarist for Midnight Shadow."

"You skated to my song." A crooked smile made him less sex-waiting-to-happen and more endearing.

Damn! Blaze's insides did a flip-flop. *Stop gawking and spit something out.* He expected more from himself than appearing starstruck by the gorgeous rock star. Where had his dignity gone? "You mean Midnight Shadow's—"

"Yeah, but I wrote the lyrics to that one." Drake blew air on his hands and shoved them into his jacket pockets.

Oh.... Oh! The guy was even sexier and more soulful than he thought. Fuck! Blaze might die. He longed to tell Drake how the song touched his cold, dead heart. Instead he allowed himself to imagine exploring the possibilities of Drake Keys between the sheets.

He'd work those black jeans down over Drake's hips, unzip and push inside him. In his dreams, lube was never necessary. Turning Drake's long hair into reins, he'd pull that lean body into his at just the right position. Drake would gratefully take everything Blaze gave him, and then they'd part ways—

"You did a Bonaly," Drake murmured with the appropriate amount of shock and awe.

Full stop. Drake Keys knew what a Bonaly was? Some people into skating didn't always know the name for the backflip. How did he tell the guy to stop being enticing? And maybe offer to tongue his lip ring so he didn't have to....

Blaze gave him a shrug. "My air splits will never be as good as hers."

"You were incredible. Though you always are," Drake assured him a bit breathlessly.

"How do you know about the Bonaly?" Maybe Drake was a blade bunny who thought he could bed Blaze for the—

That sounded not only stupid, but paranoid.

"My best friend's little sister skated when she was younger. There aren't many black figure skaters to identify with, and well, Surya Bonaly was hard-core back in the day."

"She was… is. She's working as a coach in Minnesota." Drake probably had a crush on his best friend's sister. "So, do you still see your best friend's sister?"

Drake nodded enthusiastically. "Yeah, I'm in Jasmine's wedding in July. She met this really terrific guy. Though her parents wanted her to finish her master's degree first, but I don't think she's making a mistake or marrying too young. Sometimes you know."

"Oh, hmmm." *You simply know.* The way Drake gazed at him made Drake's rambled words echo between them.

Focus. Good news, Drake didn't appear upset by her— *Why do I care? This guy is getting under my skin in the space ripped open by his damned lyrics. There will be none of the "aching and needing but always left wanting" bullshit. My heart doesn't long with desire; I simply want to fuck. Not until there was you... always. Maybe I need to bed him and move on.*

Drake shoved his hands deeper into his pockets. "So you're really going to make a list of the things you've never done? Like a bucket list?"

Blaze shrugged. He had originally been referring to a skating list, but maybe a list for outside the rink would be better.

"I think you should. I'd love to help you cross some things off your list."

Like number one, fucking a rock star? Blaze bit his tongue and settled for giving him a smile.

The pupils of Drake's stunning blue eyes were blown, edging out the indigo. His smile deepened into a grin.

What the fuck was with the perma-grin?

Drake grabbed the tote bag at his feet. "Oh yeah. I'm sorry for being rude. But she told me to have one. I've been on the road, and I didn't sleep or eat. So I kind of opened the tin of brownies a fan left for you."

"You what?" *No.*

Drake swiped his tongue over his full lips and started laughing. "Dude, I'm sorry, I was starving. I only ate two. Okay, maybe three."

"Oh God. This fan, she wore her blonde hair in braids and had a tie-dye shirt on?" Blaze's best-laid plans of crossing off rock star fucking from his list crumbled.

Drake's mouth dropped open for a moment, and then he nodded. "Yeah. How did you know?"

Shit, there went any thought of hot sex. "Donna comes to most of my home shows and exhibitions. For some reason, even though I keep telling her I won't eat them, she always makes me brownies with a ton of weed in them."

"Weed?"

"Yeah, you're not allergic, are you?"

"Nah, I've smoked." Drake shrugged. "I wouldn't have thought—"

"You'd be surprised. Now when did you start eating the brownies?"

Drake looked around for the rink clock and started to laugh. "I don't know. About an hour ago."

More than a few people in that section closest to them started to take more interest in their conversation than the little kids doing their routines on the ice.

"So everything is starting to hit your system. Come on, we've got to get you out of here."

"I'll go anywhere with you. I drove thirty-two hours straight, with only a few gas breaks, to see you." Drake's voice deepened and had a bit of a purr to it.

Just because Drake's lyrics, and now his voice, made Blaze want things, didn't mean Blaze had to give in to his desire. He cleared his throat and straightened his spine.

"I'm still pretty hungry…."

Keep things friendly and distant. Blaze chuckled. "I'm sure you are."

"I'm starving for a lot of things." His glassy eyes got a dreamy look in them. As he assessed Blaze, Drake's expression heated to smoldering. "If you know what I mean."

"Yeah, I think I do. Follow me." Blaze grabbed Drake's guitar case and exited the rink.

Chapter 4

DRAKE WAS so relaxed, it felt like he wasn't quite there, but he walked without stumbling. *Drake for the win.* But one slight bump—

"Careful, Drake." Blaze put a hand on his back and guided him into the locker room. Blaze Parker touching him—bigger win.

"Thanks. I guess those brownies and lack of sleep made—oh, wow!" Drake spun in a sloppy circle, grinning at bright white walls. There were several rows of shiny black lockers and individual white cubbies for hanging skating outfits lining the walls, with benches in front of them.

Blaze led him to one with *Blaze Parker* emblazed in gold over the top, then helped him sit down.

"Good skill, guys. You got this," Blaze called out to the young teens as he started untying his skates.

The rush and excitement reminded Drake of Midnight Shadow. "This is like backstage at a concert...."

The skaters, all except one, scurried out of the room.

"Though a lot less sex," Blaze grumbled for Drake's ears alone.

Drake pushed away, hurt slicing into his heart at being dumped by the band, then grinned. "True, but—oh, the skaters.... My God, you are the *rock stars*."

Blaze snickered. "Your marijuana-induced epiphanies should be annoying, but you're rather adorable stoned."

Shaking his head made Drake feel like he was underwater. "No! The only grown-assed man who's cute and adorable is you."

Blaze turned a pretty shade of pink. His mouth had dropped open, making Drake think of— "Cookies! Oh, Blaze. Can I have one of those cookies, man? Please. Is it okay?"

"Sure, but be warned they're zucchini chocolate chip."

Drake rushed over to the cookie jar that sat on a table labeled Reward, and it had all his attention. He opened the jar and sniffed deliciousness. "They smell incredible."

The last skater gave them a smirk on his way out.

"Enjoy." Blaze sighed and might have muttered something about Drake's enthusiasm being charming, but he couldn't be sure.

Drake shoved half a cookie into his mouth. He moaned, and his eyes rolled back. "This is delicious. Vegetabley. Is that a word?"

Blaze opened his locker and grabbed a towel as he stepped into shoes. He took off the skating guards and wiped down his blades. "These need to be resharpened."

"This is where it begins. All the glitz and glamour of skating starts right here." Drake tried to chew before talking, but he had so much to say.

He finished the cookie and touched the shiny metal locker. So sleek. He slid his fingers over the surface again and again. Guitars could have this type of sheen to them.

A woman burst into the locker room and stumbled to a halt. "What's this? And why is he petting the lockers?"

Oh, Drake knew the answer. He turned his head to her. "Lockers and guitars…."

"Oh, geez." Blaze guided Drake back to a bench. "What does it look like, Anna?"

She *tsk*ed. "That you have a stoner in the locker room."

"Got it in one. Donna's brownies struck again." Blaze opened his locked drawer. He grabbed his messenger bag and draped the leather strap around him in such a fluid movement, Drake had become sure the move was part of a dance routine.

Instead of finishing the graceful dance, Blaze glanced in the mirror. "I'm not taking off the makeup."

"Makeup on or off, you're the prettiest person I've ever seen." Drake had to tell him that. Were those diamonds pasted to his face? Blaze had better not lose those sparkles. Diamonds were expensive.

"Who is he?" she growled and put her hands on her hips.

"I'm Drake." He tried to stand straighter, then remembered he had sat down.

Anna stomped her foot while she glared at him. "How did he even get in here?"

That was simple. "If you walk like you know where you're going, and you'd be surprised—"

"Blaze?" Her tone could cut through ice.

Blaze shrugged. "What? It's true. He's Drake Keys."

She appeared more than a little bossy and kind of scary when she put her hands on her hips. "Donna needs to stop baking them for you. How many brownies did he eat?"

Blaze shrugged. "Probably three."

Brownies? He ate a lot. For the sake of clarity, he added, "Though I think it may have been four… and a half. And some of those cookies over there… but no milk. Milk would be delicious right now."

Anna chuckled. "Want me to take him to a hotel?"

"Hotel?" Who was she carting off to a hotel? How far was this hotel? And what were hotels anyway? Strangers coming together to sleep. Seemed like a dating app. He snorted.

Blaze shook his head, making his hair dance in the lights. He had pretty hair. "Um, nah. I don't want to trouble you."

"It's no problem. Viktor isn't home until later." She studied Blaze. "Ah, okay. I've been with you too long not to be able to read your *fuck-off* expression."

"Anna, I appreciate the offer, but I got this."

Drake hoped Blaze had whatever it was he needed, because Blaze should have everything. He was amazing… wonderful, smart, and—

"Drake… Keys…? Where do I know that name?" She touched his guitar case with the Midnight Shadow sticker on the side. "Blaze!"

"It's okay." Blaze held his hands in front of him as if to ward off an attack.

"Blaze, you think they'd mind if I had just one more cookie? They're delectable." Drake made sure to keep his voice even on the especially hard words.

Anna winced and *shh*ed him.

Was he yelling?

"Okay, huh? You got this?" She assessed Drake and then slowly turned back to Blaze. "You sure about that?"

Blaze rolled his eyes at Anna and smiled at Drake, who patiently waited at the cookie jar 'cause he had manners. "Yeah, Drake, have at 'em."

Drake bit into the cookie and couldn't stop a low, drawn-out moan that came out between chews.

"Well, at least we found someone willing to eat those veggie cookies. You think he's a blade bunny?" Anna studied Drake a little too closely.

Blaze snorted. "Yes, because rock stars often line up after skating events for me."

Drake nodded, swallowed his cookie bite, but he wanted to be clear. "Blaze, I'd stand in line for you."

Anna snorted and shook her head. "Speaking of lines, the finale is about to finish. So you need to go sign some autographs. Luke told me to tell you he'll be waiting at the table for you."

"Good. Thanks, um, can you take him out to my car?" Blaze handed the keys to her.

Anna muttered, "You should ignore his pretty blue eyes and dreamy perma-grin. You're creating drama for yourself, but far be it for you to actually listen to me."

Turning to Drake, Blaze touched his cheek. He had soft hands. "Anna will take you to my car. I'll be there in a few minutes, okay?"

Drake nodded happily. He wasn't going to be away from Blaze for long. "Thank you, Blaze. Again, I'm really sorry."

Blaze started to walk off but stopped and returned to Drake. He tucked a bit of Drake's hair behind his ear, sending shivers through him. "I'll see you in a bit. Okay?"

Drake smiled even bigger. His cheeks might break. "Yup. I'll be waiting for you."

Blaze turned on his heel and left.

The backside Drake had lusted over for years twitched out the door. *Wow.* Drake enjoyed the view until Anna cleared her throat. "Oh, hello. I'm going to wait for Blaze."

"Yes, I know. I'm Anna, and I get to take you to Blaze's car." Anna grabbed his guitar and used her other hand on his elbow and led him outside.

At some point he'd be pissed about eating those brownies, but right now, for the first time in what seemed like weeks, he felt relaxed. He followed her out the door and trailed after her zigzag pattern through the parking lot around numerous vehicles, and all while he tried not to laugh.

"Edibles can give a stronger high than you might be used to, and four of Donna's baked creations is a lot." She made the car alarm beep and pointed in the direction of the horn.

Shit! She keeps staring at me. I need to speak. How do mind thoughts become mouth words? "And a half. Four and a half brownies. Not on purpose, though."

"What do you mean? How did you accidentally get high?" Anna squinted at him.

"I wasn't thinking. I haven't slept in a couple of days, and I drove through the night so I'd make the exhibition."

Anna scrunched her face. "You drove from where?"

"My last concert." The conversation was getting easier.

"All the way from your last concert? Where was that?"

Drake needed to concentrate to make his lazy tongue force the meaning to come out of his brownie hole. He laughed. "New York City to here is a little over thirty hours if you add in a few quick stops."

She unlocked a silver, environmentally friendly Chevrolet Volt. "You a big skating fan?"

Was he? "More like a huge Blaze Parker fan."

"Wait, are you a stalker?" Anna clicked the fob and relocked the car door.

"No, no." Drake tried to open the door and chuckled when he couldn't. "Stalking takes too much effort."

Anna studied him, then sighed as she unlocked the door. "Why are you here?"

"That's a great question," he muttered, more to himself as he opened the car door and collapsed into the passenger seat. "Insanity… but I felt like I needed to, you know?"

The "Hmm" encouraged him as she slipped his guitar into the back, then jumped into the driver's seat.

"I've been following Blaze for a while… since I was a teenager." Now, totally embarrassed by how long, maybe *stalker* could be considered the correct term? "I've never made it to one of his competitions or exhibitions—"

"So why now?"

Her questions came at a rapid-fire pace, and his brain couldn't keep up. "Well, Brenda outed my interest in one of the guys she hooked us up with."

"Your girlfriend?"

"Ex-girlfriend… if she even was my girlfriend. You know, the more I think about our relationship, I realize it wasn't one. Since she never really talked to me. Didn't care about me. Always invited other people to join us for sex. And hated kissing me." How had he tolerated that?

"So your girlfriend dumped your kinky ass."

"No, well, yes." The weed ferreted out that truth. "I didn't want to be with so many other people. She kept telling me we were polyamorous. I'm not. I mean, that's fine if someone wants relationships with more than one person. I'm not that person. You know?"

"And?" Anna had the same look Summer got when his lyrics didn't work with the melody.

"I want one person to love and share my life with." Drake really wished he could stop smiling 'cause his face had started to hurt. "But that doesn't matter now."

Anna sat back. "Why not?"

"You're good at questions." Drake admired her conversational skills. "Why not?"

Did she need to repeat herself? Probably. "Why not what?" He tried to piece together what she asked.

Her gaze tinted with frustration. "Why doesn't it matter now?"

Yeah, the way she bit out her words meant Drake's lack of response must have made her repeat the question. He tried to answer quickly. "Bigger problems. The band, well, the manager, sleazy Frank, and Dixon, the asshole, kicked me out."

"You're out of Midnight Shadow?" Anna made it sound like a convictable offense.

"Yeah. I'd been warned I could be out as bisexual, just not allowed to be with men." Not sure why he kept rambling, other than pot did that to him if it didn't put him to sleep.

"But isn't that the bi part?"

"Exactly!" He brushed away the single piece of lint off Blaze's pristine dashboard. "I grabbed my guitar and took an Uber to the nearest rental car place. The band is on hiatus for the next two and a half months—though that no longer matters."

"So you came here?"

He shrugged. "I wasn't ready to go home, and after all the YouTube videos and Twitter clips, I got a notification that he liked my post, and saw an interview where Blaze mentioned the exhibition. I decided I wanted to finally see Blaze Parker skate live. And I can't believe he did a Bonaly. He's fantastic!"

Anna shook her head and frowned. "I discouraged him from doing that stunt, but she's always been his hero."

"I understand why. Both strive for perfection and let nothing get in their way. Like the way Blaze wiped the floor with that asshole Trent at World's."

Even high, Drake saw the lightbulb go off over her head. "Oh, so you know about the videotape."

"Trent Richards was and is a played-out wannabe who should never be allowed to share the ice with the likes of Blaze Parker."

Anna pressed her lips together. Was she suppressing a smile? Did she agree with him, or was she laughing at him?

"I'm serious. He's terrible. His routines are boring, and most of his landings are sloppy." Drake tilted his head and chuckled. "Maybe I do follow skating."

"You're right, but we're not talking about *him*. I still don't know why you're here."

Why was he here? "I don't know. I guess I felt connected—"

"To Blaze?"

"Sounds stupid when you say it out loud. But yeah. A few times over Twitter, he and I…. That's pretty creepy." Drake covered his face. How had he gone from guitar player in Midnight Shadow to ice skating stalker?

She clapped a hand on his shoulder, which forced him to drop his hands. "Look, the fact he didn't send you away means he probably wants to fuck you before he curbs you."

"Fuck me." That made him feel hot and cold, worried and excited, and maybe a bit confused.

"Yes. Sex." Anna used her finger to poke the circle made by her other hand. "But Blaze swipes right beyond Grindr, so don't get your hopes sky-high for a love connection."

Well, it wasn't that Drake had ever been opposed to a one-off, but when Blaze first saw him, something sparked between them. He felt a connection, or maybe that was just the brownies mixed with lust. What the hell had he been hoping for?

"Guess you're not a blade bunny. You don't look like the prospect of getting laid is appealing." Anna nodded sagely. "Or is it you don't like to bottom?"

"Oh no, I prefer it." He slapped a hand over his mouth and laughed. There was truth in pot. He enjoyed getting fucked more than he liked fucking. Sue him! He couldn't deny he found something enticing about taking the burning stretch as the thrusting morphed into incredible pleasure.

Blaze waltzed over to the car. He still wore his clingy, sparkly red skating costume. The way the material clung to his muscles stole Drake's breath away.

Drake pulled down his leather jacket, hoping he wasn't being indecent because he got a giant boner.

Anna must have noticed, and she snorted as she got out of the car. "Blaze, you do know all your *inconveniences* would be solved with a simple 'Yes, take him to a hotel.' Let me ask you one more time. Shall I take him to a hotel?"

Oh! Anna wanted to take *Drake* to a hotel. Right. That would make sense. Blaze shouldn't have to babysit his stoned ass, but Drake selfishly prayed Blaze wouldn't send him away. Now that he finally got here, he wanted to spend time with him.

Blaze stared at him through the windshield. "No, it's my fault he got this way."

"Oh please. You just want to fuck him." Anna shook her head.

Glaring at her, Blaze said, "There will be no fucking. He's high, and consent matters."

Did that mean Blaze didn't want him? Drake pushed aside the crushing loss of having sex shoved off the table by his greedy stomach.

Anna put her hands on her hips.

Blaze looked away from her silent interrogation and smiled at Drake, making his heart do a little flip.

Drake grinned and waved at him.

Smiling bigger, Blaze waved back. Then he turned to Anna and added, "Besides, I need to make sure he doesn't die."

Ow! Way to cut a guy.

Anna stepped closer to Blaze, and Drake couldn't make out what she said, though he couldn't miss the warning was about him.

"I will." Blaze pulled Anna into a quick embrace.

When Anna stepped back, she groaned and shook her head. "See you tomorrow at the rink."

Pursing his lips, Blaze nodded and got into the car.

He looked over at Drake with a crooked smile. "Hey."

"Hey." Drake's smile turned into a grin. "I don't want to be trouble."

Blaze pulled out of the spot. "You're no trouble."

"Not yet."

Giving him a quick glance, Blaze agreed, "Not yet."

Chapter 5

GRIPPING THE steering wheel of his car didn't help give Blaze a stronger handle on his reality. What was he doing? Why didn't he let Anna deposit the sexy guitar player into a hotel? Nope, not him.

The guy had appeared out of nowhere, like Blaze would be happy to see him. Fuck, if he wasn't over the moon about having a stoned guitar player riding shotgun. *Full stop!*

Maybe his libido took control of his world. After a skating event, he usually needed to fuck off the tension, but that wasn't possible in this case.

Not because Drake Keys wasn't fuck-a-licious, but he was high, and Blaze would never take advantage of someone in that condition. His usual mode of fuck-and-move-on wouldn't work, since they were friends, kind of, or as much as one could be friends on social media without meeting… and now they'd met.

Which brought him back to why didn't he let Anna do the more reasonable thing.

He glanced over at the wrinkled, rumpled, tangled-hair, sexy, grinning rock star—God, this already seemed too weird and they hadn't done anything.

Drake had practically stuck his head out the window, looking at the houses they passed. "Wow, this neighborhood looks so normal."

Blaze glanced at him to gauge if Drake had been toying with him. "Where did you think I lived?"

"A castle." Drake covered his mouth and chuckled. "No, I mean, I knew you didn't actually live there, but—"

"What?"

Drake sighed. "Watching you on the ice, you belong in one."

Blaze tried not to be utterly charmed by Drake's rock-star charisma, which morphed into cuteness held together by so much sincerity it soothed as much as the sweetness ripped at Blaze's heart. It couldn't be real.

Besides, this was the weed, not Drake. Guys weren't sweet.

A subject change was needed, so Blaze grasped at information he could share while keeping his distance. "Um, so I have a puppy. Well, he's seven."

"Oh! Is that the dog you hold in some of your pictures? What kind is he?" Drake bounced in his seat.

"Yes, he's a Lhaffon. He's a Lhasa Apso and Griffon mix."

Drake tilted his head left, then right. "He's very cute."

"The breeder thought he was too small." Blaze turned down onto his street.

"Too small?"

"He's got too much Lhasa in him. The breeder didn't want the dog, so Luke, my brother, rescued him from being sent to the shelter when we first moved to Colorado."

"What's his name again?" Drake's stunning smile and dreamy face distracted Blaze.

Eyes on the road. Eyes on the road.

"Ice… though Luke calls him Jack the Nipper. My Ice has no awareness of his tiny size, because he tries to take on the world, teeth first." Blaze parked on the left side of the driveway, leaving Luke room to get his car in and out.

Damn, this is weird. He didn't really bring guys home. When he hooked up with someone from an app, he'd usually go to their place or a hotel, trying to be as careful as he could to reduce the risk a little. Blaze's afterplay had always been executing an escape.

When Drake didn't emerge from the car, Blaze opened the car door.

"Oops. I'm stuck." Drake pulled at the seat belt.

"Here. Let me." Blaze leaned over him to press the button.

Drake wrapped his arms around Blaze in a…. Was this a hug?

"Hey, I'm sorry I'm causing all these problems." Drake's voice cracked.

Instead of reading him the riot act and taking him to a hotel, Blaze hugged him back. Drake had been through the wringer, according to Anna. Being kicked out of his band, driving all night—he had to be losing it. "No worries."

Unfamiliar feelings of warmth and care swirled through Blaze. Other than a few back-slapping man hugs, he wasn't really a hugger.

Drake melted into him.

Mmmmm, maybe he could change that.

Maybe inviting Drake home had been a mistake, not that Drake and he…. That wouldn't be happening. The few times he'd tried to have a guy over, Ice went on the warpath and tried to gnaw on them. But this hug….

Again, this wasn't for sex or hugging! Blaze simply wanted to be sure Drake didn't die. After all, his fan had gotten Drake too high to be left alone, so it became his responsibility. Otherwise the headline would read: *Guitar Player Drake Keys Dead Because Blaze Parker is a Selfish Irresponsible Ass*. That wouldn't play well for his brand.

Bringing Drake home was the only logical thing Blaze could have done.

"Come on. Let's go inside. Do you need help up?" Unwinding himself, Blaze ignored the regret of ending the long and rather *cozy* hug. *Cozy? What the fuck?* Blaze must just be gagging for some sex.

Drake's chiseled cheekbones were highlighted by the blush. "I got it." He slipped out of the front seat with liquid movements.

Blaze stopped drooling and grabbed Drake's guitar. All of this was surreal, but not a big deal.

Lies you tell yourself for sex— No, 'cause I'm not going to fuck him. He's a friend, or at least I know him or something, so sex is truly off the table, even when he's not high. There! Decision made and all pressure turned off.

Blaze unlocked the curtained french doors. "Ice doesn't like most people, so stand back. I'll distract him. You hurry on my signal, and then after he does his business, I'll crate him or put him in my bedroom so he doesn't nip at you."

Drake shook his head. "You don't have to do that. It's his house."

"Just be ready to move." Blaze braced himself and opened the door. There was a single low bark, and Ice flew through the air. The tiny dog launched himself at Drake.

"Ice!" Blaze froze, and everything became slow motion.

Drake caught the flying puppy and put his knuckles out for Ice to approve him. "Oh. Hi there, Iceman."

Blaze's breath caught in his lungs.

Ice sniffed twice, tilted his head to accept the petting he deserved, then gave Drake a lick on the cheek, confirming he'd received all Ice-petting privileges available. Ice barked once more and added a wiggle.

"Oh, here you go, my man." Drake set Ice down, allowing him to run around the fenced-in yard. Even in Drake's drugged state, he understood doggy speak. Not that Blaze found that fact sexy, because anyone could speak dog, right?

"Come on in." Blaze set Drake's guitar near the door.

"Nice place. You share this with your brother?"

"He lives upstairs in the main part of the house. We finished the basement and turned it into an apartment for me so I could focus on skating and not paying rent." *What the fuck?* Blaze never shared personal information.

High or not, Drake rang alert bells. He could easily become a menace to Blaze's way of life.

Blaze was already acting out of character. Maybe he needed to keep a safer distance from Drake.

The basement ran the entire length of the house. Luke had insisted they make him a tiny but fully stocked kitchen with microwave, oven, burners, refrigerator, dishwasher, sink, and tiny washer-dryer hidden behind a cabinet door. The gray granite island had flecks of silver and blue and sat on top of white cabinets. One side lined with three stools served as his dining area, but he usually ate with Luke or in front of the television.

"Sorry, I left the place a mess." Blaze had no clue why he apologized to a virtual stranger, but he rushed through the living room area, which consisted of a white love seat, two matching chairs, and a television. He put the remote controls back into the white lacquer side table drawers.

"A mess? No way. This is spotless. But since I've been living with some bandmates who think Febreze can eliminate trips to the laundromat, I might not be the best judge."

"No! Febreze? That can't be." Blaze refolded a white blanket, placed the throw over the arm of the chair, and tried not to be grossed out.

"Afraid so." Drake's frown spoke of disgusting smells and body odor.

Drake Keys was in his apartment!

Wasn't there a rule about having guys you jerked off over in your space? Always had been one for Blaze, and now—body odor to masturbation? Talk about breakneck mental topic change.

Almost tripping on his carpet, he hurried over to shut the white unit that housed a rainbow of organized fabric, sequins, crystals, thread, his sewing machine, and work table. "Thankfully, the glamour of the spotlight hides stink and small costume tears."

Drake appeared right behind him and stayed Blaze's hand. Drake's warm touch heated him.

Blaze shouldn't try to absorb the man's warmth, which now penetrated his always cold body. Drake should be required to provide a thermostat, because his heat might succeed in breaching the ice around Blaze.

Who was Blaze kidding? He'd be masochistically self-injurious and crank Drake's heat until Blaze burned to ash.

A low whistle, followed by, "Wow, my mom would love this unit. She'd fill the entire unit with scrapbooking paper, stickers, crap like that. But she's neat and orderly like you."

Blaze tried shoving and burying the familiar loss that surfaced. "My mother taught both Luke and me to put things back where they belong so we could always find them. The concept stuck more with me than Luke, because he still loses his remote controls."

Drake dropped a gentle hand on his shoulder. "I'm sorry your mom and dad died when you were so young. Both of your parents would have been proud of all you accomplished."

"Thanks," Blaze whispered as he tried to see through his watery eyes.

His mom would have wanted more for him. Of course, she'd have been proud of his skating career, and his dad would have been pleased he saved and invested his money like Luke taught him. But both his parents would have wanted him to look for happiness off the ice, not only temporary solace.

Blaze needed to escape these emotions but wasn't sure how. He stepped back from Drake.

"Do you make your own costumes?"

Did Drake read his mind? Whatever. He would enjoy the relief of shifting to less emotional topics. "Yeah, I do, actually."

Drake's eyes widened, and then he smiled like Blaze confessed to being a rocket scientist in his spare time. "How did you learn to sew?"

"My mom taught me the basics of sewing before... she died. Costumes can be terribly expensive, so I usually buy basic shirts and pants. Then I add bits of sparkle, flocking, and cutouts to the pieces."

"Come on. Most of your costumes look like you do much more than that."

Blaze didn't know quite what to do with all these heartfelt compliments. Applause from his fans only required a bow, but Drake's expression had become too full of admiration along with expectation. "Um... thanks. There's also a couple of ladies in town who taught me some more advanced techniques."

Drake pulled open the drawer housing animal print fabric. "Cool leopard print."

Blaze gasped with dramatic flair, hoping to lighten the mood further. "Oh no. You're another Luke."

"What?" Drake shook his head like he didn't get the joke.

Placing his wrist to his forehead, Blaze called upon divas both living and dead to add drama to his voice. "I can't live with such confusion."

"Confusion?" Drake's stare intensified.

"Clearly, this is a jaguar pattern." Blaze grinned and pointed out another swatch. "This one is leopard. See? Big difference."

Drake bit his lip and studied the fabrics like he would be taking a final exam on patterns. *Too cute.*

"This one is giraffe and, of course, zebra print." Blaze tucked them all neatly back in their place and shut the drawer. He pushed his sewing machine back into the unit and dropped the legs of the work tables. Finally he closed the cabinet.

Drake pointed to a Japanese screen. "What's behind there?"

Blaze wasn't sure if he should find Drake's interest in his apartment annoying or if he was weirdly pleased by the curiosity. Undecided, he gestured with his hand. "Take a look. It's where I work on my routines."

"It's like a tiny dance studio. The hardwood floor, the mirrored wall, the ballet pole, red ribbon like in your exhibition, and…. Wait, is that a stripper pole?" Drake's voice rose an octave to scandalized-but-very-interested.

After catching a glimpse of Drake's shocked expression, Blaze couldn't resist giving him a demonstration.

"I typically don't strip when I use it," Blaze snarked and strutted over to the vertical brass pole. He flipped and caught the pole between his thighs, hanging upside down for a moment, and then he jumped and grabbed the pole right side up.

Drake gasped.

Unwinding himself from the pole, Blaze twirled around with one hand out. "Placement of this pole was tricky. Too close to the mirror and I couldn't check my routines. If it's too far back, I'd have smacked my head on the sewing cabinet. Plus add the ceiling, and well, it's good that I'm short."

He held the pole with his hands and straightened his body out, perpendicular to the floor. Pulling into the pole, Blaze flipped back upside down and V-ed his legs out on either side. He checked Drake's reaction.

Priceless! Drake's bright royal blue eyes were huge, and his mouth dropped open. Then he licked his sensual full lips in a way that made

Blaze swear he could feel Drake's tongue and mouth on his cock—and that taunting little lip ring.

Enough showing off. Blaze backflipped off the pole. "It's good exercise."

Drake gasped, then stared at him with dreamy eyes. "Wow! That was incredible. You're so amazing."

Blaze waved him off. "Thanks, but I bet you tell that to all the boys and girls."

"No, I really don't." The earnestness in Drake's tone shook Blaze.

Blaze opened his mouth, then shut it. What could he possibly say?

"Um, what's that? A tiny teeter-totter?" Drake pointed at the bright orange twelve-inch curved piece of plastic.

Blaze chuckled. "That's a skate glide. It's used to practice spins. Skaters use the skate glide to teach their bodies what the rotations of certain jumps should feel like."

"Really?" Drake inspected the device.

"You want to try?"

"Sure." Drake set down the skate glide.

Maybe this was a bad idea. Though Blaze had already offered.... "You place your foot on it and turn once. Be careful."

Drake must have miscalculated the energy one needed to turn. He unsteadily spun, then started to fall.

The skate glide skittered across the floor as Drake headed to the ground. Blaze wrapped his arms around him to stabilize him.

Drake sighed and pressed flush against Blaze's body.

Damn. It had been too long since he'd had someone in his arms, but now twice in less than an hour. A couple of his skating friends with benefits were cuddlers. He tolerated those snuggles, but they didn't compare to the rightness of holding Drake. *What?*

Blaze probably missed sex. That was all. He mused at how easy it would be to guide Drake over to the love seat and.... He caught a look at himself in the mirror and touched his sequined neckline. "I'm still in my skating costume. I should go take a shower and change."

"If you insist." Drake squeezed him tighter for a moment and then released him.

Feeling off-balance, Blaze scrambled to find something to latch on to, so he asked, "Can I get you some tea or water?"

"Ew, tea tastes like twigs and dirt. I'll have some water, though." Drake's exclamation reminded Blaze he was dealing with someone who still rode the Brownie Train to Happyville.

Blaze snorted and handed him a bottle out of the fridge. "Here."

"Thanks." Drake made himself comfortable on the love seat and picked up Blaze's dragon. "Who is this?"

Blaze mentally glared at his absent dog, then rushed over to collect his treasured possession. "Flame. Ice must have snatched him off my— where I keep him. Let me put him back."

He settled the dragon back on his nightstand, where his mom used to put it to guard him from bad dreams. Silly, but he liked believing Flame protected him while he slept.

Blaze went back to the main room to… um, refill Ice's water dish.

Ice trotted through the doggy door and greeted Blaze. Then he noisily lapped water from his bowl, ensuring he'd be watering a tree soon.

Blaze needed to stop staring at Drake, though the rarity of seeing someone other than Luke and Anna in here made it impossible. Drake fit right in. Go figure. Blaze filled the electric kettle with water and started the pot. In between sneaking peeks at Drake, he got his favorite dragon mug ready with his green tea enhanced with nana mint.

Drake patted his chest. "Iceman. Wanna hang with me while your daddy cleans up?"

Right, Blaze had been heading to the shower.

Ice hurried over to Drake as quickly as his tiny legs could carry him, like the man was an old friend. Ice, the usually *not*-friendly puppy, jumped onto Drake's lap, licked his cheek, circled, and lay down on his back. The shameless dog exposed himself to Drake and got his belly rubbed for the trust.

Drake had beautiful musician's hands with long skilled fingers and…. Dragging his gaze off the impossibilities, Blaze pointed to the side table. "The remotes are in the top drawer."

Drake turned and fixated all his attention on Blaze. Geez, that was enough to make Blaze want to trade spots with his dog. Dammit if Drake's dreamy smile didn't make him positively melt. Dreaminess… right, most likely drug-induced.

"Thanks for letting me hang out with you."

"Sure." Blaze gave an awkward wave and stumbled back into his bedroom like it was his first day on skates.

Blaze fluffed the pillows on his bed and smoothed a wrinkle on the comforter. Once he reassured himself nothing embarrassing lay around, he went into his bathroom and started the shower.

He stripped, tossed his clothing into a special bag to keep his costumes separated in his hamper for handwashing, and took off his performance makeup.

Usually after a competition, he took a long bath and then used an app to find someone to fuck. That wouldn't be happening, but his cock must not have gotten the memo of the change in plans. Or maybe, since the guitar player who starred in a number of his masturbatory fantasies sat in the next room, his cock refused to accept the denial.

His cock ached. Hoping Drake had been—

He bolted the bathroom door and then stepped into the shower. Glancing down at his excited cock, he sighed. To jerk off or not to jerk off, that was the question. There had to be some edict against rubbing one out when a guest waited in the other room.

It was his house, and he needed to relax. But was that weird?

An image of Drake sprawled out on his love seat, petting Ice, made his cock harden further.

Fuck! At this point, taking himself in hand could be seen as a preventive measure against bad decisions. His mind moved Drake into his bed, and the imaginary Drake's mouth became front and center. No, he should simply turn him over and fuck him, but then he wouldn't have been able to kiss him. And God, he wanted to kiss him.

He stroked off, and as soon as their lips met in fantasy, Blaze choked back his moan and came.

Fuck, that was oddly satisfying for a solo session. Whatever. He'd needed to come, end of story.

Breathing a sigh of relief, he finished his shower.

Blaze dried and slipped into a pair of gray lounge pants with a light, slim-fitting blue top. The mirror told him he might be trying too hard. He exchanged the "top of seduction" for a dark gray T-shirt that didn't make him look like he was on the prowl for anything other than some mindless TV. Then he brushed his towel-dried hair. Leaving his feet bare because the idea of anything on them would be too much, he padded out to the main area.

On the counter sat a cup of tea. He sipped and found the tea was the perfect drinking temperature.

"You made me tea?" Blaze cleared his throat of the weird tickle he'd gotten. *I feel emotion. Who authorized this?*

"I poured the water into the cup." Drake's tone suggested what he did was commonplace.

Blaze couldn't remember the last time he'd experienced such thoughtfulness. "The only ones to ever do this for me were my mom and Luke." Unless he counted when Anna thrust a packet of tea at him, commanding him to drink some and then demanding he feel better when the doctor said he had strep.

"No big." Drake gave a glassy-eyed smile.

"Thanks." *Right! It's no big deal to the world at large; I'm making the smallest kindness into one like a weirdo.* Blaze collapsed into one of the chairs.

And stared at Drake.

Drake engaged him with his gaze.

Blaze uncrossed his arms and then sipped his tea. Why did Drake have to be so delicious sitting there with lickable earrings running along the shell of his ear? Since when were earrings worthy of his tongue? Drake's eyes held too much heat. And fuck, that lip ring….

Something sparked between them. Blaze didn't know what flashed or why it had.

Drake started to laugh, and the melody eased something inside Blaze that had coiled tight forever ago. The sound forced him to smile, grin, and soon he joined in chortling like a fool.

Ice awoke from his doggy dreams. He glanced between Drake and Blaze. Standing at attention, Ice gave a fierce defensive barking growl toward nothing in particular, which made Blaze laugh harder.

Wiping his eyes, Drake admitted, "I don't even know what I'm laughing at."

"Me either," Blaze got out, right before dissolving back into laughter. "And I didn't even have any brownies."

Shaking his head, Drake got his laughing fit under control. "I really am sorry about that. It wasn't my intention. I should have thought about the fact that I entered a legal state."

What was this feeling? Maybe contentment, and why did Blaze experience it now? How come he couldn't turn off his emotions like usual? He tried to snap himself out of his bemusement. "You must think

I'm a terrible host. If you want to shower, I can get us some food. You can use my washing machine. Or I could get you a bottle of Febreze."

Drake snorted. "You're funny."

Fearing Drake's happy sounds could easily become an addiction—even now they took hold of him—Blaze popped out of the chair. "I'll go borrow some sweats from my brother, and you can take a shower."

"Is that a hint?"

Drake Keys naked with water cascading down his— No perving on a drugged houseguest. "That or Febreze...."

"If you don't think your brother would mind, I'd love that. I left without my duffel bag."

"You okay if I leave you for a bit?" Weird, Blaze didn't even want to go upstairs.

"Yeah, I think I'm coming down. The highs that keep rolling over me are coming in lighter waves. I feel more even now."

"Good." Then maybe Blaze would stop being enamored by the delightfulness of a stoned Drake. "Shower's right in here."

Blaze trailed after Drake and gave him a tour of the bathroom to show him where stuff could be found. Drake continually kept brushing against him. The bathroom must have shrunk. Blaze needed to escape the touch before he couldn't resist touching back.

"You need anything else?" Where had the innuendo come from?

Drake's eyes glittered, and he licked his full lips. His lip ring shifted, and he raised one eyebrow in invitation to everything Blaze craved.

Holy hell. "Um, well, I'm just going to run upstairs. I'll set the clothing outside the door."

"Sure. I appreciate it," Drake said, but Blaze heard, *"I'll bend over your bathroom sink so you can fuck me."*

Blaze spun and knocked into the doorjamb. Well, that jarred him out of his delusion. After shutting the bathroom door, he headed up the steps to the main floor. He jogged past all the medals and awards Luke insisted they display there. Pictures of Blaze in all vivid, hideous, and possibly hilarious pastels to his early teen emo phase where only blacks and deep purples would do. A couple of the pictures of Blaze on the podium with those beside him cropped out—mainly Trent—gave him a good reminder of the importance of emotional distance.

Never again. It simply wasn't worth the cost.

He paused at the most recent framed photos from the Olympics. These pictures reminded him the games hadn't been a fantasy. As surreal as participating in his second Olympics felt, that photo showing him kissing the Olympic ice after his final performance, another of him receiving the gold, and one with Luke and Anna afterward, proved it happened.

For the first time ever, a small voice in his heart suggested how nice it would have been to have someone other than his brother and Anna with whom he could share special moments.

What the fuck? He huffed with annoyance. Squishing that wish, he flung open the door that led into his brother's kitchen.

Luke stood by the countertop, making sandwiches.

"Um, can I borrow some sweats?"

"They'll never fit, or are you going to shred them and make something else out of them?" Luke might have reason to be suspicious of clothing borrowing.

"No, um…." Why did Blaze want to avoid telling Luke he was going to have a sleepover with a stoned guitar player? "I have a friend over—"

"A friend? Oh, is that the euphemism now?" Luke smirked. He moved his eyebrows up and down suggestively.

"Not like that."

"Like what, then?"

"Drake Keys."

"Drake Keys… Keys, Keys…." Luke's eyes widened. "Wait! The guitar player Drake Keys from Midnight Shadow?"

"That would be the one."

Luke stared at the closed basement door. "Holy shit. Um… how—"

"All I know is he came to the exhibition and accidentally ate some of Donna's brownies."

"No!" Shock morphed into a chuckle. "She bakes them strong."

"You're not kidding. Yeah, so I just wanted to keep an eye on him."

Luke snorted. "Is that what you're telling yourself?"

"What's with you and Anna? You two are projecting your own inability to keep it in your pants onto me." Why did everyone make this a perverse thing? "I'm simply being responsible."

Putting his hands out in front of him, Luke smirked again. "I don't doubt you are, and I know you wouldn't do anything while he's high, I'm simply saying you don't usually allow strangers into your space. I find this interesting… that's all."

"Nothing interesting about it," Blaze scoffed.

"Hey, whatever, but I think you've gone off your meds."

"Medication. Ha, I don't even take aspirin." Blaze glared. The Skating Federation would try to kick him out for doping if they could.

"Maybe it's something to consider." Luke chuckled at his own joke. "Let me get him something to wear."

Blaze eyed the prepared sandwiches and put them on a tray. His perverted brother could make more for himself.

Luke bustled back with an armful of options. "Which do you think says rock star at leisure?"

They looked through them and settled on relatively new black sweats, a supersoft gray jersey, and a zip-up hoodie in case Drake got cold.

"Here, take these to your rock star slumber party." Luke added Blaze's usual celebratory indulgent pink-frosted cupcakes to the tray laden with sandwiches.

"I could come back up and share the cupcakes with you." He didn't want his brother to feel left out.

Luke shook his head. "I have one. Go downstairs and enjoy yourself."

"Thanks for the sweats and sandwiches." Once he shut the door, Blaze did something he rarely did—bolted it on his side. Weird desire, since Luke would never invade his privacy... not that he would need privacy, but when Blaze got to the bottom of the stairs, he locked that door too.

He found Drake in the living room, standing there in a towel wrapped around his waist. A sprinkling of chest hair led down, making Blaze want to see where the trail ended. Drake's wet hair waved down over his chest. Beads of water were left on his shoulders, making it impossible not to imagine Drake emerging from the sea as a merman taking his first.... What the fuck troubled Blaze's horny brain? Did he need to get laid that badly?

At that moment, he became concerned for his mental stability. Drake might drive him insane.

"Careful." Drake rushed forward and caught the tray in Blaze's hands, which had started to tilt toward the floor.

"Oh!" Blaze righted the tray.

But a mostly naked Drake in his personal space allowed him to smell freshly showered skin. "Carpet cupcakes don't taste as good as noncarpet cupcakes."

Chapter 6

DRAKE MUST have still been high when he agreed to share the bed with Blaze. Or maybe the siren's call of actually being stationary and lying flat on a cloud-like bed with fluffy soft lavender-scented sheets and plush pillows that—*nah*. After the most enjoyable meal of sandwiches and cupcakes he'd ever had, Drake wanted more of Blaze.

Of course, this wasn't how Drake's fantasy of being in Blaze Parker's bed went. Usually, there'd been the clichéd heavy breathing, accompanied by gasping moans while sheets were twisted. Add lots of fiery french kisses, some well-placed urgent thrusts, and coming to a happy conclusion together. Many condoms should be put to good use… but it was not to be.

Blaze continued to stare at the ceiling and finally cleared his throat. "Um, you have enough pillows? I could borrow—"

"Thanks, I'm good. Two is more than enough." Why did he sound tentative?

No, this chaste nervous conversation took no space in the whiplash ecstasy he played out in his mind, but as he lay there, Drake couldn't think of a place he'd rather be.

He'd suffer being frozen stiff on his side of the bed while trying not to get an erection, making this bizarre, and all for the chance to be near Blaze.

Though being in Blaze's orbit felt like existing in a constellation. Blaze was a stunning magnificent beauty who could perform, but Drake was now getting glimpses that the glitter and sparkle might be real, rather than an illusion, making his desire grow stronger.

Thank God he'd jerked off when he showered. Otherwise, between the pot and the fluid graceful movements of everything Blaze did, Drake might have died from lack of blood to the brain.

Taylor would laugh his ass off if Drake ever told him about this.

Should Drake make a move on Blaze? That question chased around his brain until he got back to square one. They were obviously attracted to each other, but he had no doubt one wrong move would shatter whatever spell had been cast, tethering them together. Maybe Drake should go for it. Maybe he shouldn't....

When no answer came, Drake stared at the ceiling. A night sky had been embedded in the panels with twinkle lights. "Are those actual constellations?"

"Yeah. I did a smaller one as a school project, and when Luke offered to help me do it in here, I thought, why not?" Blaze pointed to a slightly brighter group of stars. "That's Orion. Over by the bathroom is Ursa Minor, and Scorpius is next to it. Cetus the sea monster is near the door to the main space. Those two stars right there are part of Libra. And my favorite is Gemini, right over our heads."

"Why is that one your favorite?"

Blaze dropped his arm and glanced over at Drake. He hesitated but then said, "They're together. Not alone. I guess... I don't know, it's dumb."

"It's not." Drake wanted to reach out and hold Blaze's hand. Instead, he added, "I'm a Gemini."

"I'm a Libra."

Drake smiled. Hmm, the pot really must be leaving his system if he could actually smile beyond a perma-grin. "That fits you."

"What do you mean?" Blaze rolled to his side so he faced Drake and crossed his arms over his chest.

"You're fair, charming, and diplomatic. Libras are driven by love but can hold grudges. And you, I mean a Libra, can be a bit of a flirt."

"What about Geminis?" Blaze's voice was barely above a whisper.

"Geminis can be sociable and are always ready for playtime, but we can get serious and sometimes restless. And we enjoy a good flirt." Did he say that? Taylor would be proud.

"So you're into astrology?"

"Nah, there's just a lot of time on a tour bus. I earned the title of King of Useless Facts." Drake turned onto his side to see Blaze better. The twinkling lights highlighted the various shades of brown and gold in his hair, making it sparkle.

Gone was the confident badass skater who had given a figurative finger to the judges more than once, replaced by the real Blaze—someone who seemed lonely and in need of love and friendship. Or maybe Drake was projecting his wants and needs.

Whoever this was, he smiled at Drake, making the awkward silence become a little easier and the space between them lessen.

Blaze took a hunk of Drake's still-damp-from-the-shower hair and twirled it. "I've always loved long hair."

"It's practical. When I get too hot during the shows I can tie my hair back." Drake kept still so he didn't break the magic that fostered Blaze's touch.

"Plus, it's rock and roll. I love the waves." Blaze chuckled and started to use the ends of Drake's hair to paint invisible swirls over his palm. He sighed. "Mine is pin straight, which is why my stylist cuts my hair like this."

Drake found the courage and followed Blaze's example. He combed his fingers through Blaze's hair and let the strands sift back into place. "Your hair is extremely soft. I've always loved the color. This asymmetric style looks perfect on you."

Blaze raked his fingers through Drake's hair, fanning the strands out over the pillows. The gentle movements translated into a Zen-like contentment within Drake. He wanted to preserve the fragile bubble they floated in.

Their gazes held and then locked. In that moment they were more than just two almost-strangers sharing space. Drake could taste the potential of what could be if….

He scraped his fingernails over Blaze's scalp.

Blaze's breath hitched, and he let out a soft sexy moan. He pressed his lips together, dropped Drake's hair, and muttered, "Sorry."

Trying not to feel the loss, Drake went with no regrets. "Don't be."

The twinkling lights didn't hide the pink tinting on Blaze's cheeks when he cleared his throat. "Um… Anna told me you're no longer in the band."

"Yeah." Drake rubbed a hand over his heart. Misery seeped in as some of the weed drifted out of his system.

"What are you going to do?" Blaze's words were gentle but to the point.

"No clue. After it happened, I drove straight to see you… um, the exhibition, and then accidentally got high. And now I'm in bed with *the* Blaze Parker, Ice Dragon." His chuckle shook his body but got stuck in his throat. "I haven't had a chance to figure out my next move."

Blaze gave him a sad smile and tucked the piece of Drake's hair that fell across his face behind his ear. He brushed a finger across Drake's ear, making his earrings click together.

The tentative touch broke something inside him. Maybe he should ask Blaze for a healing kiss. Even if his mouth worked, he didn't think his brain would know the right thing to say or how to ask.

"I guess I'm not ready to deal with life. Music is… was… my life." How could Dixon and Frank kick him out? He should probably turn on his phone or at least charge the thing.

"Who you make music with might change, but you didn't lose the lyrics or your melody. They're still right here." Blaze pressed his hand against Drake's chest.

The shattered pieces started rejoining themselves at Blaze's tender words and touch. Drake caught his breath. He took Blaze's hand and pressed a tender kiss to his knuckles.

Blaze's eyes widened and his gaze skittered around the room, most likely trying to focus on something other than the affection Drake's expression must be showing. Blaze snatched back his hand and muttered, "Sorry."

"It's okay." Drake had obviously overstepped, though he hadn't misread the longing in Blaze's eyes. His tongue found the lip ring and wiggled the circle.

Blaze licked his lower lip and didn't take his gaze off Drake's lip ring until he cleared his throat and asked, "So you write music too?"

"I don't write music well. I can hear the melody when I put down the lyrics, but usually someone else puts the notes on paper. I can't distinguish all of them."

Blaze nodded. "Yeah, I get that. I don't put together all the parts of my routines alone either. I can see the big picture. I hear the jumps and step sequences in the music, but I need someone to show me how to connect them."

Drake took the opportunity to fan-gush a bit. "I think what you do is nothing short of magic."

Blaze chuckled. "Why are you so nice? Are you, like, campaigning to be the mayor of Nicetown?"

Drake belly-laughed. "What?"

"I know stereotypes are bad, but I didn't expect a rock star to be kind."

"How am I supposed to be?" Not the first time he'd heard that. Sad commentary on his fellow musicians.

Blaze shrugged. "I don't know. I guess rockstarish—arrogant, full of yourself. Instead you're sweet."

"Thanks, so are you." Drake needed to get that out there. For some reason, he felt Blaze might not have heard that a lot. Part of Blaze was the confident Ice Dragon, and the other part Drake imagined hiding in a tree, throwing as many rocks as kisses. Drake didn't mind ducking.

"Ha." Blaze bristled. "I have two moods. I'm glittery sparkle when I perform, but my usual is what Anna calls *dark death mode*."

"I don't believe that. You've been nothing but a wonderful host," Drake pointed out.

"You're easy to be around." Blaze sighed. "I don't usually do people."

Drake wasn't sure what to say, other than to ask, "Why?"

"I don't know. I guess given enough time, people will disappoint and use you, if they can." The bitter edge to Blaze's words told tales on how much hurt he still carried over the wrongs done to him.

"That's a bleak take on the world." Drake wanted nothing more than to change that opinion, but for now he simply tucked the slipped blanket back around Blaze's shoulder.

"See, dark death does fit, but let's not tell Anna. I hate that she's usually right about everything." Blaze gave him a crooked little smile.

It might be crazy, but Drake longed to reach for the stars. His dad said the only regrets are the chances you don't take.

"Are you dating anyone?" Hopefully the fact Drake lay in his bed would mean no, but after Brenda, who knew?

"Nope. I don't date." Blaze rolled onto his back and put his hands under his head. "I mean, why bother? There's hookup apps for my next mistake."

"Next mistake?" Drake frowned.

"Why spend months to figure out it's not going to work? Hookup apps jump to the reason anyone ever gets into a relationship, and you can move on before you hate each other."

The words were harsh, but the tone sliced into Drake's heart, making him determined to prove Blaze wrong. But maybe…. "Are you aromantic?"

"You mean not in need of romantic relationships? No, I just think most people are terrible, the worst, actually. So why bother?"

"But not everyone." *Not me.*

"How about you? Are you in a relationship or looking for your next ex?" Blaze lightened his voice.

Drake shifted to lie flat, folding his arms over his chest. What had he expected? That the guy he'd been jerking off to would want to marry him? Not that he…. He exhaled hard. "I'm not as fatalistic as all that. I'm looking for someone to kiss and—"

Blaze opened and closed his mouth and then snorted, "Kiss?"

"What?"

"If you said you're looking for someone to fuck, I'd have believed you, but to kiss?"

Taken aback by the negativity, Drake needed Blaze to understand. "Kissing can be everything. The last girl I saw wasn't into it, and I missed making out."

"What's so great about kissing? Okay, I guess maybe as foreplay—"

"Kissing is connection. When you press your lips to another's, it's more than just pleasure—you're giving part of yourself to that person. You're sharing yourself with them." Did that make sense?

Blaze frowned. "That sounds terrible."

"Have you ever had a boyfriend?" Drake knew the answer.

"Yeah, and some for almost twenty minutes." Blaze gave him a laugh, which Drake had trouble believing came from a joyful place.

This conversation started to make him feel hopeless. He needed to change gears. "Do you want to get together tomorrow night?"

"Tomorrow night?" Blaze turned his head and stared. His face scrunched up, and he tilted his head and stared at Drake.

"Yes, tomorrow night." Drake didn't hesitate, not wanting to give Blaze too much time to deny them a chance. He forged forward. "Where do you want to do this?"

Blaze opened his mouth, but nothing came out.

Had he mucked this up? He'd never gotten an opportunity to ask a guy out, so perhaps he overthought this and made it sound casual when the date felt anything but. "Well, I know you probably have a special diet—"

"What do you mean by that?" Blaze growled.

What the heck was with the 'tude? "I mean Summer, Midnight Shadow's singer, got me into sushi."

Blaze shook his head. "Look, I'm not into pussy, but your derogatory reference…."

"What?" Was Drake speaking a different language?

"I know you're bisexual, and that's fine, but I'm not into threesomes with women. I did two roommates once, but…. What?"

How could Drake make this better? "By sushi I meant the Japanese cuisine, though I think you jumped to sex."

"Well, that's what we were talking about." Blaze huffed and glared at the ceiling.

"I'm trying to ask you out on a date." Drake enunciated the words just in case his high still lurked and he slurred.

"A date…." Blaze shook his head. "I told you I don't go on dates."

"Well, you can add it to your Never-Done-It list, allow me to take you on a date, and then you can cross it off your list." Drake couldn't give up without a fight. The whole Gemini strong determination was a thing.

Blaze folded his arms over his chest. "Fine."

Win! But…. "Why are you mad?"

"I'm not mad." Blaze made a shitty liar.

"You sure sound mad," Drake teased, hoping against hope to dial this back from the impending cliff of no date.

Blaze sighed. "I hate I misunderstood your intentions."

"I know…. At the risk of changing the subject, you were great today. I've only watched you on YouTube or, you know, streaming the competitions because I'm never near a TV when you skate. But live, you were nothing short of fantastic."

"That's very kind." Blaze gave what sounded like a practiced answer.

"No, I really mean it. You commanded the audience to follow you, and you brought them on a journey, and—Anna asked if I was a stalker." The way Drake gushed, Blaze might think so too. Maybe he should shut his mouth.

"Yeah, she said as much to me. She didn't know why I didn't let her take you to a hotel."

"Why didn't you?"

Blaze's frown would give him wrinkles, but he'd still be the handsomest man Drake had ever seen. "I don't know."

"Yes, you do." Drake grabbed Blaze's hand and held their hands together on the bed between them.

Instead of pulling away like Drake expected, Blaze sighed. "Good night, Drake."

Go big or go home. "So we've got a date?"

"Sure, we can grab dinner." Blaze pulled his hand back and glared at him. "Stop smiling like you've won something."

"I can't, 'cause I totally did." But he restrained the fist pump of victory.

Blaze groaned. "It's just dinner."

"It's a date with Blaze Parker… *the* Blaze Parker…."

Blaze gave him a scowl, but pleased amusement danced in his eyes. "You're still high."

"I am, but not on weed." Drake reached out and reclaimed Blaze's hand. He listened to him breathe for a long while. Finally sleep took him.

SUNLIGHT STEAMING through the long, narrow windows close to the ceiling woke Drake. He rolled over, all alone except for a note on Blaze's side of the bed.

> *D—*
> *Early class and practice.*
> *See you later,*
> *B.*

Blaze had even given his phone number.

Drake would have to go on Yelp or TripAdvisor to find some restaurant options for their date.

But first, the bathroom.

After he used the toilet and washed his hands, he noticed another note on a pile of clothing.

> *D—*
> *Your clothes were dry. I figured you might need*
> *them, and a toothbrush.*
> *Hairdryer and brushes are under the sink.*
> *Have a good day,*
> *B.*
> *BTW I plugged in your cell. It's in the kitchen.*

Drake straggled into the other area. Iceman wagged his tail but didn't move from his bed. He found his phone plugged into a charger next to a croissant with an apple on a plate, silverware wrapped in a napkin, a mug, and another note.

> *D—*
> *There are eggs in the fridge, along with cheese,*
> *butter, strawberry peach preserves, and some blueberry*

jelly. I made coffee so you don't have to drink twigs and
dirt. Use or eat whatever you want. (Though be careful of
the brownies.)
    See you later,
    B

Drake smiled again at Blaze's thoughtfulness as he poured the coffee. Maybe Drake shouldn't make a big deal out of this, but the effort Blaze had made suggested… well, Drake would take it as a good sign.

In the shower, he gave up trying not to jerk off. Maybe Anna had been right and he was a blade bunny. Whatever the title bestowed, he hoped locker room blowjobs were included.

His mind took him to the rink's locker room, Blaze's skintight skating pants pulled down below his tight, rounded ass, giving Drake access to everything. Him on his knees for Blaze, sucking for all he was worth.

After the frustrated innocence of sleeping next to the man he'd most like to have babies with, it didn't take many tugs. He came quickly. Perhaps he should question whether he'd gone full-blown with his apparent ice fetish. Or he just needed to blow a particular ice skater.

He finished his shower, dried off, and dealt with his hair by brushing some of the antifrizz serum he found in the cabinet through the length and pulled the thick mass into a tail. Pulling on his purple boxer briefs, he smiled, imagining Blaze folding them for him. He put on the clean, dryer-soft jeans and T-shirt.

After whistling his way out to the kitchen, he threw the towels and his borrowed clothing in the washing machine and set it to a quick cycle.

Iceman perked up and tottered over for some petting. "Hey, little man. Your daddy left early, huh? Such a good boy you are."

Ice barked. He rushed over to a cabinet, circled to stare at Drake, and barked again.

"Ah, you're doing a Lassie, aren't you?" Drake opened the door, revealing dog food and treats.

He put one little tin of chow in Ice's dish. "There you go. Breakfast is served."

After washing his hands, he pulled together his own breakfast, slathering butter and strawberry peach preserves on the croissant and pouring another cup of coffee.

He picked up his cell and scrolled through the messages. Then he texted his mom and dad.

I'm fine. Decided to take a road trip before I come home.

Drake wasn't ready to deal with the fallout. Maybe he needed to stay off of social media for a while, and stick to texting.

He typed out the entire Brenda saga, including being booted from the band, and to avoid numerous questions, ended with *When I left she was fucking Dixon* and sent the text to Taylor.

Two bites of croissant later, he got a reply. *Fucking Dixon Fox. I always hated him.*

I know.

You deserve better. As horny a fuck as I am, I won't fuck her, and I can soak my detachable cock in bleach....

Taylor didn't have to say the words for Drake to hear them. Drake typed out, *I don't need an I told you so.*

You need to stop settling. No sticking your dick into crazy.

K. I agree. And he did.

So, D, what about the band?

I don't have a clue. Drake wanted time not to worry about it.

You know that's discrimination.

I know. But there's always that clause about participating in actions or activities that negatively impact the band.

Taylor's text came immediately. *This is crazy. You should still talk to a lawyer.*

Maybe. Drake doubted he would.

Where are you?

Speaking of crazy.... *Um... you're not going to believe it.*

Where? You're a fucking rock star. You could be on a plane to Istanbul and it wouldn't shock me.

Drake rolled his eyes, 'cause usually Taylor got on him about not cashing in on rock star perks. Not many of those would be coming his way now.

Taylor sent an impatient text. *You gonna leave a brother hanging?*

Blaze Parker's.

Dots danced, then stopped. Dots danced again, then stopped and disappeared.

Did you get my last text? Drake smirked.

Yeah.

So?

Not even I can imagine how you got there.

After everything went to shit, I saw Blaze was in an exhibition. I had the Uber take me to a rental car place and I drove.

I'm impressed, grasshopper… but how are you at his house?

I ate some pot brownies and he took me home.

How was it? Taylor's gleeful leer could be screamed through the text.

We didn't sleep together. Drake wanted that to be clear.

Okay? (And make sure you read that with a lot of what-the-fuck tone.)

Shut up. He's everything I knew he would be and more.

Oh Lordy, D. You're not serious. Have I taught you nothing? You hit that and move on with a righteous memory.

Ew. I didn't hit anything. Why you got to bring everything down to that level?

It's where I live. Seriously, though.

We slept together, but we didn't have sex. Drake wished he hadn't sent that text as soon as it went.

Having orgasms involving another person is sex.

No orgasm involving him. Or at least not his actual body.

I do not understand you.

Argh! Taylor was being Taylor. *I'm typing in English.*

But the text sounds like gibberish to me. What's the plan? Tay's irritation came through loud and clear.

I don't know, but I asked him out on a date.

A date. You, Drake Keys, asked for a date with Blaze Parker?

Drake smiled at the sound of that. *Yup. Do you think I should do anything different?*

About?

The date. I've never gone on an actual date with a guy before. Only hookups and there wasn't a lot of talking.

How would I know? I don't bang dudes.

You're incredibly helpful.

Taylor sent a cross-eyed emoji with his tongue hanging out. Followed by *Just be yourself. Let him lead. I've got to get back to work. My break is over.*

K. Later.

Ice did a doggy jig on his hind legs, then nosed his dish toward Drake.

"Ah, water." What a smart little guy. "I wish your daddy would ask for what he wants."

Well, if he was taking Blaze out on a date, he needed to wear something other than a T-shirt and jeans. He looked at the door. A set of keys and another note caught his attention.

> *Drake—*
> *Just in case you need to go out. Here's keys to the house. Please make sure the door to the yard is shut and locked. Ice can wander.*
> *Looking forward to tonight.*
> *Blaze*

Drake did a fist pump. Then he cleaned the kitchen, put the clothing and towels from the washer into the dryer, and made the bed. After grabbing his cell and wallet, he petted Ice on the head. "I'll see you later, Iceman."

Ice wagged his tail and curled up in his bed.

Drake locked the door on his way out and then remembered his rental car remained parked at the rink. *Uber.*

After securing the gate, he pulled out his phone and opened the app.

"Hey, you must be Drake. I'm Luke, Blaze's brother. You need a ride?"

Drake waved to the man jogging down the front steps. "I don't want to trouble you. I'm calling for a pickup."

"No trouble. Where are you going?" Luke stopped in front of him with hands on his hips.

"The rink."

"To see Blaze?" The guy sounded optimistic and happy about the prospect.

"Oh, um, I wasn't going to bother him. I wanted to get my rental car."

"I see." Luke's expression dropped to a frown of disappointment.

Drake felt the need to explain. "I want to get something to wear. I'm taking your brother on a date tonight."

"Blaze on a date?" Luke's mouth dropped open, and he stared at Drake like he'd claimed the Pope was getting married. "A date?"

"Well, I mean, he says it's only dinner, but I respectfully disagree."

Luke smirked. "Good. Get in."

Drake was glad to get the seal of approval from someone in the Parker family. He slid into the passenger seat of Luke's shiny green jeep.

After a few minutes of lighthearted brotherly interrogation, Luke asked, "You're touring with Velvet Touch, right?"

"That part of the tour ended." He opted not to go into the whole sordid affair. At some point he'd have to deal with next steps, but right now he had a date to plan.

"What's that like?" Luke's tone suggested he wanted the dirt.

Drake pushed aside the loss. He'd miss everything about touring with Midnight Shadow and Velvet Touch. "Exhausting, insane, and awesome."

"I imagine it's pretty crazy backstage."

"Sometimes… not always… depends who." He'd hate to give Luke the impression he was a player.

At a stop sign, Luke turned to him for a moment and asked, "Tell me, are the rumors true?"

"About?"

They were turning into the rink parking lot. "Velvet Touch's guitar player and singer being together?"

"You didn't hear confirmation from me, but totally." Drake jumped out of the jeep. "Thanks again."

"Aren't you even going to peek on Blaze?"

Drake wasn't sure if he should, but he wanted to see him. "I don't want to bother him."

"Come on. Follow me." Luke led him through the staff door and to a prime viewing location.

He saw Blaze teaching a class of tots.

"Okay. Skate to me and Mr. Panda." Blaze shook a plushie panda bear and waved it at the group.

Two out of the six made the trek on their skates, while the other four were casualties who then decided crawling might be to their advantage.

"On your blades. Up, up, up, up so big."

As if trained in utero, five out of six raised their hands to the ceiling. Mamas and a dadda came forward at Blaze's nod to help their toddlers comply.

"And now we are going to do a trick with your mommies' and daddies' help. Are you ready?"

Screams of yes echoed through the rink.

"Parents, take your skater's hands and support them as we do our big turnaround in a circle trick." Blaze demonstrated by walking his blades in a circle.

When every skater more or less finished, Blaze clapped. "Good job, everyone."

Several skaters slipped over to him to hug him and Mr. Panda. Then a couple of parents talked to him.

"I really do think you're a blade bunny," someone said from behind him. He turned and found Anna staring him down.

"I stopped to get my car."

"Hey, go easy on him. He's taking Blaze out on a date," Luke chimed in.

"A date?" She stared at Luke, then at Drake, then back at Luke. "Blaze agreed to go on a date?"

"Yes. A date. Speaking of which, I should go shopping. Thanks again." Drake slipped out of the rink.

Chapter 7

BLAZE STARED at his phone. The text from Drake said, *Pick you up at 6. I can't wait to see you. Drake*

At five thirty, Blaze started pacing, and Ice followed Blaze's path with his head.

He sighed at his dog. "Oh, Ice. I made a critical error."

Ice gave a mournful whine and tilted his head as if to ask which one.

Now Blaze had all these brain possibilities and craziness skipping through his head. "I should never have allowed Drake in my bed."

At the mention of Drake's name, Ice wagged his tail.

Blaze sighed. "I think you might be biased due to belly rubs. Sure, I mean, Drake is sexy and sweet, but I should have fucked him and sent him on his way today. But no, not me. I'm having dinner with him. What am I expecting?"

Ice joined Blaze's parade of nerves around the kitchen island as if they were going somewhere.

"I keep having all these unauthorized feelings. It's stupid. He's a damned rock star, after all. Though having all of Drake's determination and attention on me, I'll admit it's flattering."

Ice sat at his feet, staring up at him with his adorable puppy-dog face.

"Tsk, I mean that text. *He can't wait to see me.* I'm all up in my head about it. When he probably means he can't wait to have sex, right? Whatever." Blaze grabbed Ice's dish and gave him fresh water.

Ice waited for the return of his dish.

"Besides, this is the first time I'm going to meet him without him high on pot brownies. He's probably an arrogant jerk who'll talk bad about his mom tonight." Yeah, that felt… worse. Blaze returned the bowl to Ice.

Ice took a few laps of water and then joined Blaze's trek, taking his position right behind Blaze in the anxiety march.

"Well, I'm sure once we have sex all these weird anticipatory feelings will dissolve." Why didn't that give him more comfort? "It'll be good to get Drake sorted into the right category."

A doggy happy dance and bark came after Drake's name, echoing what Blaze shouldn't be feeling when he should be taking solace this thing was almost over. They'd have sex and part company.

"I can't harbor fantasies—"

Knock.

He's here! A thrill of excitement skittered through Blaze like he stepped onto the medal podium for the very first time. Ignoring his desire and fear at seeing Drake, Blaze fixated on the fact the guy showed up ten minutes early, which was rude.

He stomped over to the door. Well, he'd tell him— "Luke? Oh, hey."

Guilt slithered over him as he ate the disappointment of it not being Drake.

His brother came in and shut the door. He patted Ice on the head as he studied Blaze. "You look nice. All dressed up for your big date, huh?"

Blaze wore his perfect-fitting black jeans and his favorite gold silk shirt with the top two silver buttons undone… but not because he wanted to impress anyone. They happened to be his favorite pieces. Besides, he wore this since he didn't know where they were going. "It's just dinner. How do you—"

"He's a nice guy." Luke straightened with a disturbing smirk.

"Oh?" When did Mr. NoOneIsGoodEnoughForYou have the opportunity to form an opinion?

"Yeah, I like him. I gave him a ride to the rink to pick up his car. He's down-to-earth and smart. I guess he spends his time playing his guitar, watching science videos, reading, and stalking you."

"Oh?" He searched for other words that would get more information without indicting him as curious, but nothing came.

"Both Anna and I think he'll be good for you."

"Do you, now?" His usual modus operandi of digging in his heels rode Blaze hard.

Luke smirked. "Yeah. About time you went out on a date."

"I go out." Not on dates, but he got what he wanted, which, after all, wasn't that what dates were all about? People could pretend otherwise, but—

"Do I have to spell it out?" Luke crossed his arms over his chest and took on the big-brother tone.

Blaze refused to squirm like he had scratched Luke's jeep going through a drive-through. Though his glare probably screamed Luke should be specific.

"I think you hanging out with someone for longer than it takes to have sex is positive. Drake is a nice guy, and you should give him a chance."

He didn't want confirmation of that, since Luke was a good judge of character, nor did he seek Luke's seal of approval. Blaze growled, "Yeah, well, don't pick out china—"

Knock. Knock. Knock.

Blaze steeled himself, but that didn't stop his heart from mimicking Ice's happy circle dance at the door.

"Who are you picking out china for?" Without waiting for an answer, Drake gave Blaze a peck on the cheek, handed him one of the most sophisticated rainbow-scaled stuffed dragons he'd ever seen—he even had a rainbow ribbon around his neck—shook Luke's hand, and started petting Ice.

"Um… thanks" was all the brilliance that would work its way out of Blaze's mouth.

"Luke, I've always thought simple white china seemed good on the table. Then you could simply change the smaller plates, the chargers, or the table arrangements and linens, giving a fresh dining experience. That's what my mother does."

"A man who knows what a charger is. Explain that to Blaze, would you?" Luke chuckled and patted Blaze on the back. "And remember to invite me to the wedding so I can say I told you so."

"Wedding?" Drake gave Blaze a rock-star grin filled with sin, suggestion, and… more sin. Then he turned to Luke. "I appreciate your optimism and blessings, but let's let Blaze catch up. I don't want to scare him. Once I lock this down, you and I can talk venues."

Venues! Weddings!

Drake and Luke shared a chuckle as Blaze tried to deny this outrageousness by making a noise, which sounded like a cross between a laugh and a wheeze.

Not that he'd ever thought about weddings, forever, or any such, but he'd always seen white tuxes and bouquets of wildflowers on the tables and—

There would be no weddings!

Ice danced in a circle, barking happily like he was offering to carry the rings.

"Have fun," Luke called out as he left.

Staring at Drake didn't help calm Blaze down in the least.

The man could have stepped off the cover of *Guitar Idol* magazine. Drake's hair cascaded down in long waves over his shoulders and tucked behind one ear to highlight his lickable earrings.

He swept his tongue out and toyed with his lip ring, making Blaze want to do the same.

The royal blue jacket Drake wore, which had the arms pushed up to his elbows, was the same shade as his eyes. His indigo T-shirt was paired with tight dark blue jeans, and a shiny pair of boots added to the stunning image he made.

His guitar was the only thing missing, which might be good because that would have puddle-ized Blaze in a heartbeat. Blaze hated that he wanted to be the president of the Drake Keys fan club.

Granted, Drake happened to be gorgeous. No news there, but the comfortable humorous interaction he had with Luke meant Blaze couldn't safely write him off as a pretty face. His stomach felt even more jumpy now than before his first moments on Olympic ice. *Damn.*

Blaze swallowed, searching for words, and then realized he still cuddled the stuffed dragon. "Thank you for him. He's great."

"I thought your dragon might be lonely, and maybe Flame wanted some company."

Did he? Was his loneliness and longing so obvious? No, dammit, he had plans. Didn't he? As long as his ankles held, he'd try for gold again in four more years, and then he'd finally have a life and do all the things he wanted to do.

Between now and then, he'd get his physical needs met, and after, if he found someone he could tolerate, maybe he'd consider seeing someone. "Just 'cause Flame is alone doesn't mean he's lonely."

Drake got the message, if his hands up in surrender counted. "I know. I thought he'd enjoy Smoke."

"Smoke? Oh, the dragon's name." Blaze smiled in spite of the fact that Drake wasn't high but could still charm the pants off him.

"That was the name on his tag, but you can call him whatever," Drake hedged.

"Smoke is a great name. So, new clothing?" Blaze needed to change the direction.

Drake teased his lip with his tongue and then said, "Yeah. Can't take you out on our first date in a T-shirt, borrowed sweats, and a spritz of Febreze."

Well, actually, he probably could and he'd still look too mouthwatering for Blaze's sanity, but he needed to clarify. "It's not a date."

"As you say, but if you call it a date, you can cross it off a never-done-it activity list." Though somehow the smirk on Drake's handsome face told him Drake would consider their dinner now and always a date.

This had to be a mistake! Maybe Blaze shouldn't go.

"Ready?" Drake held out his hand.

Blaze squeezed his new dragon for support. He could do this. After setting the thoughtful gift on the counter so Ice didn't try to hump Flame's new boyfriend, he grabbed Drake's hand. "Yes."

Boyfriend?

He stared down at their interlocked fingers as they walked to Drake's car. The only time he'd held anyone's hand had been to help them off the ice, and well, last night in bed with Drake. But, hmm, this palm-to-palm hand-holding thing felt pretty nice. "Anna said you stopped by the rink during the tot class. Why didn't you say hi?"

Drake rubbed a callused thumb back and forth across Blaze's palm, sending shivers through him, along with a stab of disappointment when he let go and opened the passenger side door. "Didn't want to bother you."

Tamping down the urge to tell him he could have stopped by because Blaze missed him and it wouldn't have bothered him because…. *No, just no.* Instead he asked, "So where are we going?"

Drake drove down the almost-empty streets to town.

"We had talked about sushi. I made reservations for Tsunami, unless you'd rather go somewhere else."

Blaze didn't say *to bed and not to sleep*—even though that destination would have helped him put Drake in perspective and clear the crazy out of his mind. The meal would most likely be delicious, and begrudgingly he might want to probably, possibly, spend a bit more time with Drake before this ended. "Sounds great."

Drake parked the car in the spot right in front of the restaurant, and while he didn't make it around to open Blaze's door, he did reach a hand out. Blaze stared at the offer and almost rejected the kindness, but there was no sense in being nasty, and maybe he enjoyed the novelty of holding Drake's hand. It wasn't a crime.

He allowed Drake to guide him up the stairs to Tsunami's big red doors.

"Mr. Keys. Mr. Parker. Your table is ready. Please follow me," the hostess invited.

Candles and dimmed lanterns lit the stone path through the red room. Bamboo flute music drifted through the speaker system, giving a calming quality to the restaurant's Zen-like atmosphere. The haunting melody made Blaze think of the slow flowing movements he'd use on the ice to interpret the song.

The hostess led them past the other diners to a shadowy back corner housing the most private table, half-hidden by a shoji screen.

Drake held out the chair for Blaze. Before sitting down, Blaze pulled out a chair for Drake, then sat in the one offered.

If the hostess found musical chairs amusing, she had the good grace not to laugh. She handed them the menus and left.

"You don't have to hold chairs or open doors for me." Blaze let his frustration bleed into his tone.

"I know. I simply enjoy taking care of you."

Blaze wished he could escape the tenderness of Drake's words, but they forced him to feel. His brain was becoming gnarled with unauthorized emotion again. Finally he spat out, "You don't have to take care of me."

Drake tilted his head and studied him like there was something to see past his annoyance. "I know. I want to."

Ice would have done a backflip into Drake's lap and exposed his belly. Blaze was not his pushover traitorous puppy, so he glared at Drake.

Drake leaned toward him with a smile. "Feel free to pull out my chair, open my door, and make me coffee any time you feel like it. I rather enjoy someone thinking of me."

Blaze hid behind the menu without really seeing the meals. "What are you going to get?"

When Drake didn't answer, Blaze peeked over the menu and locked stares with the breath-stealing beautiful man across from him. Drake held his gaze for much longer than necessary. "What do you recommend?"

Trying not to shiver, Blaze mumbled, "Luke likes their rolls. Anna likes their bento box dinners."

"And you?" Drake seemed a little breathless, and his dreamy smile did nothing to reinforce this not being a damned date.

Blaze's brain scattered. "Um… everything."

"Good to know."

"Well, I mean, not everything. I have some definite preferences." They might not get very far if Drake thought Blaze would bottom for him.

"And I look forward to exploring every one of your preferences." Drake's heated expression left little to the imagination, and what had been left became filled in by him playing with his lip ring.

Fuck! Why were Drake's words and his tongue stroking his lip ring so fucking hot?

Skating being a conservative sport, Blaze wasn't around many people with piercings. The lip ring drew a person's attention to Drake's full lips, forcing him to imagine what it might feel like. Was it cool like the silver suggested or…. "Hey, how do you take out your lip ring?"

Focusing on the practical usually provided a good defense from sexiness. Though when Drake wiggled his agile tongue about and produced the open ring lying on his tongue, it became no shield from the heat.

Blaze almost whimpered when he failed to push away the thought of how talented Drake's tongue must be to accomplish that task. *Holy Blades of Glory*, he looked incredibly hot doing it. Blaze didn't want to think of what it would feel like being licked by him.

The removal hardened Blaze. "Do you tie cherry stems that way too?"

Drake chuckled as he somehow reinserted the lip ring, hands-free.

"How did you do that?"

"There's just a latch, not a ball. Again, I've had a lot of time traveling between shows."

Blaze couldn't imagine bumping along the highways unlatching a ring with his tongue. "Weren't you afraid of swallowing it?"

Drake shrugged. "It's tiny."

The waitress came over before Blaze could follow up. "What can I get you to drink?"

Blaze didn't know how long he could take this. Why prolong this with drinks, then dinner? "We're ready to order. Right, Drake?"

Drake glanced at him. "Um, sure. After you."

Fine, fine. Blaze ordered the first thing his eyes landed on. "I'll have the teriyaki chicken dinner with vegetables, the house sake, and ice water. Please ask the chef to go extremely light on the sauce."

"Sir?" The waitress turned her attention to Drake, gave him a warm smile, and widened her eyes. Ah, she figured she might have a shot with him.

Well, that didn't play well in Blaze's plan… for the evening.

"I'll have the same, except I'll have a Sprite, no sake. Thank you." Drake hadn't taken his eyes off Blaze, so he might not have noticed the waitress's interest in him or her disappointment.

She sighed but got the hint. "I'll put your orders right in."

"I usually don't do teriyaki because of the salt, or brown rice because of the carbs, but I'm going to treat myself." Blaze had enough time to lose whatever water he'd take on.

"You must have to be careful of your diet."

"To some extent. I watch what I eat, but I've been lucky with my metabolism. The thinner a skater is, the easier it is on the joints and ankles. Though Luke and Anna have always made sure I stay within a healthy range." That was an understatement. At one point, when calorie intake had almost become an issue, thankfully they nipped it before disordered eating occurred or worse took hold.

Drake nodded and leaned toward him. "Good. What is your take on religion?"

Blaze liked the change of topics. "Aren't religion and politics usually off the table for date conversation?"

"Good you're acknowledging this is a date, but I think it's a good filter to figure out compatibility up-front."

Blaze wasn't sure why the information mattered for a quick fuck, but whatever. "I don't do formal religion but consider myself spiritual. You?"

"I'm a recovering Catholic and no longer practicing." Drake's tone suggested there was a story behind his statement.

Blaze wasn't comfortable asking. "Oh."

But apparently that was enough to open up the floodgates of frustration. "I can't participate in something that thinks trans people are unnatural bombs and homosexuality is okay as long as people don't act on it. Not to mention the sex abuse that's gone on, not only unchecked, but purposefully buried. So, you might say me and my family parted ways with the Catholic Church. My parents attend a Unitarian congregation that I haven't checked out yet."

"I'm sorry." He didn't know what else to say to the reality of too many organized religious groups.

"What about politics?" Drake pushed some of his long hair over his shoulders. Blaze wanted to comb his fingers through those strands.

Happy for an easy one, Blaze answered, "I'm Independent. Stances on issues matter to me more than tribe affiliation."

"Me too." Drake grinned. "I think you've already answered the cat-or-dog question?"

Blaze could handle a rapid-fire interview. He'd done countless ones. "Oh, is that actually a question? Hee-hee, it's not that I don't like cats, I just…."

"If you could be any animal, what would you be?"

Bunny must be the wrong answer, even if Drake being so close made Blaze want to try another cuddling hug. Therefore, he went with his pat answer, reinforcing his brand. "A dragon."

Drake smirked as if he somehow didn't believe that to be Blaze's real answer. "I'd be Ice."

"A dog?" Odd choice.

Drake swept his tongue over his full lips, making Blaze's world crash down to only focus on Drake's mouth. What did it feel like to kiss someone with a lip ring? More to the point, what would making out with Drake feel like?

Nodding, Drake clarified, "No. Ice specifically, since he gets to sit on your lap and lick you."

Blaze barked out a laugh. He slapped a hand over his mouth and felt his cheeks heat when he shared, "You don't need to be a doggy to lick me."

Drake's mouth dropped open, and finally the corners of his mouth turned up. "I'll keep that in mind."

Blaze hoped his smirk counterbalanced his blush.

"I know what you've said in interviews about identifying with dragons, but what's the real reason?"

Folding his arms over his chest, Blaze asked, "Why can't that be the *real* reason?"

"Is it?" Drake actually arched his eyebrow and all. Jesus, who was this guy?

Without a clue, Blaze followed his rare need to share. "My mom and dad had given me a stuffed dragon for my birthday the year before they died. The day of my first competition, Luke insisted on bringing Flame so they'd be there in spirit with me."

Reaching across the table, Drake grabbed Blaze's hand. The firm grip settled his grief and allowed warmth to surround him. Everything got a little watery.

Blaze tried to shove the rawness back inside and shrugged. "Luke brought Flame to every competition, and some fans posted a picture of me hugging my dragon. They decided to nickname me the Ice Dragon."

"Fierce," Drake said without condescension.

Grateful for Drake's response, Blaze tried not to sniff when he added, "Anyway, fans eventually started tossing stuffed dragons onto the ice. It was like my mom and dad were raining dragons down on me from heaven. Again, dumb, I know."

"No, it's not." Drake squeezed his hand tighter. "Thank you for telling me."

Blaze shook off the stupid notion that he'd revealed too much with someone he didn't really know. He could only hope the information wouldn't be used against him in the future. Though Drake didn't seem to be the kind to do that, but what did Blaze know? "Um, yeah. When did you start playing guitar?"

"Always. I used to sit on the floor wherever my dad laid his old acoustic and plucked the strings before I could do more than drag it behind me."

Blaze could see the adorableness of that image, and he couldn't help but grin. "I guess you weren't the type of kid who needed to be forced to practice by his parents."

"Nah, they used to have to pry the guitar from my hands so I'd do other things."

The waitress gave Drake his soda. She poured the sake and set it in front of Blaze.

"Thank you," Drake said to her as she left, then tilted his glass to Blaze. "To you."

"To me?" No one ever toasted him unless he won a competition.

"For being absolutely everything I'd ever imagined you to be and more." Drake clinked his glass to Blaze's cup.

Oh.... His desire to kiss Drake took Blaze's breath away. Usually that wasn't the focus of his fantasies, but right now, taking Drake's face between his hands and gliding his lips over Drake's plush mouth rode him hard.

Speaking of riding hard, he'd like to do that too, but for some weird reason the desire to kiss Drake became a higher priority. So weirdly unexpected but kind of nice... kissing... maybe there was something to the whole connection thing.

Blaze didn't know what to say, so he drank the sake. Drake followed Japanese tradition and poured him another cup.

Finally, he was determined to drag the conversation back to the safety of Drake's passion, so he said, "Thank you. Please continue telling me about your music."

Drake studied him, giving him his entire focus. "The chords make sense to me, and music can make people smile."

"You're good at making people smile." Blaze didn't mean to say that aloud. Oops, he needed to be careful if he wasn't going to become enamored. His heart whispered, *You mean, more than you are already?*

"I like making you smile." The words weren't meant as a bold declaration. Drake seemed to be stating a fact.

That was sweet. *No! It had to be a line.* Blaze pressed his lips together.

Drake grinned at him. "You've got so many beautiful smiles."

"What do you mean?" He needed to call bullshit on this immediately. Otherwise he might start to believe this nonsense.

"There's your accomplishment smile when you win." Drake settled back in his chair.

"My what?"

"You know, your ankle is acting up yet you're still able to pull everything together and give an incredible performance."

Did he? Welcome to his life. "Which ankle?"

Drake put his elbow on the table and leaned his face on his hand. "Which year?"

Wow.... "Point taken, but I think we should circle back to you maybe being a stalker."

Drake snorted and waved him off. "There's the rueful smile that you wear when, no matter what you do on the ice, nothing works, but you continue and leave whatever you can give out there. Like two years ago at World's."

Blaze covered his face at the memory. He had hit a chip in the ice and went down, then had problems shaking off the fall. "The Gods of Ice were not kind that day. I didn't even medal."

Drake kept right on with his detailed list. "Then there's your unguarded smile I've only seen since meeting you in person when you talk to Luke or Anna, maybe a couple times last night under the stars."

Blaze caught his breath. God, he shouldn't want whatever this was because—

"There's the patient smile the toddlers in your class get when they have your full attention."

Blaze tried to glare but failed. "Well, you know my smiles or you're full of shit."

"And then there's the one I like the best."

"Which is?" Blaze didn't bother to keep the suspicion out of his voice.

"It's a little shy, like you don't know if you should smile or not."

Blaze would not melt from these observations, but his heart was totally not on board with this assessment. "When do I do that?"

"Right now." Drake reached across the table and ran a finger along Blaze's jaw.

Blaze pulled back and tried to school his face. "Our dinners are here."

As their server set their food in front of them, Drake said, "Saved by the waitress."

"YOU SURE it's no trouble letting me stay here again tonight? I really could get a hotel," Drake offered for the fifth time as Blaze unlocked his door.

"That seems silly. Why would you do that?" Besides, if he stayed, maybe they could fuck a second time, which would be after they rested from the first time. Blaze petted Ice and gave him a treat.

"I guess." Drake set down his guitar and a few bags filled with clothing he'd nabbed from his rental's trunk. "So where can I find the bedding?"

What? Maybe there was a sexy bedroom trick he wanted to do with Blaze. "On the bed?"

Drake chuckled. "No, I mean your extra linens."

"For?"

Drake scrunched his face as he pointed to the sofa. "To make this up for my bed."

"Why would you—I thought—that we would...." Blaze stared at Drake. Weren't they going to have sex, not even one time? Confusion seeped in.

"My father told me if I liked someone, to never sleep with them on the first date." Drake spouting that utter nonsense while being endearingly sweet should be against the law.

Had Blaze hit his head? Maybe he'd accidentally drunk too much sake. "What? I thought you and I…."

Images of holding Drake's hair as reins as he fucked his ass had been taunting Blaze throughout the day. Though during dinner, his wishes-and-needs list had shifted to wanting to taste those lips and to find out how the lip ring felt. Would the silver be cool or body temperature? He longed to hear Drake's pleasured moans of surrender.

"And I hope we will." Drake stepped into Blaze's personal space and smiled at him way too brightly for someone who'd rejected him. He tucked a piece of hair behind Blaze's ear.

The stroke of Drake's finger grazing the shell of Blaze's ear made him shiver with want. God, how could such innocent contact make him hard?

Hope began to—

"But not tonight."

Crash! What the fuck? Blaze bit down his desire for this idiot and tried to be logical. "I want to understand. You want to have sex with me, but you won't because you don't want to have sex on the first date because you like me."

"Basically." Drake nodded as if that was reasonable to him.

Did Blaze join a monastery without knowing? He pointed out, "You slept in my bed last night."

"But not for sex." Drake made that assertion sound perfectly logical.

"You're going to sleep out here while I'm in there." *Having sex with my hand?* This wasn't making sense in Blaze's world. Hell, he had such a nice time on their—at dinner. Why would Drake let a dumb rule stop them from spending quality time together? No, not quality time, fucking. Why would a stinking rule stop them from fucking?

How did Drake get under his skin this deep? Frustration and bewilderment warred within Blaze's mind. Absently he pulled a set of sheets from the bench storage in front of his bed. "Here are extra sheets."

"Thanks." Drake accepted them with a smile, like he wasn't bothered about not sleeping with Blaze at all.

"I guess I'll get ready for bed." *To be in bed alone.* Blaze stumbled into the bathroom and went through his nightly routine. Bathroom, teeth, moisturizer.

How was this even possible? He'd never been turned down for sex, ever.

Soft guitar music seeped under the bathroom door, relaxing him. *No, damn it.* He should be… pissed, not confused and a little bit touched. It wasn't even a date, but fuck it all if he didn't want another.

He marched back into the living room and tried not to notice how beautiful Drake looked sitting there barefoot on the sheet-covered sofa, strumming his guitar without a care in the world. "You do know I can use an app and get laid in thirty minutes, right?"

Drake glanced up at him, and his smile didn't change. "Yeah, but we both know you wouldn't be satisfied."

Why, that overconfident jerk! How dare he be right? "Well, I'm not satisfied right now. So why wouldn't I?"

"You like me." Drake grinned at him as if Blaze's emotional plight was a good thing. The bastard called his bluff.

The denial died long before the lie fell out of his mouth. When did he start liking Drake? Sure, they'd interacted on social media, but—

"What's the difference between a date and a hookup?" Drake strummed a soft tune.

"I know. One makes sure you get off and the other doesn't." Blaze's dick needed to register a complaint.

Drake chuckled. "Good one, but no. A hookup is with someone you can't wait to tell your friends who you fucked. With a date, you can't wait to tell your friends who you met."

"What are you saying?" Lack of orgasm combined with sake might be creating a block in Blaze's ability to use logic to make sense of things.

"I can't wait to tell Taylor about you."

Blaze's frown evaporated even as he tried to keep the grimace in place. The sweetness of Drake would be his downfall and he'd end with a broken heart. But…. "Mind if I hang out with you?"

"I'd like that." Drake patted the seat next to him.

Even if they weren't going to have sex, at least he could listen to him play.

"And I'd like to ask you out for tomorrow."

Another date? "Okay," Blaze's voice squeaked.

Chapter 8

I DON'T know why you don't believe me, Drake texted Taylor.

How could nothing happen? You're both guys.

Stereotype much? Taylor could be totally open-minded, but at times his determination to ride gender norms and expectations all the way to the binary station made Drake crazy.

Whatever. You & Papa Keys' dating rules are very 1850s. The words of the text didn't block Taylor's scoff.

How could he make Taylor understand? *Exaggerate? I really like him.*

No kidding. Look, from all you've said, maybe he's aromantic.

He says he's not. I don't think he's used to dating. That might be an understatement.

This morning, when they'd woken up together on the sofa, twined around each other, Blaze had rushed upstairs to his brother's, making an excuse about needing to exercise with him.

He may see your rule as less about respecting him and more about rejecting him.

I'm NOT rejecting him. Drake couldn't think of a person he'd ever wanted more.

Meet him where he is comfortable.

I could do that. An idea began to form on how he could start their date. *Later, Tay.*

Drake decided to meet Blaze where he usually resided, which might be a risk, but maybe if Drake played in that realm, giving Blaze a little of what he was used to, it might be something to build on.

The basement door cracked open, and Blaze peeked around the corner. He didn't quite meet Drake's gaze. "Um, so yeah… I see you've already showered. If you're done in the bathroom, I guess I'll take mine."

Drake had hoped the distance Blaze put between them would shrink, but without him doing something, it looked like that wouldn't be happening.

"Okay. I'll clean up out here." He folded the sheets, then stacked them and the pillows onto one of the chairs. After putting his cup and plate from breakfast into the dishwasher, he glanced around for something else to tidy.

He gave Iceman a nice ear rub for a bit, and when the sounds meant Blaze had finished dressing, Drake walked outside. Through the french doors, he watched Blaze search the living area and his practice space.

Drake knocked on the door.

Blaze spun around and dashed to the door. "What are you doing outside?"

"Thought I'd start off date two properly." Drake enjoyed Blaze's shy smile, meant just for him. He stepped inside, then shut the door.

"Date two, huh? You still want to go ice skating, then out to lunch?" Beneath the snark a wariness lurked, reinforcing Drake's instinct that he needed to ease Blaze by meeting him at his own comfort level.

"That sounds great."

Blaze huffed out a breath. "Should I even ask how many dates until—"

Drake wrapped his arms around Blaze, dragged him close, and stared into his eyes. "I want to kiss you."

Blaze squeaked, "Okay," as he jumped out of Drake's embrace. He clasped his hands in front of him and stared at the space between them.

The distance yawned like a chasm between two mountains. Drake tried to bridge the gap by taking Blaze's hand. Not wanting him to feel trapped, Drake clarified, "Unless you don't…."

Shifting from foot to foot, Blaze claimed, "No, I want to."

Did he?

Blaze peered at him, and anticipatory excitement flashed past his worried expression, luring Drake to move close enough to feel Blaze's body heat.

"I don't want to go too fast," Drake reassured him.

"You're not. Jesus, we haven't even had sex yet. This is definitely not too fast." Blaze's voice rose.

Somehow a lot of pressure fell onto this single kiss. This was his chance to show Blaze the magical power of a kiss, and it would be their first kiss. The one as a couple you'd always remember.

No matter what, he wasn't going to let Blaze down. He'd pour all his affection and lust into the kiss, and maybe Blaze would understand how much he hoped this would be only the beginning for them.

Drake caressed Blaze's smooth-shaven cheeks, then cupped his face in both of his hands. He tilted Blaze's head a little to the right.

Licking his own lips, he paused in his descent to those lush pink lips to savor his growing anticipation.

Blaze's breath quickened.

He let his breath mingle with Blaze's minty exhale and went hard from relishing the potential. Shared air passed between them in a way almost more intimate than a kiss.

Blaze pushed closer, his light aftershave enticing Drake to act.

Drake wrapped an arm around Blaze, and a tremor ran through Blaze, but he remained pliant.

Sweeping his tongue along his lips, Drake made them wet for what he hoped would be the best first kiss ever. He traced his lips over Blaze's, barely touching him, until Blaze whimpered.

Drake couldn't take the temptation a second longer and pressed their lips together.

Sparks flashed between them like the first explosive notes of a rock anthem. He dropped his hands to Blaze's waist and hauled him closer. The rub of Blaze's hardness against his own created a delicious friction.

A soft needy moan escaped Blaze and burrowed into Drake's soul, making him want to give Blaze everything he desired. Those expressive hazel eyes widened and then slowly slid shut as Blaze parted his soft lips, offering Drake more.

No longer hiding his intensity, he kissed Blaze like he owned him.

On a whimper of surrender, Blaze tangled tongues with him.

Yes! Thrilled Blaze didn't retreat, Drake guided him toward the chair and teased a finger over the bulge in Blaze's jeans. A desperate gasp rewarded his efforts. "How about I start our second date by answering your original question?"

Thrusting his hips, Blaze groaned with lustful confusion that excited Drake. "Question?"

"How many dates until…?" He let the potential reply hang over them as he tantalized with his fingers along Blaze's zipper again.

"Oh God." Blaze shifted restlessly against Drake.

Gliding his lips over Blaze's, Drake teased his fingers along the bulge behind Blaze's zipper.

"That kiss makes me believe you could really be mine." Drake ghosted tender kisses on his neck.

"What? I'm not yours," Blaze sputtered. He panted, but Drake couldn't tell if he was turned-on beyond his erection or if he was looking for an escape.

"Not yet." Drake shared what lurked in his heart as he traced his lips over Blaze's jaw.

Blaze offered his neck to Drake's mouth. "There's nothing to hope for unless it's sex you want. I'm good at that. I can give you that."

"Blaze." Drake relished his name as he grazed his teeth along Blaze's neck.

"No, Drake. There's nothing for me to give you other than an orgasm."

Drake heard Blaze's statement as a challenge. Blaze played the part of the untouchable ice prince to perfection.

"Bite." Blaze pressed his neck against Drake's teeth.

He nipped along the column of Blaze's neck, licked over his Adam's apple to finally tease his tongue against Blaze's pulse point.

"Please," Blaze gasped.

Moaning, Drake gave him what he wanted and bit down on his neck. Blaze's knees buckled, but Drake tightened his arms around him and held him upright.

"I don't know what I'm going to do with you, Drake."

Deciding clarity would be best, Drake explained, "I know exactly what I'd like to do with you."

"What's that?" Blaze's voice was filled with seductive suggestions.

"Take you in my mouth and suck on you until I make you come. Then I'm going to swallow."

Blaze's mouth dropped open, but nothing came out. He squeezed his eyes shut.

Assessing the reaction, Drake added, "Unless you don't want me to."

Blinking his eyes open, Blaze shook his head. "I've never... I haven't...."

Full stop. "Haven't what?"

His honeyed brown eyes widened as Blaze admitted, "I don't.... I haven't. Only topped."

All of the countless encounters Blaze'd had, but no blowjobs? Pieces began to fall into place. Blaze hadn't been embellishing his lack of boyfriend activities. Hate for Trent Richards multiplied in Drake's heart.

He squeezed Blaze's shoulders, hoping to get him to look into his eyes. How did you get someone to believe in you? He'd take his cues from Blaze. "Blaze?"

"I never wanted to make anyone feel the way I felt." Blaze folded his arms over his chest, hugging himself.

"We don't have to…. I didn't think—" Drake started to backpedal harder.

Blaze stared at him and then shook his head. "No, see, um, I want to… with you. I know I shouldn't, but… I thought you should know."

The admission cost Blaze. Vulnerability and worry fought for dominance in his expression.

"So you'd like me to—"

"Yes." Blaze added a nod.

Drake dropped to his knees and glanced up at Blaze. "You tell me if I do anything you don't want or don't like."

Blaze put a hand onto Drake's shoulder. "Wait… um—"

"What?" Drake stopped trying to unbutton Blaze's jeans.

"Maybe you shouldn't do this, because I'm not ready to do it back." Blaze's voice cracked as he frowned.

"I never expected you to." Blowjobs were great but never an expectation. If anything, the whole idea of a returning-the-favor type of thing was kind of gross to Drake. It should be natural and loving and not a forced obligation.

Blaze squinted his eyes and tilted his head. "But then why?"

"Why would I want to blow you?" That couldn't be Blaze's question, could it?

"Yeah, I mean, why would you want to do that? I'm not doing anything for you, so what are you getting out of it?" Blaze's tone held skepticism laced with disbelief.

Drake didn't even know how to approach that sad mind-set. The belief had to have been formed in tremendous amounts of hurt and shame. He went with honesty. "I want to make you feel good."

"Oh." Blaze's cheeks tinted a deep red, and he didn't meet Drake's gaze. "I guess… it's stupid. I didn't even think of that."

"It's not." Drake shook his head. It was heartbreaking that Blaze couldn't imagine someone simply wanting to make him happy. "I'm sorry I wasn't more careful with my words."

Blaze scoffed. "Who would imagine someone getting weird about receiving a blowjob?"

Drake ran his hands along Blaze's thighs, not to stimulate but to comfort. "Hey, it's a big deal for you to let down your guard like this."

Blaze sighed, but there was no denial forthcoming.

"We can go directly to lunch," Drake offered.

"Oh… um, yeah…."

"Unless you want me to?" Drake licked his lips as he stared up, hoping Blaze would give him the go-ahead.

Blaze shifted restlessly. "If you're still offering, I really do want you… to."

"I definitely do." The trust being placed in Drake made him feel weightless and made his fingers tremble.

Blaze wiggled his hips side to side as Drake worked the jeans and black silky underwear down to knee level.

His dick jutted out from a nest of neatly trimmed pubic hair. Blaze was probably about average-size, but his slender frame made his cut cock appear huge.

Drake blew a stream of warm air against Blaze's shaft.

"I think I should sit down." Groaning, Blaze shivered and sat.

"Please." He pushed Blaze's shirt out of the way. Out of the corner of his eye, something on Blaze's upper thigh drew Drake's gaze. "A tattoo? May I taste?"

Blaze nodded.

Drake outlined the colorful rainbow dragon on skates with his tongue, and then he joked, "The reds, oranges, yellows, greens, blues, and indigos all tasted the same."

A snort and a hand in his hair told him Blaze was amused.

When Drake finished playing lick-the-dragon, he couldn't prevent a smile as he concentrated on Blaze's cock.

The tip glistened with anticipation of Drake's attention. "May I?"

Blaze gasped and tried to exhale, but only a wheeze came out. He gave a jerky nod. "Are you really going to…?"

The catch of uncertainty in Blaze's voice made the affection growing in Drake's heart expand. Boundaries and time frames were smashed. Keeping his intense feelings to himself, Drake blew another gush of warm air over Blaze's throbbing cock.

Blaze shifted closer to Drake's mouth.

"Yeah, I'm going to suck you off." Time to live out a fantasy. Even though they weren't in a locker room, this was still Blaze Parker.

"God, yes." Blaze exhaled hard.

The longer Drake stared, the wider Blaze's eyes became until finally the message flicked a switch, because Blaze's expression softened, and he ran tender fingers through Drake's hair.

Drake inhaled Blaze's amber bath gel and his excitement and then blew yet another stream of air over the tip of Blaze's cock.

"Oh." A long-suffering moan echoed through the space as Blaze pushed forward, giving Drake more access.

Ducking his head lower, Drake swiped his tongue over Blaze's balls. Adding plenty of spit, he teased his tongue across Blaze's sac. In long, wet licks, he trailed his tongue around the root of Blaze's cock.

Blaze's head knocked against the back of the chair as he gasped.

Encouraged, Drake lashed his way along Blaze's shaft until he reached the crown. He circled the tip with quick flicks of his tongue.

Hissing, Blaze tossed his head back and forth, but kept his gaze fixed on Drake.

I'm the first to give him pleasure like this. The truth gut-punched Drake. Blaze never having the selfish pleasure of someone's mouth on him was miserable, but humbling that he allowed Drake to give it to him.

He trailed his tongue down to Blaze's balls in one long lick, then dragged back to the tip.

Drake, who'd never had much opportunity to give head, would be Blaze's first in this one thing. The trust, which wasn't easily given, weighed a million pounds while making Drake feel as light as air.

Determined to make this great for Blaze, he used every skill he had and some he'd only seen in porn. He wanted to kneel between Blaze's knees and worship his cock for hours to convey how much he cared.

The soft mews of Blaze's building pleasure grew more perfect than any music Drake had ever made, and served as a warning that Drake had only a couple of minutes.

He swiped his tongue across the top of Blaze's cock, collecting the precum droplet there, moaning as he finally tasted the essence of Blaze.

Another drop appeared and Drake licked again, relishing the sweet saltiness.

Blaze dug his fingernails into the arms of the chair as he let Drake tease his cock. He writhed in his seat but asked for nothing.

Drake almost begged Blaze to ask him for whatever he craved, whenever he needed it. But until he could, Drake would try to give him what he thought Blaze wanted.

He wrapped his fist around Blaze and gave him a stroke.

Thrusting, Blaze hissed, "Yes."

Drake slid his mouth over the top of Blaze's cock and licked at the little circumcision scar.

Attention to that bundle of nerves pulled sexy whimpers from Blaze. Then he locked his lips together and remained silent.

Drake longed to listen to the music of appreciation Blaze made, so he whispered, "No, please. Let me hear you."

Enough teasing—Drake started sucking him off for real.

Blaze trembled and inched forward even more in the chair. He hooked one leg around Drake's back and secured him.

God, Drake had always loved giving a blowjob. The taste and feel of cock on his tongue. The familiar rush of power that he made a man helpless and dependent on the skill of his mouth to bring him pleasure. The total surrender when the man shot off in his mouth.

But having Blaze in his mouth took the activity to another level. Tasting and touching Blaze with his tongue… it passed incredible and entered the realm of indescribable.

"Oh God. I can't control this." Blaze whimpered and trembled but allowed Drake to go at his own speed.

Drake's mouth filled with saliva as he plunged down, sucking Blaze halfway to the root and dragging his lips back to the top. He tugged Blaze's tightening balls away from his body in rhythmic pulls and jerked him off with the other hand right into his mouth.

"So good. I've never…." Blaze's eyes glazed over, appearing lost in a sea of sensation and lust, but yet he watched every suck, lick, and stroke. His fingers were uncoordinated, but never once did he tug Drake's hair or try to force him to go faster or deeper.

For all the adoration Blaze received, it was directed at what he did on skates. Did anyone ever pour affection over him just because?

More affection burst in the region of Drake's heart. This man….

Panting, Blaze simply absorbed every touch Drake gave him.

Gorgeous and gentle, Blaze's tone changed into sex-filled begging moans. "Drake. Oh. Drake."

Drake set about to bring satisfaction to what Blaze craved. He sealed his mouth around him and sucked while moving his lips up and down in time with strokes from his hand.

Blaze shivered and then froze. "Drake. Yes. God, yes. Drake."

Everything became a sensual blur as Blaze filled Drake's mouth with his warm cum. Drake continued to suck and stroke him through his orgasm, timed with the pulses he shot.

When Blaze sagged into the chair, Drake licked him clean, trying to pull air into his lungs.

Yes, this was exactly what Drake had wanted to give him. Sitting back on his heels, he grinned at the completely relaxed and peaceful Blaze. He had done that. Drake was equal parts happy and proud, and maybe a bit astounded.

Blaze tugged him into an unexpected hug and whispered, "Why?"

"I wanted to make you happy." And maybe he wanted to show him how he felt. Drake melted into him.

"You did. You really did." Blaze released him from his death grip.

Drake wiped his mouth on the back of his hand and could feel the tension in Blaze return and start to percolate. Trying not to look at a Blaze sans bottoms, Drake said, "If you want to get dressed, we can head out."

Blaze stood on unsteady legs and wiggled his pants up to his hips, then zippered them. He studied Drake with a tilted head. "Um, a… what about you?"

"I'm good." No one ever died from an unsatisfied erection. Besides, Blaze needed to be convinced Drake wasn't going to use him.

Blaze's mouth dropped open, and he stared at Drake through squinted eyes. "What do you mean you're *good*?"

"What I said." Drake leaned in and pressed a kiss to each of Blaze's pink cheeks. "Shall we?"

"I don't get you," Blaze grumbled. He stepped into his shoes and held the door for Drake. Once they were outside, Blaze locked up and followed Drake to his rented car.

Drake opened the rental's passenger side for him and shrugged at the semiconfused glare Blaze directed at him. He shut the door once Blaze settled in.

Blaze reached over and unlocked the driver side. Oddly touched by the gesture, Drake cleared his throat and said, "Thanks."

He headed down the street, remembering where to make the one and only turn to the rink. "Um, why do you keep staring at me? Do I have breakfast on my face? Or am I going the wrong way? Or—"

"No, I… I can't believe you did that." Blaze shook his head.

"Did what?" Was Blaze really so freaked out by affection?

"You know. And then you *really* didn't even expect me to do anything back." Blaze sounded put out and even more mystified.

Drake sympathized as he pulled into the skating rink parking lot and found a spot right next to the door. "Like I said, I wanted to make you feel good."

"Mission accomplished." Blaze jumped out of the car.

The parking lot was empty. Shit! The sign said the rink had closed for the next two hours. "I should have checked the hours."

Blaze grinned. "It's fine. I have rink privileges."

Chuckling, Drake teased, "Oh, you win Olympic medals and you get what you want?"

"Not everything." The leer combined with a bit of come-hither made Drake's unattended-to parts throb as the *yet* hung in the air between them.

Once inside, Blaze led him to the rental shop. He hopped over the half door, looked at the bottom of Drake's boots, and handed him some skates. "Here. Put these on while I get mine out of the locker room."

Drake pushed his feet into the skates. He started lacing his left foot and stopped once he got halfway to the top and tied a bow. *Good enough.*

Blaze appeared with his skates on. Drake hadn't even gotten his second skate finished.

"Um… why did you stop halfway with the laces?" Blaze had his arms folded over his chest like there was a serious violation happening.

"I don't want them too tight." Drake shouldn't have to point out the logic to a skater.

Shaking his head, Blaze dropped to his knees and started retying Drake's skates.

Drake tried to ignore what the position conjured in his horny mind. He licked his lips, still tasting Blaze's cum.

Blaze tied Drake's left skate, then the right, and finally proclaimed, "There."

"Ow, Blaze. Are you sure skates should be this tight?" Drake couldn't help but whine.

"They should be one size smaller than your shoe size. As long as the boot isn't pinching and is giving your ankle firm support, yes, they should be that *tight*." Blaze stood, grinning as he pulled Drake to a standing position.

Drake wobbled. He clutched on to Blaze.

"Have you ever been on the ice before?"

"Um, a friend's birthday party?" Blaze's scrunched-up face made Drake confess, "I was six. I fell and my dad took me home."

"You're going to be fine. Walk around on the mat a bit. Get a feel for the skates." Blaze peeled Drake's fingers off the wall and sent him on a circuit around the benches.

He didn't feel stable, but he could balance.

Blaze drew an imaginary arc. "You have two edges on the blades. Inside and outside. When we hit the ice, you'll bend your knees slightly and stay on the inside edges. Let's try this."

But the mat was so comforting. Drake sighed and tried not to suggest they remain on the rubber haven.

Blaze slipped off his skate guards and glided onto the ice. He did a quick turn, and returned to stand in the entranceway. "Step onto the ice and use the boards to stabilize yourself."

Drake followed his instructions.

"Great. Now let go, put your arms out, and bend your knees."

"Argh! How?" *Was he crazy?* Drake latched on to the railing tighter.

"Keep your middle centered over the skates."

Drake pinwheeled his arms a little and then grabbed back on and stabilized somehow. "Oh. I got it."

"Nice, now use your right foot to push yourself forward to me."

He'd become addicted to the railing in the short time he'd been introduced to the ice. "That means I'll have to let go."

"Yes." Blaze admirably kept a straight face.

"Or I could live here."

Blaze snorted. "Come on, you're doing great. Now put your arms out and bend your knees."

"Look, I'm doing it!" Drake was very pleased with himself.

"Yes, you are. Well done."

"I think if balancing became an Olympic sport, I'd be a contender!" Maybe Drake shouldn't say that out loud—he might jinx himself.

"You got this. Time to try marching."

"What? No. I'm a balancer. See?" Drake saw no reason to change since he'd perfected this skill.

Blaze laughed. "And you're great. Take baby steps toward me."

"Oh my God, I can't." There was no way that would be happening. He'd face-plant for sure.

Holding his hands out, Blaze said, "Yes, you can. Trust me."

The word hung between them.

"It's all about trust." The lightbulb over Blaze's head went off, and his eyes expressed a new understanding of what he'd asked Drake to do.

"How about we both try to trust each other?" Drake wasn't willing to give away the opportunity to bring his agenda home.

Blaze took his two hands and squeezed. "Deal."

Chapter 9

"GOD, YOU make me laugh," Blaze got out between gasps for air. All through his lunch with Drake, he found himself smiling, laughing, and happy. Drake regaled him with stories of the tour, his childhood, and his best friend.

Drake gave him a heart-stopping crooked smile that made affection seep into Blaze. "I'm glad someone appreciates my stories of—"

His cell vibrated.

"If you want to get that…," Blaze offered.

Drake turned over his cell and grinned. He showed a picture of a middle-aged woman holding a balloon bouquet and a big sign that said "We love you, Drake" written in rainbow colors. "It's my mom. If you really don't mind, I probably need to let her hear my voice, because apparently texts don't confirm that I'm alive."

"Sure. Sure." Blaze gestured for him to take the call.

Drake kissed him on the cheek and stepped away from the table so he wouldn't disturb other diners.

Blaze traced his fingers where Drake's lips had brushed across his cheek. How could such a small gesture mean so much to him?

Jealousy of Drake having a living, breathing mother quickly transformed into feeling pleased for him still having parents around to love him with balloons.

Drake paced in front of the restaurant, laughing and talking to his mom like they were good friends. Once again, Drake's persona refused to allow Blaze to categorize him as anything other than terrific.

How fucking frustrating! Blaze should be filing him away like he'd been able to do with every other encounter, but his heart whispered that Drake wasn't like any of his one-time hookups.

That kiss….

Holy hell. That had been an epic first kiss. How could the press of lips and licks from Drake's tongue melt Blaze's mind? Granted, he didn't have many—okay, any—real make-out sessions to compare to the kiss, which made a lot of weird feelings happen. He didn't want to name the emotion as affection, though he might *like* Drake.

This was a disaster! To like Drake, who selflessly blew him, simply asked for trouble.

Oh, but the blowjob. He didn't want to even get started on Drake's mouth and how the gentleness made him feel, but the word "cherished" bounced around his brain anyway.

Again, he didn't do feelings, but right now he was drowning in them.

Fuck! Cherished? That wasn't something he'd ever attached to sex, or anything, before. Why couldn't Drake have demanded Blaze return the favor? Then he could have resented him and been done with all this, but no. No! Drake had to be gracious and shit, and didn't that muddy the situation?

Other than family, no one gave without expecting something in return.

Trust. Blaze had agreed that he'd try to trust Drake, but holy fuck, he didn't realize the obstacle course his brain had organized to keep him from doing that. His procedures of never getting too close reinforced his walls and always felt like a perfect barrier between him and heartbreak.

Drake grinned at him through the window and waved.

Blaze smiled back.

Goddammit, now those walls were cracking, especially in the region of his heart?

Something needed to change in this insane dynamic.

Blaze handed their passing waiter his credit card. He knew exactly what he had to do to stop all this foolishness.

"WHAT DO you mean you *should* blow me?" Drake's twisted expression looked like Blaze had suggested he shove a firecracker up his ass right here outside the café.

"Exactly what I said." Wasn't he clear? Blaze fought against seven years of protocols and protections he established to get that question out. Drake should be courteous enough to hear the offer of head when it was given.

Drake scrunched his face as if he tried to assess Blaze's intentions. "Do you even *want* to do that?"

Did he? His instinct told him no, he shouldn't! The humiliation of what Trent did to him rushed to the surface. Him on his knees offering himself to his crush and being used and ridiculed across the internet for that trust.

But fuck, if his shitty experience would force him to forego giving Drake pleasure…. Wasn't it time to let go of the past? Besides, this blowjob would even things up between them so Blaze could alter his perspective and his wayward feelings would realign.

Glancing over at the gorgeous man, he couldn't deny the cock he longed to suck was Drake's.

"Yes, I want to." He freaking gagged for Drake with a disturbing desperation.

Drake took his hand and pressed a kiss to the knuckles. "Why don't we go back to your place and see where things go?"

He could do that. Though he needed to set the right expectation. "I don't bottom."

Shrugging, Drake grinned. "Perfect. Just so you know, I do."

The ease with which Drake agreed worried Blaze. "Why?"

Drake opened the door for Blaze and kissed him into his seat. The kiss had started soft and gentle, then stoked the embers that burned at the surface to fucking smoking hot.

Going from agitated to horny in the time it took Blaze to get his ass on the seat must be a record. Goddamn! It must be the man's lip ring, highlighting how delicious his mouth and tongue felt.

Deepening the kiss, Blaze wreathed his arms around Drake's neck. Trying to pull Drake into the passenger side with him didn't quite work.

Drake stepped back. His hand partially hid the small smile that turned up the corners of his mouth. "I don't want to stop kissing you, but we shouldn't do this here."

Blaze glanced around. Shit, they were in the middle of town, on Main Street, and he had been ready to have at him. He promptly buckled his seat belt. "Point taken."

Jogging around, Drake slid in behind the wheel and pointed the car in the direction of home.

The kissing haze started to vanish, allowing some reason to return to Blaze's brain. "So why do you like bottoming?"

Of course, Blaze had never done it. The whole thing looked rather painful, but the men he'd fucked seemed to enjoy taking his dick well enough.

Drake gave him a glance and then pulled out of his parking spot. "There's something about letting someone that close to me that I... I don't know. It feels great and I just like it."

"Have you done it a lot?"

Shaking his head, Drake clarified, "Some. A few times."

"So usually you're with women?" *Bisexual my ass! Drake is probably straight but likes to be fucked every so often. Though usually the heteroflexible don't enjoy kissing and touching a guy the way Drake does.*

He shrugged. "So far that's how it's worked out."

"Have you ever been in a relationship with a guy?" Relationship? What the hell kind of question was that, and why the fuck did Blaze want to know the answer so bad?

Drake frowned and gripped the wheel tighter as he turned down Blaze's street. "I haven't found a lot of guys interested in more than a fuck, and then with the tour, relationships are usually impossible."

"You'd be interested in more than a fuck with a guy?" Blaze didn't keep the disbelief out of his voice.

Glancing quickly at Blaze, Drake nodded. "Absolutely."

Blaze folded his arms over his chest. How could he...?

Drake gave him a smirk that twisted Blaze's insides. "If I haven't been clear, I like you, and I want to get to know you better."

What in the fuck was this?

Blaze worked on shutting his mouth, yet he muttered, "Don't you understand the concept of hard to get?"

"Sure, but I don't play games. I enjoy spending time with you." Drake was completely unapologetic, in that honest way of his that confounded the fuck out of Blaze.

"Why?" The question fell out of Blaze's mouth, highlighting his insecurities and doubts.

Drake pulled into the driveway. "You're fun, funny, sexy, sweet, intelligent, clever, loyal, and independent."

Ice slipped out the doggy door and into the yard, barking greetings to them on the other side of the fence.

Blaze sat in the car until Drake opened the door. He hated to admit it, but he liked the unfamiliar feeling of someone taking care of him.

After opening the gate with care, Drake caught a flying Ice and nuzzled the dog's neck. "And you have the world's greatest dog. Right, Iceman, right?"

Ice licked Drake's face, then wiggled to get down. As soon as his paws hit grass, he barreled over to dance and bark in front of Blaze.

Kneeling down, Blaze scratched him behind the ears and exchanged doggy kisses. "I missed you too, Ice."

Ice barked once and ran off to patrol the perimeter of the fence.

Blaze opened his french doors and let Drake in.

Whoosh! His back hit the wall, and Drake pushed flush against him.

Blaze traced his tongue along Drake's mouth. Teasing, maddening little licks sought to drive him insane.

After slamming the door, he manhandled Drake into the love seat.

"God, you're strong," Drake mumbled. Blaze shoved him down flat on his back.

Pride flared through Blaze. He always enjoyed kicking down stereotypes that his smaller stature meant he couldn't control a larger man.

Blaze slid over Drake's body to get to those taunting lips. Pressing his mouth to Drake's, he might have growled because the kiss wasn't enough. He had started to crave things he swore he'd never want, like needing to swallow Drake's pleasure.

When Drake's lips parted, it only encouraged Blaze to swipe his tongue into Drake's mouth. Tasting the sweetness made Blaze's desire for full possession rage.

He skimmed his hands under Drake's T-shirt along his sides and up to his nipples. Blaze circled them with his fingertips, which seemed to ignite Drake.

"Please." Drake arched his back, pushing his chest at Blaze.

Blaze yanked the offending barrier of the T-shirt out of the way and firmly licked the dark red nipple closest to him.

Groaning, Drake begged, "Bite."

Ignoring the request, Blaze kept circling his tongue around the dark rosy tip. Maybe he enjoyed being contrary, but he loved the feeling of power flowing through him. Drake under him, begging and ready to lose his fucking mind.

"Blaze," Drake groaned.

Taking pity, Blaze used his teeth to give him a nip.

"Oh yeah." Drake held Blaze's head against his chest.

A new excitement ripped through Blaze. He had never played with anyone this way before. There was something enthralling about Drake's helpless reactions to him. He took Drake's nipple between his teeth and ever so slowly tightened his jaw.

Drake writhed, breathless and restless. His hardness teased Blaze, and it was as if Drake searched for something only Blaze could provide.

He bit again, then licked the bitten peak. Trailing his tongue to the other nipple, Blaze circled the peak, laving the point with his tongue, and gave him three nips until Drake trembled in his arms. Sucking the point into his mouth, Blaze caressed the abused nipple while Drake twisted beneath him.

Blaze longed for more but wanted to stay in control. He had offered a blowjob, but God, making Drake surrender delicious raspy cries excited him. He needed to focus.

Crawling along Drake's torso, he got close enough to whisper, "Can I suck you off?"

Drake pulled back. "You sure?"

"Yeah. I hear if someone keeps sucking, eventually the suckee gets off," he snarked. He could do this if he minimized how important being with Drake had started to feel.

"Ha-ha. You know what I mean." Drake traced a gentle finger down his face, being way too tender, and gave him a sweet kiss on the mouth.

"Yeah. I wanna." And he really did. The thought made him nervous as hell but excited. He needed to share this with Drake. Grabbing Drake's finger, Blaze sucked the digit into his mouth.

Drake's pupils had blown huge, chasing the intense blue to the outer circle of his iris.

Pulling his mouth off Drake's finger with a noisy pop, Blaze whispered, "I want to make you feel good."

A number of emotions washed over Drake's face, all of which made Blaze uncomfortable because he might be feeling some of them too.

"Stop acting like it's a big deal. This is only a blowjob. Hell, I've done reach-around hand jobs plenty of times, so this isn't much different. Right? I'm simply adding my mouth." There, that sounded normal.

Drake raked his fingers through Blaze's hair. "Have you ever given head since…?"

Blaze grimaced, not wanting to relive that, but he needed to make it sound like less of a deal. "No. Usually the guys I meet want to be fucked."

"I'm sure they did, but I want you to do what you want." Drake scraped his fingers against Blaze's scalp, raising feel-good goose bumps. He tugged Blaze into a quick kiss.

Maybe Blaze should stick to fucking. He pressed his hips against Drake one more time to enjoy the friction against his dick. No, a blowjob would even things up, so he rolled off Drake.

On unsteady legs, Blaze stared down at Drake sprawled out in his living room.

Holy hell! Drake's long hair fanned out over the pillows and arm of the love seat. His shirt was rumpled and pushed high on his chest while his jeans strained at the zipper. His lips had become puffy and red from Blaze's kisses. Fuck, if he didn't look every bit the rock star his pictures on Instagram suggested.

Blaze longed to please him, craved sucking on him way too much. Not wanting to overanalyze and make this into something more than an attempt to right his equilibrium, he quit staring.

"Stand." Blaze wanted to be gruff, but his voice came out all soft, so he pulled Drake into a sitting position, then tugged him until he stood next to him. Drake was at least a head or so taller than Blaze.

Blaze eased Drake's shirt off the rest of the way. He dropped the fabric while getting lost in the depths of Drake's gaze.

God! Drake stood there like a confident rock god ready to do Blaze's bidding.

Endless emotions swirled in a tidal wave, threatening to pull Blaze under, but then Drake laced their fingers together and smiled down at him.

That was it. Calm, cool clarity seeped in. Blaze could do what he wanted without judgment. Right now, he wanted to mark Drake as taken, even if it was only as temporary as a hickey. Making the bruise would feel good, if he could ignore how unsettling the idea of Drake slowly fading away made him.

Blaze concentrated on action, went onto his toes, and trailed kisses along Drake's neck. On a moan, Drake twined his arms around Blaze and bent closer.

Grazing his teeth over Drake's pulse point, Blaze teased his tongue back and forth. He dragged his teeth across the spot until Drake pressed into the nip, requesting a bite, which he gladly delivered.

"Oh, Blaze," Drake wheezed out and shivered.

Blaze sucked a mark onto his neck.

"Mmm, yeah." Drake wrapped his arms around him tighter, almost lifting Blaze off the ground.

Taking that as a wish for more, Blaze marked his collarbone again and again.

Drake ran his mouth along Blaze's jaw and bit gently on his chin, as if asking permission to lay claim to Blaze and mark him.

Blaze tilted his neck and bit his own lip to prevent begging. He quivered when Drake's tongue was replaced by his lips. Incredible suction that went directly to his cock surely marked his neck, thrilling him. "More."

Drake sucked on his neck until Blaze's fingers trembled as he unbuttoned and unzipped Drake's jeans.

"You sure?" Drake whispered.

Blaze settled onto his knees, ran his hands up Drake's thighs and around to his ass to give it an appreciative squeeze. *Nice!*

Then he dragged every scrap of clothes below Drake's waist to his feet, and peeked at Drake through the curtain of his hair. He wanted to see what lay beyond the barriers he created.

With tender touches, Drake tucked Blaze's hair behind his ears. His erection stood at attention, waiting for Blaze.

Blaze's mouth watered, and he shifted to adjust his own dick before he injured himself from lack of circulation. He inhaled Drake's musky smell, which must be filled with sex pheromones, because each inhalation reinforced that he definitely wanted to do this.

He might not have had much practical experience, but he'd watched thousands of hours of blowjob tutorials on YouPorn, and it was past time to taste the delicious-looking cock in front of him. "Sit."

Drake plopped back onto the love seat.

Wiggling closer between Drake's knees, he got an up-close view of Drake's dick. His cock blushed a dark red, jutting out from neatly trimmed pubes. The shaft curved to the right, and several veins bulged out close to the surface and begged for a tongue to trace them.

A clear drop of precum glistened from the tip.

Leaning in, Blaze swiped his tongue over the droplet. Smiling at Drake, he didn't hide his appreciation. "Mmm."

Drake gasped, then panted, "You have no idea."

Blaze's confidence grew as he licked along the veins and then around the underside, teasing his circumcision scar. "About?"

"You… doing this… is…."

Wrapping his hand around Drake, Blaze stroked the lower half of his dick.

"Is what?" Maybe he happened to be evil, but he liked making Drake lose his ability to speak in whole sentences.

Digging his nails into the cushion, Drake gasped, "A fantasy."

Blaze didn't know what to say. He covered Drake's tip and let the round head fill his mouth. He licked the tip, and then sucked.

Drake groaned.

Liking the noise, Blaze bobbed his head, letting Drake go deeper each time. Blaze gagged a little when he hit the back of his throat, so he pulled off. He went back to trailing his tongue along the length of Drake's shaft in slow, wet licks.

Another droplet formed at Drake's tip. Blaze hurried to cover the mushroom head with his mouth, tasting the sweetness. He pushed his tongue into Drake's slit to get more.

Drake whimpered.

Blaze sucked more of Drake into his mouth. Suck followed by a lick—he enjoyed the taste, texture, and feel of Drake in his mouth.

Yeah, this was so good. He loved giving Drake… no, he loved giving head. Blaze shouldn't personalize the activity. It could be anyone he sucked off, right? *No* bounced around his brain, denying his need to lie to himself.

"I, um…. You okay?" Drake moaned around the words.

Blaze nodded, and with the hope of dismissing more worry, he poked his tongue back into Drake's slit and then sucked on the tip.

Drake stared down at him with wide eyes, and tormented sounds fell from his lips along with words. "I just, I need you to know I'm grateful you feel… mmmm, God, Blaze… comfortable enough to share this with me… but if you want to stop at any time…."

His concern reinforced the fact that Drake deserved Blaze's trust, and that made *like* bloom into affection, causing nervousness to scatter through Blaze.

This was uncalled for…. He pulled his mouth off Drake's dick. "I know I haven't done this much, but are you always this chatty during a blowjob, or am I not sucking you right?"

Drake's lips twitched, and his eyes sparkled. He might suspect Blaze's need to downplay what was happening between them. Whatever. "You're doing everything plenty right. Trust me."

"I do." That careless but very true admission made Blaze's heart beat faster. He did.

Here on his knees, sucking Drake, he... trusted him. Blaze attempted to avoid the soft emotions trying to knock down the protective ice around his heart, and to concentrate on the physical.

But the terrible and wonderfully amazing thing was that the physical morphed into an outlet for Blaze's unauthorized emotions. His affection for Drake transferred to his mouth and tongue. Giving pleasure became his way of saying he... he... fuck... he might care about Drake.

Drake shifted this way and that but never once thrust. He reached out with a shaking hand and tucked Blaze's hair behind his ear again. His careful tenderness with Blaze continued to smash some of Blaze's negative expectations.

Daring to meet Drake's gaze, Blaze's whole body felt hot and on edge.

Panting, Drake warned him, "I'm not going to last. Where?"

Yanked out of his musings of feelings, Blaze was back to his wheelhouse of sex. Though no expert in blowjobs, there could be only one real answer to that question. "My mouth."

Drake gave a weak wheeze, and his entire body froze. He hung suspended over the precipice.

Blaze covered the tip with his mouth and got right to work. He quickened his strokes, timing them with his sucks, dragging his mouth up and as far down as he dared. Hollowing his cheeks, Blaze gave Drake even more suction.

A gasped "Blaze" was his final warning.

Sweet saltiness flooded in pulses, filling Blaze's mouth to overflowing. *Swallow! Swallow! Swallow!*

How could he forget one of the basic tenets of Blowjob 101? At least he followed Drake's rhythm and slowed his sucks.

He'd done it. Proud, horny, but happy, he licked Drake clean and then rested a cheek on Drake's thigh.

Drake's taut muscles relaxed. He sighed contentedly and smiled down at Blaze. "That was the best ever."

Giving him a quick nod, Blaze turned away to hide his blush. "Good. Want something to drink?"

"Well, if you're offering." Drake grabbed on to Blaze's hands and pulled him into a hug.

Drake unbuttoned and unzipped Blaze's jeans with deft fingers, and then Blaze found himself sitting with his pants around his ankles on the love seat. "What are you…?"

Drake's eyelashes fluttered as he flirted and toyed with his lip ring. "You offered me a drink, and I'm thirsty for you. Is that okay?"

As corny as that should have been, Blaze's dick throbbed and was more than ready to quench Drake's thirst. Somewhere his mind threw an obstacle to avert the offered pleasure. "You don't have to."

"I know, but I really want to." Drake grinned and gave Blaze's cock a wet, incredibly long lick from his balls to the tip of his cock. "May I?"

Dear gods in heaven, yes! Blaze nearly injured himself by nodding so hard.

Drake covered Blaze's cock, and he started taking soft, teasing pulls on Blaze. Each bob of his head allowed his lips to reach farther than the last trip.

"So good," Blaze moaned.

Amazing how far down his shaft Drake could go, and when he got to the tip, he lashed his tongue along the ridge. Again and again. Blaze lost count of how many times Drake's mouth followed that path.

Now he couldn't help but notice Drake's lip ring as it glided along his cock. The tiny piece of silver was body temperature and looked sexy as fuck touching his cock.

When Drake wrapped his spit-slicked palm around him, Blaze understood the battle had been lost and he was going to win big very soon.

Drake sucked, bobbed his head, and kept his gaze locked on to Blaze's. Blaze couldn't have looked away even if he wanted to, but what reflected in Drake's eyes was more than *like*.

Blaze couldn't help but feel the whisper of their shared strong affection like a boot to the head. He couldn't escape the emotion, so he grabbed Drake's hand and pressed their palms together. With Drake's firm grip, Blaze found he could handle the emotions that threatened to overwhelm him. Because he didn't have to deal with them alone. Drake was in this with him.

Drake added more heavenly suction.

Blaze's body shook and he came hard, grunting as waves of release separated Blaze from everything except the glorious pleasure Drake gave him.

Perfectly paced swallows, head bobs, and suction finished him off with perfection. Drake licked him with a caring affection that made Blaze's heart expand again.

Bliss relaxed every part of him. The barriers of ice protecting his heart were not only cracking, they had begun to melt.

Holy fuck.

Blaze's carefully erected walls were being liquefied, and he hoped his trust in Drake wasn't misplaced.

Chapter 10

THE NEXT day Drake strolled along Safe Haven's downtown with Blaze. The peaceful street was filled with boutiques, restaurants, art galleries, and specialty cafés. He must have inherited his parents' love for interesting shops filled with art, souvenirs, and kitsch. "This reminds me of a condensed version of New Haven."

The sun shone and the temperature headed to the high seventies, and he was glad he'd listened to Blaze about not needing his leather jacket.

"You're from Connecticut, right?" Blaze didn't sound like he asked a question. Maybe Drake wasn't the only would-be stalker.

Might as well get this part over with. "Yup, born and raised. Yes, I partied in the woods. I did go to the Meadows to see Dave Matthews. My mom works for General Electric as an engineer, and Dad is a kindergarten teacher. I don't know that we have better pizza than New York, but don't tell anyone I said that or I'll never be able to go home again."

Blaze laughed at Drake's proud claiming of Connecticut stereotypes, making sparkles of carbonated joy burst around the region of Drake's heart. He grabbed Blaze's hand and kissed his knuckles.

The blush tinting Blaze's cheeks felt like a win to Drake as well as a surprise, considering what they'd done together in the shower a few hours ago. After he'd sucked Blaze off, Blaze demonstrated how talented his fingers were and how incredible the combination of mouth in front and fingers in back was, which made Drake look forward to more. But he'd be patient and not push Blaze for more than he wanted sexually.

He released Blaze's hand with a smile.

The small, simple gesture of affection left Blaze opening and closing his mouth. Finally Blaze spat out, "Um, so… um, yeah. What do you mean by condensed version?"

Wanting to resettle Blaze back into his comfort zone, Drake willingly returned to discussing his hometown. "Well, New Haven is more spread out. There's no proper Main Street like this."

Drake played stadiums and arenas filled with screaming fans, but it didn't even come close to the simple thrill of meandering with Blaze down the pristine street lined with benches and trees. He pushed the stab of betrayal about the band out of his head and focused on the happy contentment that calmed and soothed his weary soul.

"My dad would love these old-fashioned wrought-iron lampposts with the flower baskets. He's got a garden and would go crazy for these flowers." Drake snapped pictures of the baskets dripping with colorful blooms to send to his dad.

"Yeah, the town really tries to keep things looking good and everything easy for tourists to enjoy. Most of the shops and restaurants are on this block and two other streets that run parallel between Main and the river."

"A river?" Drake took a picture of the mountains shadowing the street and the wildflower-covered hills surrounding them. Made sense they'd have a river, but could this town be any more storybook?

Blaze pointed down a side street. "Let's cut down here, and I'll show you."

After two short blocks, they crossed a wooden bridge decorated with a riot of lavender plants and bright red flowers in boxes hanging off the railings. Drake stopped in the middle to inhale the lavender.

"What are you doing?" Blaze asked.

Chuckling, he stated the obvious. "I'm stopping to smell the flowers. Come here and take a whiff of these."

Pressing his lips together, Blaze trudged back to Drake and stared at him.

"Smell." Drake gestured to the heavenly flower. "They are almost in full bloom, but you can smell them."

Blaze pushed his face in the potted bush. "Mmmm, that's good."

Drake picked out a couple of leaves that decorated Blaze's hair, and smiled. He looked down at the slow, meandering river. Several little kids with parents waded in the crystal-clear waters. Others lounged on the huge rounded boulders dotting the water and its banks.

"There's three bridges crossing this river. In the spring and summer, everyone relaxes here." Blaze's tone suggested some level of confusion.

"What are we doing standing here?" Drake rushed over the bridge and found a free rock away from people so he could pull off his high-tops and socks.

Blaze stood in front of him with his hands on his hips. "What are you doing?"

"What does it look like?" Drake rolled up his jeans. "You are coming in, right?"

"Um, I've never…. Yeah. I will." Blaze sat and pulled off his footwear.

"Another thing to add and check off your list." Drake kneeled in front of him and folded Blaze's jeans up to his knees. He restrained himself from wanting to rub and kiss Blaze's battered ice-skating feet.

"Thanks." Blaze's voice sounded unsteady, but when Drake glanced up at him, they shared a heart-stopping smile that lasted several beats longer than normal.

"Come on." Drake grabbed his hand as they trudged unsteadily down the small bank, then stepped into the cool water.

"Oh!" Blaze's exclamation evolved into a moan.

Drake grinned at him. "Feel good?"

"Much better than the ice baths I use at home or at the rink." Blaze squeezed his hand as he led Drake farther down the river. "I can't believe I've never done this."

"Well, you're doing it now." There were too many things Blaze hadn't done, but then again, most people didn't win Olympic medals.

"Hey, I've always wanted to sit on that rock down there." Blaze pointed out a gray boulder with a nice ledge, perfect for relaxing.

Such a simple desire having gone unfulfilled made Drake sad but even more determined to help Blaze enjoy the world beyond the skating rink.

"Let's go." Drake tried not to get splattered as he trudged through the water, grateful all the rocks at the bottom were worn smooth.

Blaze slipped on one of the rocks, giving Drake a reason to tighten his hand around Blaze's. "Oops, some of the rocks are slippery."

A mother, gathering her splashing son and daughter to the river bank to dry off their feet, smiled at Drake as they passed, giving him a stamp of approval. Why would…? Oh, the hand-holding. Some places were still backward and asinine about public displays of affection between same-sex couples. But her easy acceptance felt good.

"Blaze, this is okay here, right?" Drake squeezed Blaze's hand twice to indicate what he was talking about.

"Yeah, Luke picked this artsy town because Safe Haven is very LGBTQIA friendly. They have a huge Pride celebration every year. The library does periodic free movies, lectures, and classes on LGBTQIA issues."

Drake followed Blaze's lead to the large boulder in the middle of the river downstream. "That's important."

No one else was near them.

With fluid grace, Blaze hopped onto the ledge of the boulder. "Yeah, especially if you're like me."

"What do you mean?" Drake sat down on the smooth space next to him. The boulder encompassed them with high back and sides, giving them more privacy than he'd expected.

Sunshine made the highlights in Blaze's brown hair sparkle as he shook his head. "Femme gays aren't always popular. You know the saying 'No femmes need to swipe right.'"

"Huh? I don't understand." Drake didn't use hookup apps so only had a sketchy understanding of how they worked.

"In hookup apps you swipe right if you're interested to make contact."

"That's terrible. That shit is based in misogyny. People are way too comfortable suggesting female qualities are a problem. Sexism at its finest. As Taylor likes to say, 'Just 'cause you're on the rainbow doesn't mean you can't be a stupid asshole.'" Drake didn't mean to preach, but that attitude pissed him off.

Blaze stared down at his feet, which barely dipped below the water's surface. "Ah, then you've never had the problem of turning the heads of straight or closeted men. That tends to cause a stir."

"I've never understood all the labels." Drake could hear Taylor in his head explaining how labels could be good to find community, but they could all too easily be used to pathologize and create the "other." Then Taylor wouldn't even take a breath before he pointed out Drake's privilege for *passing* as straight, which would evolve into a discussion on bisexual erasure. God, he hated that word—*passing*.

Blaze readjusted his ever-present messenger bag. "Shorthand sexual preferences."

"Sounds more like sexual prejudices to me." Drake was insulted for Blaze and couldn't hide it.

"I'll admit that sometimes I'm grateful. I know that sometimes these labels help me weed out guys who are threatened by being attracted to my more feminine qualities. It keeps me safe, at least so far." Blaze sucked in his cheeks, accentuating his bone structure, and puckered his kissable mouth.

Drake held his tongue on what he thought about hookup apps and meeting strangers with possible dangerous intentions. Maybe that's why he asked, "You've gotten a lot of shit from judges because of this, huh?"

"What do you think? Ha, funny when you're thirteen and told not to act so gay in a sport that's dominated by people on the LGBTQIA spectrum." Blaze frowned and pointed at no one. "But you… you're too gay. Act *straighter* like Insert Any Male Skater's Name Other Than Me."

"How fucking awful." Anger slashed through Drake at the unfairness Blaze had to tolerate to participate in competition.

Blaze gave him a small smile and patted him on the arm. "It is what it is. If I hadn't made peace with the stupidity long ago, I wouldn't have been able to function on the ice."

Leaning into Blaze, Drake searched for something to say that might comfort him. What he must have gone through. "I'm sorry you've had to experience such homophobia. Prejudices suck."

Blaze sighed. "Whether preferences or prejudices, I prefer someone to be up-front if they don't want a femme top. I don't waste my time, energy, or risk my safety."

Kicking at the water, Drake added, "It still sucks."

Starting to chuckle, Blaze added, "Well, I do that too now. At least for you."

A burst of affection expanded Drake's heart even more. He certainly did.

Drake trailed his foot through the water to caress Blaze's foot.

"And I'm sorry the band was shitty to you because you're bi."

Closing his eyes, Drake didn't want to think about the two assholes who kicked him out of Midnight Shadow. "I've been luckier than most. This is the first real time biphobia affected me, and I know many are bullied, not believed, called stupid things, and even erased."

Blaze pressed against him. "I wish we were all born with acceptance. I know I'm learning about checking my own expectations and stereotypes based on what bisexual means."

Drake imagined sitting here pressed against Blaze forever, just listening to the birds chirping, the river's babble over and around the rocks, and the wind rustling through the trees. Nothing else. No one else. "Thanks, I—"

"Blaze Parker? I've never seen you here taking the time to enjoy the river." Drake opened his eyes to see a woman who appeared to be in her early seventies. A stripe of purple cut a swath of color through her white hair.

"Hi, Mrs. Reynold. This is—"

She put a hand to her cheek and stared at Blaze with concerned tunnel vision. "Sweetie, I've never seen you sitting down unless you were putting on your skates. Seriously, I'm worried. Are you feeling all right, honey?"

"I'm feeling fine," Blaze reassured her.

"Good. Good. You need to find a nice man to settle down."

Blaze sighed in a way that indicated this wasn't the first time she'd given him that particular recommendation.

Mrs. Reynold's smile dropped a bit, and her attention turned to Drake. "Oh, I'm sorry, my dear. I didn't mean to ignore you. This is just extraordinary.... So, do tell. Who are you?"

Drake jumped into the water and held out his hand. "Hopefully a very nice man. Glad to meet you."

Shaking his hand, she giggled when he raised hers to his lips and kissed her knuckles. "Oh, Blaze, he's charming."

"This is my friend, Drake Keys. Drake, this is Mrs. Reynold. She runs the bakery in town."

"Well, Mr. Keys, I hope you are a *nice* man. That would be marvelous." She turned her laser-focus back onto Blaze. "Well done in the Olympics. We're all so proud of you. You training again?"

Blaze shrugged. "Never really stopped."

"You don't sound excited the way you used to. My Ronny, that's my husband, always says life is too short to do anything but what makes you happy."

Was he really that unhappy? Would Blaze retire from skating?

"Well, I'll leave you to enjoy the river, but if you two ever need a rainbow wedding cake, I'd be thrilled to bake the cake of your dreams. Not like that narrow-minded S.O.B. in Lakewood." She winked.

The offer flooded Drake with elation, but one look at the paling Blaze made him say, "Oh, um, thank you, but—"

"Stop by the bakery, because a balanced diet should include a cookie in each hand." Giggling, she made her way to the shore.

Blaze shook his head. "Sorry about—"

Jumping back into his place, Drake said, "Don't be. Is she right?"

"About skating?" Blaze asked like he was stalling.

Drake nodded.

"I've been skating seriously for almost twenty years. Practiced until my feet bled, been in countless competitions—"

"Went to the Olympics, where you won silver and gold medals." Hard to believe he sat next to a two-time Olympian instead of just streaming him on YouTube.

Blaze sighed. "It's what I do."

Drake totally got that. It's how he felt about music. And until a few days ago, music had always accepted him and made him happy. Though Blaze had fought through discrimination and prejudice, and even after winning and bringing home Olympic gold, Drake could tell Blaze still questioned his worthiness.

"I mean, at times I've thought about how many years and how much I've sacrificed for skating. I can't help but wonder if all those hours were a waste." Blaze laid his head against the rock.

"You followed your dreams. Those Olympic medals say you didn't waste your time, but that doesn't mean your needs and wants can't evolve past your original dream."

"I know the past shouldn't decide the present or the future."

Drake trailed his foot through the water. "Sometimes events shape our perspective and warp our current."

Sitting upright, Blaze pressed his elbows into his legs and dropped his head into his hands. "True. You know, I nursed and carried that grudge against Trent for the last seven years. I've done terrible things because I couldn't move beyond how he humiliated me."

"What do you mean?" Did he sleep with a judge or dope or—

"I revenge fucked Trent Richards." Blaze's tone sounded tired and resigned.

Did he expect Drake to criticize him for it? Other than the possessiveness of wishing Blaze had never touched anyone but him, Drake would never condemn Blaze's past actions.

Needing to remind him, Drake pointed out, "I guess you feel like that was a really shitty thing to do. Maybe it was, but you were hurt by that video. He betrayed you and tried to end your career."

"In some ways, I think that's one of the main reasons why I've stayed on the ice so long. I don't know."

Drake attempted to fit that information into everything he believed about Blaze. He couldn't be serious. "But I've seen you on the ice, especially with those kids. You love skating."

Blaze shifted to stare at Drake. "I love parts of it, sure. I mean, exhibitions are like playing and showing off what I've practiced—no pressure, just fun. And teaching, well, that's simply helping other skaters find the joy in flying across the ice."

It needed to be said aloud even if only this once. Drake did the honors. "You deserve to have all the good you get from skating and none of the bad. You're incredible on and off the ice."

Blaze touched his heart. "That means a lot."

Grabbing Blaze's hand, Drake kissed the knuckles and held it. He then rested his eyes.

Blaze sighed. "You're right, I didn't waste my life, but it sucks that there's a lot of things I haven't done or haven't had time to do in forever."

Drake opened his eyes and grinned. "That's why you've been crossing things off your list. Let's make an official list and write it down. Then we can do them all."

Blaze stared at him for a long minute. Worry that he'd overstepped flooded Drake, making him start working out how to backpedal.

Shrugging, Blaze didn't even notice Drake's quandary, and warned, "Some of these things are dumb."

"Bring it." Drake pulled out his cell phone and tapped his list app. "We'll name it Blaze's I've-Never-Done-It List."

"Okay. I've never played a video game, gotten drunk, or goofed off by sitting in a coffeehouse people-watching like they do in movies. I haven't sung karaoke or gone to the summit of Pikes Peak. Haven't been to the movies or ridden an actual bike in years."

Jesus. "Great. Those are good things to try."

"I've never really explored the towns I've been to for competitions. It's always airport, rink, hotel, rink, airport." Frowning, Blaze huffed out what sounded like irritation. "Do you know I haven't even really seen this town? I've never partied in the woods, and I don't even know what that means."

"Hey, since I've got nothing going on, I'll happily be your guide on these ventures," Drake offered. His heart hoped Blaze would want him to do these things with him.

After a long while, Blaze smiled at him. "I accept. We both seem to be at a crossroads."

"Maybe relaxing and doing some shit will help both of us figure out what our next steps should be." Drake truly wanted Blaze and him to share the path for as long as possible, but he kept that wish to himself. Wish or goal, he wasn't sure, but either way he wanted Blaze in his world.

Chapter 11

DRAKE'S CELL buzzed with a text from Taylor. *You've been in Colorado for three weeks. When are you coming home?*

I'll be there for the wedding. Not the first time Taylor let him know he was missed, but Drake was having an incredible time with Blaze.

How's the domestic bliss? Did he fuck you yet?

Ignoring the rude question, Drake texted, *All is wonderful here. How R U?*

Finally! How was it? Tay was probably leaning forward staring at his phone, waiting for the dirt.

Drake sighed. *I told you I'm not pushing him.*

Pushing him? You're living with him.

Fuck, was he? Over the past three weeks of working down Blaze's I've-Never-Done-It List, he'd earned his place at Luke's kitchen table, where he and Blaze shared dinner with Luke almost every evening. And best of all, he slept next to Blaze, holding him every single night. *Nah, we're hanging out, taking it day by day.*

Whatever. Denial's not only a river in Egypt. Though how have you not done the deed together?

We've done lots of deeds, just not the one you're talking about… that hasn't come up. He hoped Tay would drop the subject.

Maybe he doesn't know if you'd be into it….

That couldn't be the case. Drake mentioned the joys of bottoming once or twice, but Blaze changed the subject. No way would he pressure Blaze. When he was ready, they would. Until then, he wasn't exactly suffering with two and sometimes three orgasms a day.

He texted back with a subject change. *I want deets on that girl you're seeing. But breakfast here. Got to go. Later.*

Drake smothered his yawn into his shoulder as he opened the door to Luke's kitchen. His job became drinks, so he set his and Luke's coffee cups at their places. *His* place.

The kettle hissed, cutting off his musing, so he made tea for Blaze.

Luke put scrambled eggs on each plate. "Did you drag Drake out of bed early to take him to the rink with you?"

Adding a slice of buttered toast to the plates, Blaze denied, "Nope."

"You two have a cozy routine down. I didn't expect to see you until tonight," Luke fished for details.

They did have a routine; that much was true. Blaze still practiced early. Drake would run errands, like filling up Blaze's refrigerator with things on Blaze's to-try list. He would make a late breakfast—brunch technically—they would eat when he returned. Usually the conversation would morph into a make-out session, with so much kissing Drake no longer felt bereft in that department. Then they would get each other off in the shower. If Blaze had an afternoon class to teach, Drake would play his guitar and work on songs. If not, they would bum around town, working down Blaze's list, which grew daily, go for a drive, or hang out watching movies. Then they went upstairs and made dinner together so they could eat with Luke, ending the day twined in bed, sucking each other off. All in all, their routine felt perfect.

Fuck! Tay was right. He was basically living with Blaze. Luke hadn't even raised an eyebrow at him. The closest he'd come to discussing the arrangement was when Luke told him, "This is the happiest I've ever seen my brother. Keep up the good work." And several times he teased, "Make sure I get an invite to the wedding."

In a way, the acceptance was odd, but in another way, he and Blaze fit.

Blaze shoulder-bumped Drake—shoulder-bumped him! "We're taking a day trip and need an early start."

"You're taking the day off from training?" Luke made it sound like a first as he shoveled cereal into his mouth.

Drake couldn't help himself. "Listen, Luke. I can skate backward now with *almost* no help. I don't want to burn myself out by training too hard."

Luke snorted.

Blaze shook his head with a grin.

Success! Drake lived to make Blaze smile, grin, laugh, chuckle, giggle. Anything, really, that meant Blaze was pleased had become an addiction for Drake.

Once Blaze swallowed his mouthful of egg, he told Luke, "Actually, I did a few extra hours yesterday, and I'll probably do a couple extra tomorrow."

Although Drake didn't think skating at a snail's pace, stealing kisses, and making sure he didn't fall on his ass when he skated backward could really count as training for Blaze, Drake sure enjoyed their time on the ice.

"So, where are you off to?" Luke, still finishing his cereal, was on his feet. He then rinsed out his bowl.

Drake finished the last of his coffee. "Garden of the Gods and then Pikes Peak."

Luke swallowed, and then his mouth dropped open and he stared at Drake like he rinsed his plate with gutter water.

Blaze growled.

Drake scrutinized Blaze, then studied the brothers, trying to figure out the issue between them. "What am I missing?"

"I'm driving; it'll be fine." Blaze did not meet his brother's laser stare as he put the dishes in the dishwasher.

Luke handed two bottles of water to Blaze. "Be careful."

"No worries. Since you have class tonight, we'll grab you a chicken sandwich on the way home." Blaze finished wiping down the table.

"Thanks." Luke followed them outside, opened his car trunk, and pulled out a blanket. "Here, take this."

Drake took the blanket because Blaze's folded arms said he certainly wasn't accepting it.

Luke shrugged. "In case he gets cold."

"Thanks, man." Drake put the blanket on the back seat and slid into the passenger seat.

Blaze said something to Luke, resulting in a brotherly hug. Then he put the water in cup holders and started the car.

Drake decided not to ask. He'd learned to give Blaze time. When he wanted to share, he would. Pushing him resulted in retreat and distance.

"Anything you want to listen to?" Blaze asked as they pulled out of the driveway, waving to a concerned-looking Luke.

"How about classical? I'm in the mood for no lyrics."

"Still having trouble with the song you're working on?" Blaze spared him a glance while at the red light.

Drake had two songs written, but the current one was all stops and fits of confusion, and he found hearing someone else's beautifully constructed lyrics compounded his problem. "Yup."

"I'm sorry." And that's all Blaze said. He didn't dig, and Drake truly appreciated someone not needing to analyze everything. Blaze simply accepted what he said and didn't push him to open up.

Drake tuned the satellite radio to a classical station. "How's this?"

"Fine. Anything but jazz."

Surprising. "You don't like jazz?"

"Reminds me of my first skating routine. The teacher forced us into a lackluster number that, would you believe, included jazz hands during the finale? I think she was trying to be ironic, but... no. I avoid the reminder when I can."

"Duly noted." Drake smiled. He loved all the little stories Blaze revealed to him. All the bits and pieces fit together and helped give him a better understanding of Blaze. Bad experiences meant he'd choose to avoid the thing, person, or experience in the future instead of trying to make it better.

The music surrounded them as Blaze drove them down the mountain and onto a straightaway.

Blaze reached his hand out.

Drake stared at the offering. His heart skipped a beat for what the gesture meant. Blaze wanted to connect with him, and the fact that he had asked for the affection felt huge.

Pulling himself together, Drake clasped Blaze's hand but couldn't stop smiling.

Blaze glanced over, giving him a small shrug, and squeezed Drake's hand as if it were nothing.

The miles of peaks with purple and gold flowers filling the meadows melded with Mozart, Bach, and Vivaldi, until they arrived at the Garden of the Gods.

"The park just opened, so we should beat most of the crowds." Blaze drove into the park.

Grass, trees, and bushes decorated the ground, and towering red sandstone formations soared three hundred feet into the sky surrounding them. Drake had long ago decided Colorado was one of the most beautiful places he'd ever been, but there were concentrated spots with awe-striking beauty.

Drake whistled. "The Garden of the Gods. The name fits."

"We'll get out here." Blaze turned into the first parking lot.

He followed Blaze out of the car and onto the paved footpath that looped through the stone forest. They started walking among the red sandstone giants.

"Look." Blaze pointed to a deer eating in the small meadow. He took a picture with his phone.

Drake kissed Blaze's cheek. "Thank you for sharing this with me."

Blaze opened his mouth but then shook his head and led Drake over to a red wall of rock. "Take a picture of the whole thing, and then I'll take one of you pretending to climb it."

Taking Drake's phone, Blaze chuckled. He crouched low and took a picture of Drake acting like he scaled the formation. "Okay, one more. Go stand on that rock and snap a picture down at your feet."

Drake did as instructed, then accepted his phone back. He scrolled through the pictures. "Ha-ha. Damn, Taylor's going to flip out. This perspective gives the impression that I climbed the formation."

With Drake trailing after Blaze, they got to the angle where one of the formations resembled two camels kissing.

"Shall we?" Blaze held out his cell phone and seemed to be daring him.

"Absolutely." He wasn't the one with commitment issues and relationship phobias.

Drake turned to face Blaze. They tried to mimic the kissing by pressing their lips together. The first picture came out crooked, but the third try was the charm. The two of them were framed perfectly under the kissing camels.

"It's a pretty sweet picture." If Drake's mom ever saw the snap, she'd probably deem it romantic.

"I've never posted a picture of me with someone else, but do you want to post it?" A definite challenge echoed in Blaze's voice. Who was he daring, Drake or himself?

Posting any picture of them together would be a declaration, like changing one's relationship status. But this? They were kissing, so there would be no question.

Holy shit, Drake really loved the idea of letting people know he was *with* Blaze.

Though what did with *mean? Focus, obsess later.*

Drake tried to keep his feet on the ground. This really didn't mean anything. "I have no problem with it if you don't. Also, you can add that to your list and cross it off if you do."

"You still staying off social media?"

Drake wasn't sure when Frank would make the announcement, but Drake wanted to avoid the pity, rage, anger, and possible celebration over him no longer being in Midnight Shadow. Plus he'd been having such a great time with Blaze, he'd barely noticed. "Pretty much. It's been nice only texting my mom and Taylor. But I have no problem with you posting and tagging me on it."

Blaze stared down at the picture. "Okay, then, I'll post it to Instagram and tag you."

"Sure." *Hmmm, just to Instagram….*

A few thumb-clicks later and the deed was done.

Dare Drake ask if this meant they were together? He'd learned to tamp down his need for talking about how stable his relationship was with Blaze. In his head they were together, but would the suggestion of being more than friends with benefits send Blaze running for the hills? It seemed like as long as he didn't mention their relationship, he could have it.

One look at Blaze prowling back and forth with his brows knitted close together, the muscle under his eye jumping as he studied his cell, told Drake timing was everything. And now was not the time. Besides, he only put the picture on Instagram, where it would make less of a stir, and not Twitter or Facebook, which would prompt relationship questions.

He suggested, "Let's head to the car."

They circled back to the car in silence, listening to the crickets and birds.

"There's another stop in this park we have to make." Blaze drove them at a snail's pace, following the park's strict speed limit through the outcroppings of red rock.

He pulled off to the side of the road. "It's just a short walk from here."

At almost the exit of the park stood a misshapen round rock perched precariously on a flat but angled formation jutting out of the ground.

Blaze took silly pictures of them from the perspective of holding the rock up or pushing the rock down.

"You're a master at these optical illusion pictures." Drake loved these dumb pics.

Snorting, Blaze explained, "When we first moved here, I found it fascinating how you could make something look one way even though it's nowhere near reality."

"My dad always said reality is done with smoke and mirrors."

"Exactly." A line started to form of tourists waiting to take their own pictures with the rock. Blaze asked the first one in line, "Hey, could you take our picture?"

"Sure." The guy took Blaze's phone and listened to his instructions on how to operate the camera.

Blaze grabbed Drake and hurried into position.

Drake didn't have to fake a smile when Blaze threw an arm around his waist and leaned into him. He slipped his arm around Blaze's shoulders and tugged him close.

"Nice." The guy handed the phone back.

Once Blaze returned the favor for the guy, taking several of him and his girlfriend with the guy's phone, they returned to the car.

Blaze started the engine, rolled down the windows, and stared down at his phone. The most recent picture of them in the most coupley couple picture filled the screen. He stared at Drake.

Drake held his gaze. He'd prove to Blaze he could be steady, stable, and trustworthy.

Pointing at his phone, Blaze said, "You know what people will think if we post this, right?"

"Honestly, all I'm interested in is what you think." Drake held his breath.

"We do look good together." Blaze tried going for the joke but failed to reach the standard for humor to apply. "I like you. I do...."

Yes! Fucking yes! Wait.... "Is there a *but* coming?"

Blaze snorted.

Drake rolled his eyes and tried not to join in with a snort of his own, but his inner thirteen-year-old wasn't having the pretense of maturity. He chuckled. "Mind out of the gutter."

Blaze waved him off. "Okay, okay. It's just that I like you. It's been three weeks, and I don't want you gone."

"Good." Impressive admission. Drake was surprised Blaze remembered how long they'd been together and didn't seem to be counting the seconds to get rid of Drake... well, doing whatever this happened to be.

"I mean, do you like me?" Blaze fluttered his hands about as if he were casting a spell.

Drake opened his mouth, ready to terrify the relationship-phobic Blaze with exactly how much he *liked* him, but shut that shit down. He answered with an even "Yes. Very much. I like you a whole lot."

Blaze stared at the steering wheel.

Meeting no resistance, Drake gently turned Blaze's face to him. Their gazes locked.

Blaze licked his lips. It might not have been an invitation, but Drake received the gesture as one.

Drake leaned toward him, giving Blaze plenty of time to retreat. Instead Blaze closed the distance between them. Blaze's lips glided against Drake's. He had been going for a quick stolen kiss, but he got one filled with affection. He parted his lips, and Blaze swept his tongue in.

With mischief-filled eyes, Blaze pulled back. "I'm glad you like me."

Drake grinned, savoring a huge victory. "Onward."

Sighing, Blaze gave him a nod and drove out of the park.

After a restroom stop, they continued up the twisty mountain road. Blaze had turned off the radio and had a death grip on the wheel.

Drake tried to enjoy the fresh air scented by the pine trees they were driving through, but he was getting concerned about Blaze, whose breathing came in rapid huffs as his tension grew. Maybe the whole relationship thing had been too fast for him. So Drake kept making inane observations as they climbed higher with every switchback turn.

"Wow, looks like we are starting to drive beyond the tree line. From here you can see for miles," Drake commented as they made the turn on mile fifteen of the snaking road.

There were no guardrails and only three feet of dirt between the road and nothing but air. It was magnificent, an infinity pool that filtered off the cliff.

Blaze whimpered, and the car started slowing down, but there didn't seem to be any engine trouble.

Drake kept quiet until Blaze steered the car almost into the center, way over the line, into the terribly unsafe category.

"Blaze? Blaze! You're in the middle of the road."

"No guardrails." He clutched the steering wheel with white knuckles and panted. He didn't seem able to catch his breath.

Was this a panic attack?

Luckily, this early in the day, no one was starting back down the mountain… yet. But this was dangerous.

"Blaze, listen to me. Do you trust me?"

He wheezed. "Yes. We're going to die. I don't want us to die like this, but we will."

"No. You'll signal and pull off into that lookout up ahead." Drake talked over the honking horns of the worried and annoyed drivers behind them.

Blaze shook his head. His face had drained of all color. "There's not enough room."

There were two bikers in the turnoff taking pictures, but there was an additional ten feet for their car to fit. "There is. Just signal and slowly pull into the empty space."

"We're going to die. We're going to die," Blaze chanted as he followed Drake's instructions.

"You're doing good. You got this." Drake channeled his dad's calm voice.

"I can't. We'll go over the cliff." Blaze trembled, shook his head, and kept rolling down the dividing line of the road at a glacier's pace.

One motorcycle guy pointed their car out to the other, and they hurried to pull back onto the road.

"Do you trust me?" After the last three weeks of getting closer, and finally the admission of *like* today, Drake hoped he knew the answer. He held his breath all the same.

Blaze whimpered, "Yes."

"Good. Pull off onto the dirt."

"Drake!" Blaze inched the car into the space, and their vehicle rolled to a stop.

In a precarious move, the gravity and Blaze's light foot on the gas did the work of the brake.

Drake needed to secure the car. "Blaze, put your foot on the brake so we can put the car in Park."

"Okay." Blaze's foot didn't move.

Lacking a dominant bone in his body, Drake channeled Taylor's dominant tone. "You can do it. I've seen you do a Bonaly. Take the foot you land on and put it on the brake. Now."

"Okay." Blaze pressed the brake with his foot. The car lurched, but Blaze didn't unclench his fists from the wheel.

Drake put the car in Park. "Good job. Now we're going to switch seats."

Blaze stayed frozen.

"I'm going to come around the car and help you." Drake jumped out and glanced over the edge. Damn, that was a long way down.

"Don't fall off the cliff. Please. Drake, don't die. I don't want you to die." Blaze's eyes were closed, and a big fat tear rolled down his cheek.

Drake opened the door and unbuckled Blaze's seat belt. "I'm right here. Everything's fine."

Blaze latched on to Drake's shoulders.

Drake hugged him into an upright position. He walked a clinging Blaze around the car. Blaze's eyes were squeezed shut, which, considering how near they were to the railless edge, might have been a good thing.

He settled Blaze into the passenger seat and fastened his seat belt.

His gaze fell on the blanket, and he now understood why Luke insisted they bring it. "You're safe. But I'm going to put the blanket over your head so you don't have to see the drive."

Blaze grimaced, but he didn't argue.

"Tell me, do you trust me to get you up to the top? We've only got four more miles. Or do you want to go back down?"

Blaze's hands twitched where they had clutched at Drake's shirt. He stared at Drake with big eyes. "Can you really drive us to the top safely?"

Drake felt exhilarated and energized by the height, not afraid. "I can."

"I trust you." Blaze kissed Drake with a desperation that screamed these were his last moments on this earth, while all the affection he hid from Drake leaked through without his usual filters.

Drake reached back and handed Blaze the blanket.

Blaze sniffed and said, "Thank you." He released Drake's shirt and put the soft cotton over his head.

Drake felt ten feet tall and unstoppable. Blaze trusted him! He almost waltzed around the car, and then he joined the slow caravan inching toward the top. The drive certainly wasn't the most comfortable in the world because every one of the switchback turns put their car in the lane closest to the edge. Guardrails really would have been a great thing to invest in, but at this height with this little space between the road and death, maybe a piece of metal wouldn't have stopped a car going over the side.

He breathed a quiet sigh of relief when they reached the summit. Even though it was summer, there was a dusting of snow on the flat plateau that consisted of a parking lot, a small building, and lots of lookout points. Drake pulled the car into a spot away from the edge.

"We're here."

Blaze peeked out from under the blanket. "We made it?"

"Yup."

"Oh God, you must think I'm the biggest dope ever." Blaze covered his face and ducked his head deeper into the folds.

"No, not at all." Drake tugged the blanket off his face.

Blaze scowled and ran shaky fingers through his hair. "Why are you all grins?"

"Am I?" Drake shrugged.

"See, even you're laughing at me," Blaze growled.

"No. I'm not. I never would." No sense trying to hide the reason for his smiles. "I feel pretty fucking good, you know? You trusted me to get you here."

Blaze's pretty pink lips opened and closed several times. Finally, he nodded. "I did and I do."

Drake's face hurt from his smile, but it kept getting bigger.

A tad indignant, Blaze sniffed. "Well, we like each other."

"Yup." *Not sure where Blaze is going with this.*

"So are we in a relationship or something?" Blaze shrugged, probably trying to convey he didn't care how Drake answered.

"Which would you rather, something or a relationship?" Drake held his breath, waiting for the answer.

Blaze pulled his Facebook app up. "Currently it doesn't say anything. Would you mind if it said 'in a relationship'?"

By unknown superior strength deep within him, Drake restrained his fist pump. "I wouldn't mind that at all."

"So does this mean we're boyfriends?" Blaze gave him an intense stare.

Happiness backflipped in Drake's heart and then skittered to a stop. "If you're good with that, yeah."

Blaze tossed the blanket into the back seat, clicked on his phone, and then got out of the car. "Well, at least that's what my social media pages say."

"If it's on Facebook, it must be true," Drake teased, not letting Blaze back away from coupledom as he followed him into the brisk air. The cool temperature almost made him wish he'd brought a jacket.

Blaze's mouth twitched as if he were trying not to smile. "We're at fourteen thousand one hundred and ten feet. Seems much higher."

Drake held his hand as they meandered to one of the lookouts. "This is stunning. It's like you can see forever. Are you okay up here?"

"Yeah, fine. Heights don't bother me; it's edges and the pull."

"The pull?"

Blaze shrugged. "Feel drawn to go off over the edge."

Drake grabbed on to his arm, just in case.

Blaze rested against Drake. "Not if there's a rail there. It's really odd. Sorry you had to witness my insanity."

"Don't be. Again, you trusted me to get you here."

"And you did, and it's gorgeous. I'm glad I made it to the top this time. Last time I made Luke take me back down while I covered my head."

"Ah, at least I figured out why Luke gave me the blanket."

"Yeah. Thank you." Blaze grinned.

"You're welcome. I think it was pretty brave of you to come up here."

Blaze snorted. "Yeah, with a damned blanket over my head."

"You were terrified, but you didn't avoid something you were afraid of. You dealt with it. And you get to check another thing off your list." Slipping his palm down Blaze's arm to his hand, Drake laced his fingers through Blaze's.

Happiness threatened to overwhelm Drake. Shouting out *I'm with Blaze Parker and he's my boyfriend* would probably annoy Blaze, so Drake once again put the brakes on his fantastic idea.

Drake stared out across the mountains, valleys, and fields below. He didn't point out the road that snaked around the mountain, because the drops on either side were nightmarish from this angle.

Blaze took some pictures of them and the scenery. "Let's go over to that lookout." They crossed the lot and walked down the steps to a railed enclosure with a plaque dedicated to Katharine Lee Bates and the words to her song.

"I can see why she wrote 'America the Beautiful' up here." Drake wished he could leave a small portion of the gift she left. Her poetry had inspired generations and would for a long time to come.

"Well, I can see the purple mountain majesties, but where are the amber waves of grain?" Blaze teased. The color had returned to his cheeks.

Drake pointed at the building. "The Summit House promises the world's best doughnuts. I guess this used to be a weather station, though they've been serving doughnuts here for over a century. Oh, and hot dogs and fudge."

"Doughnuts of death, totally not worth it," Blaze snarked.

No one was around as they entered the building. Drake spun Blaze around in the tented entryway that separated the outside door from the inside one, and pushed him up against the canvas wall.

"You haven't tasted them yet, so you don't know." He covered Blaze's mouth, kissed him breathless, and stepped away like nothing had happened.

Blaze's eyes sparkled, and he traced a finger over his lips. "Now that kiss… had I known I could get that up here… screw the doughnuts."

Drake laughed and followed Blaze into the cafeteria-styled room. "Should we bring doughnuts home for Luke?"

"Sure, though they say they won't taste as good as fresh, but it's a damned badge of honor. Proof I did it." Blaze grinned.

"Want a hot dog?" Drake didn't know how long they'd been there, but he'd eaten worse on the tour.

Blaze leaned back, his expression making it clear old-hot-dog-flavored kisses were not acceptable. "No hot dogs. How about some fudge, doughnuts, and a diet soda?"

Drake ordered the doughnuts, then said to the person behind the counter, "He'll pick out the fudge."

The server handed Drake two cups and pointed to the dispenser behind them, then started tossing the doughnuts into the bag. She handed them to Blaze with the warning "Careful, they're just out of the oven."

Blaze studied each of his fudge choices carefully, and only then did he speak to the server. "May we have quarter of a pound of the peanut butter fudge and the same of that colorful rainbow fudge?" He paid for the doughnuts, drinks, and calorie-ridden hunks of deliciousness before Drake got back from getting their fountain drinks.

"Thanks." Drake smiled at their feast.

They sat down and dug into their sugar-filled carb fest.

Blaze stuffed the last of his doughnut into his mouth. "Okay, these are delicious."

Drake looked up from the pamphlet with all sorts of facts about the area. "The bakers use a secret recipe. Though I don't understand why they don't have more flavors."

"I think the celebration of surviving the drive up here is enough flavor." Blaze cut a sliver of fudge and savored the goodness with closed eyes and a shivering moan.

"Wow," Drake let slip out.

"Mmmm, what?" Blaze didn't even open his eyes.

Drake shrugged. "Either that fudge is incredible or I need to up my game."

"Huh?" This time Blaze did open his eyes to stare at Drake.

Keeping his voice low, Drake said, "That's the face you made last night when you came."

"Do you know how often I have fudge?" Snorting, Blaze grinned at him.

Somewhat pacified, Drake said, "I guess we can check it off your list."

Laughing, Blaze cut some for Drake, and he popped the rainbow fudge into his mouth. The colored vanilla fudge was delicious.

Well, that might be as good a segue as Drake could have hoped for. "Speaking of crossing things off your list, I have a question for you."

"Sure." Blaze sprinkled half a sugar packet on a second doughnut and took a big bite.

"What are your plans this summer?"

Blaze chewed, swallowed, and then sipped his diet soda like that would counterbalance the doughnuts and fudge. "You mean if we live to see the bottom of this mountain?"

Drake snorted. "Yes, if we survive the drive down."

"I don't know. I guess perfect next season's routines. Though I haven't decided if there should be another season."

Again, he was gut-punched and couldn't imagine Blaze not skating. "Wow."

"Yeah. I'm basically doing the same old, same old out of habit. And all this exploration and working down my Never-Done-It list has been eye-opening."

Drake smiled and hedged, "I told you about Jasmine's wedding."

"Yeah? Your best friend's little sister, right?"

"Yup. I wondered... you know, if you had time... maybe you might want to go with me?"

Swallowing the last of his doughnut, Blaze asked, "And be your plus-one?"

"You are my boyfriend. It says so on social media," Drake reminded him.

Blaze's eyes widened, and he straightened in his seat. "I am... and if we live—"

"So, if we live, do you want to go to the wedding with me? It's over Fourth of July weekend, so there's a bunch of other stuff going on along with the wedding. A brunch, the reception, fireworks...."

Sitting back in his chair, Blaze toyed with another doughnut. "Do you think that's wise?"

"Do you trust me?" That's what everything boiled down to in a relationship.

Blaze didn't meet his eyes, but he spread his arms, waving his doughnut around. "I'm here, so yes. I'll go with you."

Over the last three weeks, Drake had fit into Blaze's life, but did Blaze want to fit into his life?

Chapter 12

"FIRST YOU go to Pikes Peak. Now a few days later, you're going on a road trip?" Anna acted like Blaze was heading off to Mars.

Maybe inviting her to dinner was a bad idea. "Yeah. Drake's taking me to his best friend's sister's wedding."

Anna handed over the plate of cupcakes she made for dessert. "You're going to a wedding? You? As his plus-one?"

Luke's and Drake's chuckles echoed into the dining room, confirming they heard the conversation.

Blaze cleared his throat, hoping the kitchen help heard the "*Shut the hell up*" he infused in his cough as he set the cupcakes down on the window seat. He pulled out a dining chair for Anna. "Yes, and we decided, instead of flying, to go on a road trip. It should be fun."

"Again, I don't understand. You on a road trip to a wedding?" Anna sat at the dining room table.

Sitting across from her, he smacked his hand on the table. "Why is this so hard to imagine?"

She scrunched her face. "You don't like long car rides, weddings, or—"

"I'm expanding my horizons." While that was true in the past, it had been years, and with Drake he loved doing just about everything.

"What about your training?" Mother Hen Anna morphed into Coach Anna the Strict with breakneck speed. "To get ready for next season's competitions, you've got—"

"I've got a list of rinks on the way, and I've already booked ice time at the first stop."

"When will you be back?"

That was a good question and one he didn't want the answer to yet, because what then? Would they stay boyfriends? Not that he wanted— *oh, fuck me sideways!* Who was he kidding? He did… shoving aside the impossible—maybe they should simply fuck and then they could move on. It had always been easy before to hit and then quit.

He rubbed a hand over his heart, hoping to quiet the ache. "Not sure. Sometime after the wedding."

Drake and Luke carried in plates of shrimp and vegetables. Luke set the serving dish down and said, "Dinner is served."

"I want to know more about this road trip." Anna spooned more broccoli onto Blaze's plate.

Blaze bit his tongue, partly because, as usual, she was right… again. He needed more green vegetables. "What do you want to know?"

"You guys said you'd be breaking the trip up with some side trips. Where are you going to go?" Luke added shrimp to his dish.

"Here's our proposed route." Drake handed Luke his cell phone with their plotted course, thanks to Google Maps, and Luke then passed it to Anna for her to glare at the screen.

"We'll be doing longer drives spaced between activities. If we go the Nebraska route, we'll probably hit Omaha for the Henry Doorly Zoo."

"The zoo even has an aquarium and desert dome." Blaze had never gone to a zoo before.

"And if there's time, the Joslyn Art Museum." Drake grinned at him.

Excitement raced through him about the upcoming adventure. "In Iowa, there's the Grotto of the Redemption."

"The what?"

"The Grotto of the Redemption, which is a shrine that took forty-two years to build. Father Dobberstein devoted his life to its creation because he promised if he survived an illness, that's what he would do."

Blaze grabbed Drake's hand and kissed it. "And the Lost Island Waterpark."

"A water park?" Luke arched his eyebrow at Blaze. "Who are you and what have you done with my brother?"

"Ha-ha. I've never been to a water park." Blaze shrugged and tried to rise above the memories of fearing the other kids laughing at his skinny body.

Luke looked at the ceiling and shook his head. "That's 'cause you refused to take time off of the ice."

"Granted, but now it's time I live life a little, don't you think? I should see something beyond the ice rinks."

Anna frowned at Drake like this was all his fault.

Ice trotted up the steps into Luke's dining room. Without acknowledging any of them, he beelined to the bowls that Luke kept for him. He munched on some dry kibble and drank some water.

"What about Ice?" Anna acted like the road trip meant his puppy would have to be put down.

"The little nipper will stay with me like he does when Blaze goes on an overseas competition. We'll have a great time together." Luke smiled over at Ice.

"Ha, you just want him as your wingman at the dog park," Blaze pointed out.

"While Ice is a chick magnet, that doesn't mean we won't have fun together." Ice walked over and curled himself around Luke's feet.

"Ice will be fine," Blaze concluded as he gestured to his dog, who now tenderly gnawed on Luke's pants cuff.

"Tell us more about the trip," Luke invited and then continued eating.

Not noticing the daggers of ice Anna was throwing at him, Drake stopped giving Blaze that dreamy-eyed look and sighed with a smile. "When we get to Chicago, we're planning on a couple of days to hit the Magnificent Mile, the Art Institute, and Navy Pier."

Luke swallowed and nodded. "Good choices."

Drake continued, "Indiana and Ohio are up in the air in terms of activities, but in Pennsylvania we're definitely doing Philadelphia."

Anna stopped glaring and said, "Beautiful city. What parts?"

"The historical section with the Liberty Bell, South Street, and of course we've got to race up the Rocky Stairs to the Philly Museum of Art and see the Science Museum."

Anna folded her arms and asked, "How will you book the hotels?"

"Through the HotelTonight app—"

Before anything came out of Luke's open mouth, most likely giving voice to the worry written all over his face, Blaze chimed in, "We'll also be checking each choice with review sites so we don't stay in a murder-bedbug sanctuary."

"Good." Anna huffed out a breath of air and slowly unfolded her arms.

Luke shrugged. "That's very road trippy and flexible of you, Blaze."

"It is." He smirked. Blaze was pretty impressed with himself that he would really be doing this. He was going to do something other than skate.

"He's very bendy." Drake grabbed his hand and kissed the knuckles.

Blaze snorted along with Luke, while Anna gave Drake the stink eye.

"Make sure he stays that way." Anna scowled.

Blaze and Luke laughed harder while Drake let the curtain of his hair fall to cover his blush. "I will."

"How did you cook the shrimp?" Anna asked.

Relief swamped Blaze when the conversation changed directions. Sometimes, contemplating the road trip too long made him irrationally sad. Maybe because it highlighted the obvious expiration date on him and Drake. It caused too many questions to circle. The biggest being how could their relationship work?

Pushing away his melancholy, he dug into his food. And he focused on pressing his leg against his boyfriend's…. It had been less than a week since he accepted the *boyfriend* title, but the idea no longer felt like a foreign concept and didn't strike terror. The title made him happy.

After the delicious cupcakes Anna had made and tea, she hugged Blaze and told him, "Be well. Have fun. Email me which rinks you'll be at and the times."

Blaze rolled his eyes. "Why, so you can have your friends spy on me?"

"Absolutely. I don't want you to reinforce mistakes we fixed." Anna stated her intentions without an ounce of guilt.

There was no arguing with her, so he hugged her again and promised, "I'll send you the list."

"And you." She stabbed a finger at Drake. "You make sure he's safe and happy."

"Will do." Drake almost saluted, but her frown seemed to force him to drop his hand before it touched his forehead.

She pushed a piece of paper into Drake's hand and then pulled him into a hug. "Make sure he has fun, but call me if he's favoring either of his ankles."

After the door shut, Drake whispered to Blaze, "I'm afraid I will rat you out. I'd be scared not to."

Blaze snorted.

THIS WAS their third day on the road. How was Drake still asleep? Blaze ran three miles, took a shower, and dried his hair with a noisy hairdryer. He even chatted with Luke and Ice on Skype. Pacing right next to the bed didn't help, so he cleared his throat, and then he even coughed, but nothing worked.

Drake turned onto his stomach and continued to sleep.

Blaze opened the motel curtains. "Time to get up."

Nothing.

Running out of patience with *subtleties*, he bounced on top of Drake and then settled right on his boyfriend's ass.

Instead of rolling over or pushing him off, Drake wiggled his ass back against Blaze's jeans-covered dick in the most enticing way possible. He moaned, "Well, this is a good morning."

Fear skittered through Blaze's belly. The contradiction of not doing what they both wanted played with his mind.

He jumped off Drake and grasped at straws. "Zoo's going to open in an hour."

"Plenty of time." Drake arched his back and grinned over his shoulder at Blaze. Whatever he saw on Blaze's face made the sexy grin morph into a sad but resigned smile. He shifted and leaned toward Blaze's cheek with a kiss. "Let me just get myself together, and I'll be ready to go in five minutes."

Stupid relief flooded Blaze. The avoidance was becoming pathological. Shit, clearly Drake was more than up for *it*. Not wanting to think about the whys, he started yammering. "I packed us up so after the zoo we can continue driving."

Drake put paste on his toothbrush. "Great."

Since Drake had showered last night, he was good to his word, and they were in the car, heading to the Henry Doorly Zoo in five minutes.

"Dare we go through another drive-through this morning?" Drake asked, as if he didn't know the answer.

"Yes! I want to try another one of those muffins with egg in it."

"Your wish is my command."

Happiness skittered through Blaze. Not the first time Drake said those words to him, but he liked that Drake really cared about what he wanted. He felt the same way.

Once Drake parked in the zoo lot, Blaze was out of the car and dragging him toward the entrance.

Drake chuckled. "Anxious to cross another thing off your list?"

As long as it didn't involve fucking Drake, the answer was "Of course. So, um… did you go to zoos growing up?"

"My mom was strictly against animals in captivity, but my dad believed animal ambassadors who were kept as free range as possible helped promote conservation and education. So he took me to one or two of them."

As they approached the admission booth, Blaze pulled out his wallet. "My turn."

"Thanks."

They had an understanding and simply took turns. There were no macho fights about money. Blaze appreciated the ease between them… on so many things. After he paid, he asked, "Where to?"

Drake gestured to him. "You pick the direction. I'll follow you."

Blaze fussed with the map, but decided to pocket it. He set off down the dirt path lined with plants and trees. When they came to a bridge over a tiny river with a little waterfall, Blaze leaped onto the large rock and hopped over the water from rock to rock.

"You always do take the most difficult path." Drake grinned.

"It's usually the most rewarding." Blaze accepted Drake's hand and jumped back onto the path.

Drake pulled Blaze into a quick kiss, then mumbled, "Don't I know it."

Blaze gave him an arched brow but didn't respond further, because who knew where the conversation would end? A sign caught his gaze. "Look, the butterfly pavilion."

He let Drake open the first door, and once that barrier to the outside was closed, a sign asked to scan for winged escapees. None were on the run, so Blaze opened the second protective door to a veritable paradise. Colorful fragrant blossoms and flowering bushes were on either side of the path. Lush green foliage almost hid all evidence he had entered a screened cage.

An orange butterfly with brown spots floated by, followed by a saffron-colored one. A shiny black butterfly with red under its wings danced in the air with brilliant blue butterflies fluttering around. Many were gathering at bowls of fruit soaked in a thick nectar throughout the enclosure.

Glancing at Drake, he motioned for him to stand still. "You have a friend on your shoulder."

Drake looked to his right shoulder, and his face lit with pure delight.

Blaze snapped a picture.

At a snail's pace, Drake reached down and dipped his finger in the nectar. He held the droplet up to his winged friend, who unfurled its tongue to taste.

"You're feeding him." Blaze restrained his squeal.

The butterfly stepped onto Drake's finger, and he moved the butterfly toward Blaze.

Blaze touched the nectar to his finger and held out the drop, hoping to tempt the butterfly.

Drake gently pressed their hands together, and the butterfly straddled both their fingers and slurped the sweetness. "I got to try to get a picture of this."

With one hand, Drake captured their hands touching with a butterfly uniting their fingertips and snapped a picture.

As the butterfly fluttered away, Blaze continued to hold Drake's hand and was struck by his overwhelming affection for Drake. The emotion was powerful, wonderful, all-encompassing, and pretty freaking amazing. He interlaced his fingers with Drake's and hoped he'd never have to let go. "You really are magical."

A DAY later, Blaze pulled into the parking lot of the Grotto of the Redemption. Almost an entire city block was taken up by the towers of stones, mounds of rocks, and statues. At the summit stood a big cross with Mary holding a dying Jesus.

Drake got out of the car and put his hands on his hips. "One man's devotion built this."

Blaze grabbed the pamphlet from the glove compartment and leaned against the car next to Drake. "It says Father Paul Dobberstein was a German immigrant."

As they walked to the entrance and the closer they got to the structure, the more the crystals, rocks, and semiprecious stones dazzled in the sunlight.

"Let me get this one; you can get the next two." Knowing Drake's mixed feelings on religion, Blaze gave the eight-dollar requested donation for each of them.

"Look, the date—1912." Drake pointed to the cornerstone.

Blake led them onto a concrete path. They passed the stations of the cross, each lovingly displaying a picture surrounded by rocks and semiprecious stones. "Remember that one YouTube video we watched? It said these rocks came from around the world, arriving by train and carload."

"Oh yeah. And Father Dobberstein would close the school so the kids could help unload the trains. Then he would affix each stone to a slab that the parishioners secured in place."

"Ignoring the child labor issues, it's pretty amazing how the entire community seemed involved."

Drake took the steps two at a time and gestured to a pond. "This must be where the caretaker said the priest would puff a cigarette, hold the smoke in his lungs while he swam underwater, and then release it after he surfaced in the bathhouse."

Blaze chuckled. "Yeah, great exercise, that. Him inhaling another cigarette in the bathhouse, then swimming back out to where he kept his other one."

"I can't even imagine doing that. My lungs hurt from thinking about it." Drake shook his head and studied the archway that led into one of the nine caves that comprised the grotto before entering.

Chuckling, Blaze stepped inside after him. "Well, that's devotion for you."

Drake remained silent as he stared at the stained glass window that cast reds, blues, and yellows into the cement floor. When he turned and faced Blaze, the look he wore was filled with too much longing. "You ever want that kind of devotion?"

Yes! Yes! Yes! His heart pounded like he'd finished doing ten quads, so he focused on the gleaming crystals that formed rosettes, as if geology was his new passion. He cleared his throat. "Well, I mean we both have that—you know, with our fans."

Taking a step closer, Drake touched his shoulder. "Blaze…."

Blaze turned toward him.

Drake's expression told Blaze he wasn't going to let Blaze skate around the question. "You know what I mean. Or would you rather I spell it—"

"No." Blaze's voice broke a little. He wanted to get lost in Drake's mesmerizing blue eyes, but he was in too deep. This man in front of him had single-handedly reprioritized the schedule of his life. Sure, he'd always thought he might find someone to date after he couldn't compete any longer, but not before. Of course, he didn't believe in forever or even love… or at least he didn't before—

"So do you think you could be devoted to someone who was devoted to you?" Drake pressed him.

The answer should have been an easy "*No fucking way!*" But nothing was clear-cut anymore. Especially when a piece of him really wanted…. "Maybe… someday."

Drake's expression erupted into a huge smile. He did a little happy dance. "Yeah, me too."

DRAKE TOOK the first leg of the drive out of Dubuque, Iowa, where they'd stayed after driving from the water park, and into Illinois. "Well, it's day six of our road trip. Chicago is three to four hours from here. Do you—"

His cell jiggled with a Midnight Shadow tune.

"Do you want to pull over to get that?" Blaze offered. Earlier that morning, he had seen the band's apology on social media. He wanted to find a way to bring it up to Drake along with the upcoming tour.

"Nah, it's probably just the lawyers contacting me or something." Drake handed him the cell. "Could you put the thing on silent?"

"Yeah, but you've got a lot of texts." How could someone ignore all of these texts and calls? What the hell was he thinking?

"I don't want to deal with it now."

What Drake probably meant is he didn't want to include Blaze in a discussion about his future plans.

"But don't you want to stay in the loop?" Blaze hated himself for grasping at the proverbial straws—in this case guitar picks. There was no way Drake could ignore so many texts, especially not with everything going on with the band. Or maybe he did deal with them but not around Blaze? Clearly he didn't want Blaze's thoughts on the situation.

"That ringtone is Midnight Shadow's business number. Summer is working with a children's organization in the Middle East without much cell reception. Amanda and Artano don't do social media or texting. They started a program to schedule posts on Instagram just to shut Frank, the manager, up. Jessie keeps to herself, and I don't expect the jackass Dixon to reach out unless it is to stab me again."

Blaze needed to stop thinking there was something special between them. Enjoy what time they had and stop expecting more was the smart thing to do. He should be careful about overstepping, so he'd back off. "Got it."

"I really need a break. I like focusing only on the present moment." Those were the words Drake used, but Blaze heard them as the ticking down of their relationship, which made sense....

Right. Blaze needed to stay in the present moment and not think about the future. He hated he had allowed himself to feel too much for Drake and now he kept getting ahead of himself to being alone again. He would do without—he'd be fine.

Drake glanced over at him. "What's the matter?"

"Nothing. I'm just tired." Blaze adjusted Drake's cell to silent mode and turned on his road-trip playlist.

Drake began to sing in his deep baritone.

Fuck it. Here and now is all they had, so Blaze decided to enjoy it. He couldn't resist the pull, and soon they were belting out everything from happy '50s songs to heavy metal ballads together.

AT LUNCH, Blaze pulled out the chair for Drake and then waited for his chair to be pulled out before he sat. Drake didn't comment, though he gave him a pleased smile, which made Blaze's heart do a Bonaly.

After they ordered, Blaze's phone vibrated, drawing his attention to the screen. He rolled his eyes.

"What?" Drake asked.

"I keep getting questions about our relationship status, especially after I posted the butterfly and our two hands together." He wiped his hands on his jeans and took a sip of water.

"Oh, so you haven't changed your relationship status?"

"I did." How to get off this conversation path before he crashed.

Shrugging, Drake said, "I thought we agreed we were boyfriends, so what's the problem?"

"People asking stupid questions—"

"Like?" Drake tilted his head and studied Blaze like he was a puzzle with a piece missing.

Blaze swallowed hard and shrugged. "Like how serious we are." A bizarre need to scream *"He's mine now and always!"* made Blaze choke on his water. *Where the fuck did that come from?* "Um, yeah... I said we're just having fun."

"Oh... okay. Whatever you're comfortable saying." Drake's calm grated on Blaze's nerves.

How could he be so serene? He'd be going back on tour soon and leaving Blaze behind as a *nice* memory.

Fuck, that hurt way more than it should. Blaze rubbed his hand over his heart. This was why he had always sidestepped entanglements and never considered coupledom.

Drake turned to him, and their gazes locked. So many emotions swirled across his face, Blaze was relieved when a small smile settled. "You okay? Anything you want to talk about?"

What could he possibly say? Drake's silence on the news spoke volumes. Blaze grabbed Drake's hand and lied, "Nah, I'm fine."

"I'M GOING to pull into that rest stop and grab a soda." Drake pointed to the sign.

"Sounds good. I'll also take the final leg into Philadelphia, because you know I don't do navigation."

Drake snorted. "You did fine."

"I told you to go down a one-way street in Iowa Falls." Blaze enjoyed driving but not navigation duty.

Pulling into the empty lot of the rather upscale Welcome Center, Drake parked closest to the vending machines. Drake turned off the car, handed Blaze the keys, and hopped out. "What kind do you want?"

"Diet Sprite if they have it or a water." Blaze slid out of the car to stretch. He locked the doors.

Drake hollered back from the machine, "Both are out."

He meandered over. "Hmm, I guess I'll take a diet peach Snapple. I've never had one of those."

Drake punched in the number.

Before Blaze could collect the bottles, he found himself pressed against a wall, which gave them a little privacy from the lot.

Drake whispered in his ear, "You know what else you haven't had?"

Going from flaccid to wood in seconds bent Blaze's mind. He hadn't been this constantly horny since… ever. He tried to sound sexy, but instead his voice broke. "What?"

"Me. You've never had me."

Red alert! Duck and avoid.

He craved everything Drake offered, but his twisted mind rebelled with apprehension and wouldn't let him have what he wanted. He headed to safer ground where there was still a lot to enjoy.

"Um, but I noticed there were woods out back. No one's here this early on a weekday. I know you've had a hand job in the woods, but how about a blowjob?"

Drake studied him a bit too closely and then sighed. "Only if you want one too."

"Deal." Blaze kept their pace slow as they ambled past the empty picnic area to a well-worn path….

THE PINKS and oranges of dawn were beginning to color Philadelphia's skyline, and there wasn't a soul in sight.

"Come on!" Drake pointed to the stairs of the Philadelphia Museum of Art.

Laughing, they began sprinting up the stairs until Blaze couldn't resist and took off at a run. The concrete was solid under his pounding feet, but in truth he was flying.

Joy and elation had always been connected with skating, but now halfway up the stairs, he glanced over his shoulder and found Drake eight steps behind him. He shifted directions and ran the steps backward so he could keep Drake in his sight.

"Show-off," Drake gasped.

"Catch me if you can," Blaze teased.

Drake took the steps two at a time, and when he got to the top, he grabbed Blaze and swung him in a circle. "Gotcha!"

"You did." Blaze felt like he was in a movie. He pressed his mouth to Drake's and gave in to everything that admission meant.

Rocky be damned!

Now if only Drake had wanted to keep him.

Chapter 13

"THIS PREWEDDING do is much fancier than I expected," Blaze whispered to Drake as he took in the white tent and tables and chairs, all overlooking the grand expanse of beach carrying in the fresh ocean air. "Thanks for having me take a sports jacket in addition to my suit."

Blaze would have been mortified as he gawked at all the well-dressed people. This event felt more like an international skating-sponsored event, rather than a prewedding brunch—though Blaze hadn't been to any weddings.

"Prewedding brunch in Connecticut." Drake said it like Blaze had any idea what that meant.

Drake scanned the crowd. He nodded at several people engaged in conversation but kept guiding Blaze through the crowd with a hand on his lower back.

"Oh, there's Mom and Dad. Come on, let me introduce you." Drake pointed out a handsome couple wearing coordinating colors. The man's shirt under his charcoal jacket matched the woman's royal blue dress.

Blaze gasped as terror flooded him. "Wait. What, now? I'm meeting your parents?"

Did Drake not get the memo? Blaze wasn't exactly a meet-the-parents kind of a guy. Why would Drake even think he was the sort of man parents wanted to meet? How did Blaze not know Drake would expect him to meet his parents?

"Don't say it like I've tricked you." Drake grabbed Blaze's hand and gave a quick smile, but his words were laced with concern.

Well, too late now. The couple rushed over like birds homing in on their wayward chick.

"Drake, honey. It's so good to see you. I've missed you." The woman enveloped him in a hug, forcing him to let go of Blaze's hand.

Blaze could escape.

A familiar ache made Blaze's heart throb. Usually he only got this particular salt in his gaping wound around Mother's Day, but Drake's mom made the typically controlled longing spring to life. She even smelled flowery and safe like the memories he had of his own mother.

"Oh, and the lip ring works for your rock-star image." His mother touched the silver ring gently.

Well, Drake's lip ring worked for Blaze too… probably for different reasons.

As soon as Drake broke free from his mom, the guy who looked like an older version of Drake with shorter hair nabbed him into a backslapping man grab. "Glad you're home, son."

When Drake stepped back, he captured Blaze's hand again, cutting off any hope of Blaze heading for the hills. "I'd like you to meet my boyfriend, Blaze Parker."

Boyfriend? Temporarily….

Blaze clamped his mouth shut, pasted on a smile, and awaited judgment. This felt ten times more intense than the kiss and cry.

Drake's mother smiled at him, then grinned at her son. Returning her focus onto Blaze, she said, "So you're the reason it's only been quick texts and vague answers. I know all about you."

Drake's sputtering didn't really provide more information.

She waved her son off. "How could I not notice those pictures Blaze posted on social media tagging you, and that Blaze's relationship status had changed?"

Blaze held out his hand. "Nice to meet you, Mrs. Keys."

She bypassed the offered handshake and tugged him into a hug. "Call me Julia. Thank you for making Drake's smile reach his eyes."

What did one say to a grateful mother? "Um…."

"I'm Drake's dad. Call me Matthew." The older version of Drake treated Blaze to a less smacky version of a man hug.

Mrs.—Julia cupped his chin for a moment. "No lip ring. That's probably good. You might get tangled with each other. Though I don't think either of you would mind."

"Mom!"

Julia chuckled. She waved off Drake's embarrassed plea and asked with an intensity that couldn't be missed even if one would rather not look, "Will you be staying with us after the wedding, Blaze?"

"Um…." Blaze didn't know where to focus. He couldn't stare at Drake, because they had purposefully avoided numerous conversations about anything beyond the wedding. There were too many things to resolve that seemed to have no solution other than goodbye.

He couldn't meet Mrs. Keys—Julia's—hopeful gaze.

Somehow he had a rock star for a boyfriend. That was overwhelming and quite enough. He didn't know what would happen next.

"Mom, we're not sure where we're going to head next. As soon as we figure it out, I'll let you know." Drake to the rescue with the truth.

A rescue but still not much hope for a future between them? However, the *we* did sound kind of nice. And this might be one of those boyfriend things he'd never really experienced... or expected to.

She smiled at Blaze and combed Drake's long hair over his shoulder. "Of course, dear. You let us know when you figure out your plans... all of them. I'm curious about—"

Drake's father tapped his mother on the shoulder. "Let's not worry about that until after the wedding. There's Isaiah and Sam. Honey, I told them you'd speak with them about that opening in your department."

"Certainly." She nodded to her husband. "We'll see you boys later."

Mr. Keys—Matthew—led his wife toward the two men, but not before throwing a wink over his shoulder at Blaze.

Blaze turned to Drake and didn't know what to say.

Giving him a sheepishly sexy smile, Drake said, "See, that wasn't so—"

"Drake, my man." A guy with a passing resemblance to Will Smith when he sported his close-trimmed goatee sauntered over. He gave Drake a combo handshake chest bump with a man hug chaser.

"Tay! Good to see you, buddy." Drake tapped him on the arm and said, "Dude, how much have you been working out?"

"Hey, the ladies love it." Taylor smirked at Drake, making a dimple come out, then turned his attention to Blaze. "You must be Blaze Parker."

"That's me." Blaze happily settled for Taylor's nonbruising handshake.

"I'm your man's best friend. So if you need dirt, let me know. I've got a bunch of shovels and piles of facts," Taylor offered with a smirk.

Blaze snorted, feeling instantly at ease with the man. "I'll remember that."

Drake adjusted the collar of his shirt.

Taylor stopped him and pulled the neck of Drake's shirt to the side, revealing a ring of hickeys Blaze'd had a very good time making. "What's with the bouquet of love bites?"

Drake pulled away, and his face had gone bright red.

Taylor glanced at Blaze. "You part vampire?"

"Maybe." Blaze chuckled. He couldn't help it.

Pointing a finger at Taylor, Drake said, "Hey, I've seen women after they've dated you. Between the beard burn and the hickeys—"

"Nah, man. Blaze, don't listen to Drake. I'm a real lady pleaser." Taylor rubbed his hand over his close-clipped curls and flashed a sinful grin that Blaze believed would work on any woman Taylor set his gaze on.

Blaze liked this guy. "I'm sure you are. So can I ask you an important question?"

"Yes, I'm trans." Taylor studied Blaze.

Didn't see that coming. "Oh, um, okay. Thank you for sharing. But my important question was, can I get you a drink?"

Taylor snorted. "What?"

"Hey, I just met this guy's parents, and now I'm with his best friend. Don't know about you, but I need some fortification. Stress is my middle name right now." Blaze rarely drank, but he could stand to loosen up.

Drake folded his arms over his chest and glared at Taylor. "I know you use gender as a fucked-up litmus test to determine good and bad people, but maybe add some other markers to the examination?"

Taylor rolled his eyes. "Oh, do shut up, Drake. Blaze, I'd love a sex on the beach."

Blaze held his hand out in front of him. "Dude, I didn't ask for your wishes and dreams list, only your drink order."

"Hee-hee. Fair enough. Though I like it sweet, so that's what I drink… too." Taylor wrapped an arm around Drake's shoulder and declared, "I like him. You've got good taste in men."

Blaze caught Drake's eye before his boyfriend could go off on the rant he appeared poised to do and asked, "And whatever's on tap for you?"

Drake grabbed his hand and kissed the knuckles. "Thank you."

Maybe it was cowardly, but Blaze didn't stick around for the ribbing Taylor was under the bro code obligated to give Drake.

Blaze tipped the bartender a twenty, so hopefully the man would be generous with the alcohol. He was.

Blaze carried the three drinks back and held out Taylor's drink. "Here you go."

"Thanks. Oh, you like sex on the beach too?" Taylor accepted his and pointed to Blaze's drink.

"Do we know each other well enough to exchange these kinds of preferences?" Blaze snarked.

"Yeah, we do through Drake. Though sex on the beach…." Taylor grimaced. "Man, the sand gets everywhere."

Drake shook his head. "Don't encourage him."

"Who?" both Blaze and Taylor asked.

Doing his best glare, which, oddly, reminded Blaze of his puppy when Ice attempted to act tough around bigger dogs, Drake snapped, "Either of you. I can see you both need adult supervision."

Taylor gently elbowed Blaze in the ribs. "Where do you think he's going to find that?"

"No clue. I'm not from around here," Blaze added.

Drake shook his head but raised his beer. "To the happy couple."

Blaze and Taylor clinked glasses with each other, then with Drake.

"Oh, I did not tell Jasmine who your plus-one was." Taylor leaned in. "And little sister's been so busy pulling the wedding together and getting ready for grad school, I don't think she's up on her social media."

"Speaking of the bride…." Drake pointed across the lawn at the giggling, squealing woman in a yellow dress, running toward them—handcuffed to a nice-looking guy in a yellow polo shirt and cargo shorts.

"Drake!" She leaped into Drake's arms and held him close even as her handcuffed partner twisted and turned to give her maximum movement. "Drake!"

He gave her a big kiss on the cheek. "Jazzy Jasmine. Are you ready to get *married*?"

Her smile and eyes sparkled as she glanced toward her prisoner. "Absolutely. I love him with all my heart."

Taylor might have grumbled, "You're too young," but Blaze couldn't be sure.

Drake fist-bumped the guy she was handcuffed to. "Good to see you again."

She jumped off Drake, dragging her fiancé with her. "Taylor, shut—Blaze Parker?"

"Yup." Drake chuckled.

She elbowed Drake and pointed at Blaze. "No, seriously. Is this a joke? You found a double of Blaze Parker as a wedding present?"

"Nope. That is Blaze Parker. He's my plus-one."

She put a hand on her hip and glared. The wind blew her midnight waves, making her look more like a goddess than anyone's little sister. "Yeah, right. Sex-on-ice at my prewedding brunch? Tell me another."

Sex-on-ice? Blaze squirmed under the weight of her curiosity.

Drake put a finger to her mouth. "Jazzy, he's standing right there."

Her fiancé held out his hand to Blaze. "I'm William Jones."

Blaze shook it, glad of something to do. "Congratulations, William."

William didn't bother to hold back his smirk when he asked, "So should I call you Sex or Mr. Ice?"

Chuckling, Blaze replied, "Blaze will be fine."

Jasmine's face twisted into a grimace, and she smacked Drake's middle. "Wait! That's really him?"

"Ow. Yeah, I just said he was." Drake held his stomach and frowned at her.

"Oh! My! God!" She spun away from the group, dragging William with her.

William stopped her retreat, put his forehead to hers, and talked softly to her.

"Oh, no. No." Her words erupted, and then she crashed her head into her fiancé's shoulder.

"Pull it together, sister of mine," Taylor called out.

She straightened, took a deep breath, and whirled around to Blaze with her hand out. "Mr. Parker, it's an honor. Your skating has always been an inspiration to me, and your ability to do a Bonaly… well, I think we share a hero."

"Indeed we do." Blaze grasped her hand, hoping the weirdness would evaporate. "Best wishes on your upcoming marriage. I wish you both every happiness."

She fluttered her free hand around. "I'm sorry about… well, being stupid before."

"No worries." Trying to ease the tension, Blaze prayed for a topic change.

"The way Drake used to drool over you, that's the nickname I gave you. I'm sorry for objectifying you," Jasmine explained.

Blaze was taken aback. Lesson learned. He needed to be careful with the power of prayer. "Drake? Drooled over me? Details, please."

Taylor snorted. "You could say that."

"But we won't, will we," Drake growled.

Not being able to hold back the tease, Blaze asked, "Was Anna right all along? You're a blade bunny."

Everyone laughed. Even Drake, who kissed him on the cheek. "I'm totally a blade bunny for you. I'll show you later."

Blaze didn't even spare Drake a glance, because he felt his cheeks heating, so he threw out a distraction. "Well, if no one is asking the obvious question, I will. How and why are you handcuffed together? Or is this a Connecticut thing?"

"One of my bridesmaids thought it would be hilarious." Jasmine glanced at Taylor. "Mama was not pleased."

"I bet." Taylor leaned toward Blaze. "Our mom isn't uptight, but things should be a certain way… hers."

"And me handcuffed to her daughter like a ball and chain is not that way. I'm enjoying the benefits." William smushed Jasmine tight and kissed her cheek. "I hope she doesn't expect these cuffs back until after the honeymoon."

Jasmine grinned and giggled. "Exactly what I was thinking."

"Oh my God. Too much information, people." Taylor groaned.

"Jasmine! Come here. Question on the ceremony tomorrow," someone called out. Several women waved to her.

She sighed and gave Blaze a big smile. "I'll talk to you later."

"Hey! What about your brother and me?" Drake complained.

William shrugged as she tugged him away from the group.

"Just make sure he's at the parties tonight!" she called over her shoulder, tugging her groom-to-be up the small hill.

"That mister is going to be henpecked." Taylor shook his head.

Blaze added, "But from the grin on his face, I don't think he minds one bit."

They lapsed into a comfortable silence and drank while people-watching.

Taylor shrugged. "Hey, Blaze, I want to say I'm sorry I sprung the whole trans thing on you. I guess it's a bit of a shitty habit of mine."

"I think you needing to test people suggests how much further we all need to go with understanding what transgender means. But let me know if something I say bothers you."

Drake rolled his eyes. "Oh, you don't have to tell him. He's got no problem calling someone out. You might say he enjoys it."

"Teaching moments are good for all, and I do it with love." Taylor's mouth twisted into a smirk. Then his smile dropped. "Because gender's such an issue for my family—clearly—both Drake and I are standing up with my sister and her bridesmaids. William's sisters and a couple of his cousins will be at the altar with him."

"Cool. To be honest, I never really thought much about the gender identity, the binary… skating took up most of my brain, but it sucks to push people into boxes based on what's in their pants or their outward appearance. I look forward to your *loving* education."

Taylor nodded with a grin.

Drake said, "Oh, and the bachelor and bachelorette parties will be attended by anyone who wants to stop by."

Taylor slapped Drake on the back. "Except this man. My sister requires him through her entire party."

"That's only 'cause you refused."

"And miss a bachelor party? Nah, not me. I'll stop over *after* some fun at William's with your man here."

"You okay with that, Blaze?" Drake asked.

A piece of him wanted Drake to step in to save him from the new experience, but Taylor seemed to want to spend more time together. Blaze gave Drake a wink and said, "I'll miss you, but a bachelor party for a straight guy might be interesting. Besides, it'll give me time to get some of that dirt Taylor offered me."

Taylor grinned, then finished off the last of his drink as he sobered. "Oh, I should warn you. One of Jasmine's bridesmaids is bringing Dixon to the wedding."

Drake's mouth dropped open. "No. Fox is going to be there?"

"Isn't he the guy who encouraged the manager to kick you out of Midnight Shadow?" Blaze kept his voice down.

"Yup. This should be fun." Drake's grim expression said it would be anything but.

Taylor tilted his head. "Not what I'd call it, but yeah, the asshole will be there."

"WHERE'S THE strippers?" Taylor opened his second beer and handed Blaze a diet soda.

"Strippers?" One of the partygoers glanced around with hope on his face.

William snorted. "Why would I want to invite strippers?"

Taylor glared at him. "It's a damned bachelor party. Strippers are a requirement."

Blaze bit back a chuckle, because to laugh at someone's pain was wrong.

William unglued his gaze from the TV and stared at Taylor. "Maybe back in the day, but I'm marrying your sister tomorrow, and that's such a pre-MeTooMovement thing to do. Don't get me wrong, I'm not against strippers, or sex workers, for that matter—just not my thing."

Several guys nodded, along with two women.

"Your sister, she's my thing. Now shhh, this is her favorite part." William pointed to the screen, and the elf Legolas leaped from rock to rock while shooting his bow.

Taylor groaned and rolled his eyes at Blaze. "He's a bit of a nerd."

"What's your sister doing?" Blaze whispered so as not to disturb the others.

Taylor gave Blaze a long-suffering sigh. "Drake confirmed by text, the same as him."

"A *Lord of the Rings* marathon?" Blaze added, "I'm glad. They clearly are meant for each other."

"I guess," Taylor grumbled.

A few minutes later, Blaze's phone vibrated with a text from Drake. *I miss U.*

He sent back, *Miss you too.*

This movie is endless. Drake drew the same conclusion as he had.

LOL

When can you sneak—

"Hey, take his phone. William is texting Jasmine," one of the guests ratted out the groom-to-be.

A struggle ensued, but William kept his cell and promised not to text her after midnight.

We just tried to stop the bride from texting. Epic fail.

Blaze snorted. *Here too. There's no rule against it.*

Come over.

On my way.

Blaze whispered to Taylor, "I'm going to head over to Jasmine's party."

"Take me with you," Taylor whined.

"Of course."

Taylor tapped William on the shoulder. "Enjoy, man. We're going over to Jazzy's wild night."

William shook Taylor's hand and Blaze's. "Thanks for coming."

Taylor grumbled, "No one *came*."

Blaze chuckled.

Chapter 14

THE NEXT morning, Drake stood next to Taylor. Man, he hoped the purple flowers filling the altar wouldn't trigger Jazzy's allergies. The organ music could have used a little bit of guitar and some bass, but he knew Taylor and Jazzy's mother well enough not to suggest veering so far from tradition.

He smiled over at the groom, who didn't look nervous at all, just happy and excited.

While trying to ignore the music, Drake studied Blaze, who was two rows back with Drake's mom and dad.

At first, when his mom had lassoed an arm around him, Blaze appeared to be counting steps to the exit, but he had settled and now laughed at something Dad said.

It had been a risk bringing him to a wedding. A wedding celebrated commitment. Beyond Blaze's dedication to skating, commitment seemed to be frustratingly out of his wheelhouse. So having Blaze attend a wedding as a plus-one, which suggested a level of coupledom that Drake hadn't been positive Blaze would be okay acknowledging on such a scale, he skated on thin ice.

This was real life and far past couple status in their social media spheres. Drake couldn't help but measure how easily he fit in Blaze's Colorado existence. Even with skating, Luke, and Ice, there was plenty of room for him and them as a couple.

Since Drake considered them to be serious, he needed to see how Blaze would feel in his world. His parents gave Blaze the seal of approval even before they met him, and when Drake mentioned him in the limited conversations he'd had with his parents, that approval was reconfirmed. For Drake, the most impressive thing was seeing Blaze not only pass Taylor's fucked-up tests, but make a friend out of him.

It troubled Drake that Blaze wouldn't discuss plans beyond the wedding. Somehow today had become a make-or-break thing in their relationship. Though in fairness, he hadn't exactly brought the subject up either, because what exactly did he have to offer? Some royalty money if Midnight Shadow used his songs.

But between all the time he'd spent with Blaze and how Blaze's comfort zone had expanded, maybe there was hope. And newsflash, Drake wasn't planning to let Blaze toss what they had aside without a fight. He wanted them to work.

On the first notes of Pachelbel's "Canon in D," everyone got on their feet. Blaze caught Drake staring and gave him a small smile, which sent his heart into overdrive.

Jazzy looked magnificent in her white lace gown. While the dress hugged her curvaceous body, the flowers covering the material made it almost innocent. The tiara she wore raised her look to regal until she saw her groom and broke out in the big silly grin of a woman totally besotted by her man.

His attention darted to Blaze. Drake feared he drank in Blaze the very same way the bride and groom ogled each other.

Their gazes locked, and the corners of Blaze's mouth turned up.

Oh yes, Blaze Parker, you're mine. Now, how to convince Blaze of that?

DRAKE STOOD in the reception hall with his champagne glass in hand and pointed at Taylor with the microphone. "Leave it to Taylor to make everything hard on me. How do you follow a toast like that? I'll try."

"That's right. You got this, Drake," Jasmine called out.

Drake smiled as he tried to remember she wasn't ten years old. "That's my Jazzy. She encouraged me to never give up on my dreams.

"She said, 'If you want something, you go after it and don't let anything stop you.' I've always lived by that." A quick gaze at Blaze told him he'd continue to do so.

He paced in front of the dais. "Now I've known Jasmine, or Jazzy, as I have called her, since she was born. In every way, she's my sister, same as Taylor's my brother born to another mother."

Knowing he'd get flak from Taylor, he couldn't help but add, "I even helped Jazzy win the spelling bee."

Taylor whined, "Hey, I helped too."

Drake held up his index finger at Taylor. "No, I'll take all the credit for her seventh-grade win."

Jasmine snorted. "You're so silly, Drake."

"She's the type of person who knows what she wants and goes after it. I respect that. But together William and Jazzy have done something many of us could only dream of, finding that one perfect person we want to spend the rest of our life with." Drake darted his gaze to Blaze, who immediately stopped staring at Drake and pounded back his drink.

Drake refocused on the toast. "Oh, I know you two have been given a lot of grief by people worried about you being too young, who question how could you possibly know this is the one. But let's be honest, you know. I know just by looking at the two of you. You are meant to be together."

William pulled Jasmine into a kiss that spurred the glass-tapping tradition to begin. Jasmine shrugged, slid into his lap, and kissed him on the mouth one more time.

Someone yelled, "Save some for the honeymoon."

Once the laughter and applause died down, Drake continued. "Though I do need to report you both to your friends and family. During their bachelor and bachelorette parties, they were texting each other. They even synchronized watching *The Lord of the Rings* the director's cut extended version. Yeah, if you missed the wild event, they each had a marathon of elves, hobbits, and wizards. But for me, their parties confirmed they were meant to be."

Drake smiled at the happy couple, hoping he'd be allowed the same kind of romance. His gaze skittered back to Blaze as he said, "It won't always be easy, because love wasn't meant to be easy, but if you fight for the two of you and protect what you have, you'll find happiness together."

Raising his glass to Blaze, he spun in a circle to the rest of the crowd. He stopped when he faced Jazzy and her groom. "Congratulations. I wish you both the very best life has to offer. May love, happiness, and romance be yours always."

"NOT SURE if it's the open bar or the company, but I'm having a great time," Blaze whispered to him after dinner.

"I'm hoping it's the company," Taylor declared.

Blaze kissed Drake on the cheek. "I'm sure of it—oh, they're doing the cake bit. We have to watch."

"Why?" Drake was curious to see Blaze completely enthralled.

Blaze whispered, "I think it's telling of the relationship," and then he craned his neck to see the event.

William gently fed Jasmine a piece of cake, and she daintily did the same. Then they kissed stray icing off each other's lips.

"Aw! Perfect. They'll be happy together," Blaze declared, like he could see into the future.

Taylor *tsk*ed. "What do you mean? I know people who shoved the cake in each other's face and they're still happily married."

Blaze nodded. "It depends if the couple is like two playmates getting married. It's different if they both do the shoving lovingly and both have fun. But when there's a casual disregard of the other's feeling that—what?"

Drake shook his head.

Placing his elbow on the table, Taylor leaned into the palm of his hand. "You've given this some thought."

"Well, yeah. I guess." Blaze blushed a bit and shrugged.

"Does that mean you're the marrying kind, Blaze?" Taylor asked with a smirk.

Blaze's mouth dropped open, and he blinked rapidly. He turned toward Drake and said, "I hope so."

Oh? Drake tried to school his elation so he didn't dance around doing fist pumps to the relationship gods who graciously smiled down on him.

Blaze swallowed with a gulp and glanced away from the table.

Taylor stared at Drake with big eyes and tilted his head. He mouthed, "Slow your roll, bro."

Sighing, Drake mouthed back, "I didn't do anything; you did."

Taylor tapped Blaze on the arm. "Hey, Blaze, this is that line dance I told you about. It's yesterday's news, but you want to try it?"

Jumping to his feet, Blaze said, "Of course," and escaped toward the dance floor without looking at Drake.

Taylor laid a hand on Drake's shoulder and warned, "Chill. Don't push him."

"You were the one who asked. I didn't say anything. Not my first rodeo side-stepping Blaze's commitment phobia." The truly frustrating thing was Blaze triggered himself more than Drake did.

"You didn't have to, but my marrying-kind joke turned real by the hope and excitement written all over your face, which translated into major pressure for him. Be cool." Taylor headed off to the dance floor.

Dammit, he was, but how long could he skate on thin ice? Drake polished off the rest of his drink.

Dixon meandered over to Drake. "Surprised to see you here."

Fuck! Damn, Drake's luck on avoiding the asshole ground to a halt. "Why?"

"Thought you'd be getting ready," Dixon slurred.

"For…?"

Dixon gave him a stupid smirk. "Like you don't know."

"Whatever." Drake needed some air or maybe a safe haven away from jackasses.

Blaze now danced with Jasmine, pretending to pair skate. Jazzy giggled up a storm. Her new husband clapped them on as they glided around the floor. Drake caught his attention on a quick turn and a twitch of Blaze's hips. He held up a finger, letting him know he'd be back, and stalked out of the ballroom.

He searched for peace and found a quiet hallway with some chairs. No one was around, so he plopped down and closed his eyes for a minute.

"Or are you trying to say you haven't seen what Midnight Shadow has been posting?" Dixon's shrill voice invaded his solitude.

Dammit, Dixon had followed him and now stared down at him.

"Well, have you?" Dixon demanded.

Why would he? "No, I've taken some time away from social media."

A bitter laugh barked out of Dixon. "A cleanse?"

It sounded dumb when said aloud, which was why he hadn't really announced his status of not looking at Twitter, Facebook, and Instagram. Besides, Blaze kept him too busy to even miss his infrequent checking, and Blaze even posted and tagged Drake's page so he didn't feel any guilt about not keeping people informed of his life.

"I needed a goddamned break." Drake stood because he didn't like looking up at Dixon.

Dixon glanced down the hallway and shifted from foot to foot. "Hey, remember that guy in science class?"

The bastard reeked of alcohol and sweat, but Drake asked, "What guy?"

"You know, he showed up sophomore year. Super smart, like an incredibly hot nerd."

"*Incredibly hot* nerd?" That confirmed Dixon's lack of sobriety. He shouldn't be driving.

"Yeah, you remember. Steward Fudson? He had longish hair, always tangled, and the kindest amber eyes… like real soulful and shit… and his mouth…." Dixon's voice sounded weird and wistful somehow.

"The one you used to pick on?" Drake had vague memories of the kid—intelligent and really nice. Where was Dixon going with this?

Dixon stuffed his hands into his pockets. "I didn't… yeah, him. He wore his hair like you do now. So long you could pull it, and he'd make these cute little whimpers—" Dixon wobbled and then lunged mouth-first at Drake.

What the fuck? He tried to step back, but Dixon held him in place.

Dixon's mouth plastered against his, kissing him.

Fuck, what was happening? Was this an alternate universe? Drake tried to pull away.

Grabbing Drake's shoulders, Dixon clung. He even tried to part Drake's lips with his tongue.

That was it. Drake shoved him away. "No, Dixon. Stop. You're drunk."

"And I'll thank you to take your lips off my boyfriend." Blaze's voice had a sharp edge.

Dixon stopped his alcohol-soaked mouth from going back for Drake's lips. He glared at Blaze. "Why? He'll never be faithful to you, so you should get used to it."

Blaze folded his arms over his chest, and when Dixon didn't fill in the blanks, he asked, "Why do you think Drake is unable to have a monogamous relationship?"

"As beautiful as you are, he's *bisexual*." Dixon enunciated Drake's sexuality like he proved evidence of a crime.

Blaze gave him his are-you-stupid smile. "I don't think you understand what bisexual means."

"Whatever." Dixon wiped a hand over his mouth.

"No, not whatever. Definitions matter. Bisexuality means you're attracted to two genders."

"Ha, we'll see how faithful he is when he's back on tour." Dixon scoffed and started to stumble away.

Drake ignored the asshole and grabbed Blaze's hand. "Thank you for not thinking I would—tour? What the hell are you rambling about, Dixon? You got me tossed out of the band with your stupidity."

"Don't play dumb." Dixon clenched his fists.

Blaze tilted his head and stared at Drake like maybe he was drunk.

Why did both Blaze and Dixon look at him with expectations that he knew what the hell Dixon was referring to? "What tour?"

Dixon turned and scoffed, "Do you really not know?"

"Know what?" Strangling Dixon would get him into trouble, and he didn't want to cut his hair for jail.

Blaze cupped Drake's face and turned it toward his. "Is this why you haven't mentioned it?"

"Mentioned what?" Drake only had a couple of drinks, so he wasn't drunk, but *what*?

"Midnight Shadow's tour, it's all over social media," Blaze explained.

Dixon folded his arms over his chest and meandered back toward them. "Apparently your media cleanse was a bit too thorough."

"Shut up, Dixon." Drake stared at Blaze.

"Wait, you really don't have any clue about the band? Summer Simpson made a huge apology to you. She fired Frank and this dumbass who can't keep his lips off my boyfriend." Blaze gave Dixon a rather scary glare.

What the fuck? Had he been that much off the grid?

"Well, I'll leave you to your fuckery." Dixon turned and hurried down the hallway.

Drake cupped his hands and called out, "You're not driving, are you?"

Dixon stopped but didn't look back. "Nah, the bridesmaid I'm fucking did, and she's a vegan nondrinker or some shit," and then he continued on down the hallway.

Blaze stared at Drake with big eyes. "You really didn't know? How could you not know?"

"I didn't want to think about reality. Tay tried to bring up the band once or twice, but I nixed the discussion, and he respected that. My parents never mentioned anything, but they aren't on social media unless they are looking for pictures of me. I didn't want to deal with anything but being with you. Do you think the band called or texted?"

Pointing to Drake's cell, Blaze chuckled and advised, "Check."

Wow. "Twenty-five missed calls and a ton of texts."

"Listen to a message," Blaze suggested.

Drake put the message on speaker phone. "Hi, Drake. It's Summer again. Look, I'm super sorry Frank acted like a dick to you. I didn't know about any of it until I got back into town last week. I don't know if you got my last messages, but the band fired Frank, and when Dixon tried to justify what Frank had done to you, we got rid of him too. Please call me back."

He stumbled over to the chair and sat down. The band wanted him back. Drake stared at Blaze as if he might have the answers.

"Is this why you didn't bring up anything after the wedding?" Pieces were falling into place, and Drake could fill in the blanks, having learned how Blaze's mind worked.

Blaze shrugged and sat down. "I thought you knew about the band and weren't saying anything. By not talking about it, I thought you were sending me a message. I didn't know what to think, other than you didn't want to share it with me."

Drake couldn't believe Blaze and he were that stupid, but there it was. "So of course instead of asking me about it—newsflash, I love you."

Blaze's eyes widened. "You what?"

No more skating on thin ice. It was time to rock reality. "I love you. I'm sorry if that scares you, but that's all my cards on the table. I want no more confusion between us."

Blaze stood, yanked him out of the seat, and pulled him close. He tugged Drake down so he was in kissing range and pressed his lips against Drake's. He delivered the sweetest, softest kiss in history.

Drake's toes curled as the affection wound its way through his body and into his heart.

When the kiss ended, Blaze whispered, "I must like you a whole bunch if I can enjoy your lips even with Dixon's homophobic and biphobia flavoring on them."

Drake couldn't be disappointed Blaze hadn't said "I love you" back, because for now the confession of "like you a whole bunch" was a huge win.

He grinned and went with "Do you really taste him?"

Blaze chuckled. "No, not really… only in my head."

"Let's go into the bathroom." Drake pointed at the door a few feet away.

Blaze purred, "Oh? Hand jobs in the bathroom?"

Shaking his head, Drake clarified, "There's mouthwash in there."

"Oh, right, fancy hotel, and probably an attendant," Blaze mumbled with a frown.

Drake didn't want him to think he wasn't interested in anything and everything Blaze could come up with to do, but not in a bathroom. "But later."

"Yeah?" Blaze's smile would win any competition. His smile made him sparkle brighter than all the stars in the sky.

"Definitely… anything you want." As they walked into the bathroom, Drake added, "Not for nothing, but thanks for not thinking I would willingly kiss Dixon."

Blaze rolled his eyes and did a quick spin, showing off all his best bodily assets. "I may have some insecurities, but I do think highly of myself in some regards. You choosing Dixon over me… not in this lifetime."

"Taylor would have liked seeing you put Dixon in his place about bisexuality." *Hmmm, maybe I should speak to Taylor about pansexuality, because that's a more accurate account of where my attraction falls. Or maybe queer might be the best label—not the time.*

After he and Blaze used the urinals, washed their hands, and used the mouthwash, they headed back to the reception.

The band played "Flightless Bird, American Mouth" by Iron & Wine. Drake led Blaze onto the dance floor. He'd never slow danced with a man before, but when Blaze spun into his arms, nothing had ever felt so right.

He was breathless by the way Blaze didn't exactly follow. They partnered each other, flowing from spinning to stepping in perfect time with the music and each other.

Blaze asked, "Isn't this the song in the prom scene from *Twilight*?"

Drake smiled at the memory of Blaze curled up in his arms, enthralled by the vampires who sparkled in the sunshine. There were so many gaps in Blaze's experience, and Drake happily guided him. "Yeah, it's also in a later movie we haven't watched yet."

"I look forward to watching the rest with you." The words fell from Blaze's mouth without hesitation.

Drake fought down the excitement that skittered through him over Blaze mentioning doing something together after the wedding. He breathed a sigh of relief that his "I love you" hadn't put distance between them.

He pulled Blaze close, moving to the haunting melody. Staring deep into Blaze's eyes, knowing he'd never get tired of this or Blaze, Drake knew in his heart of hearts he never wanted this to end.

As the song finished, Taylor danced over to them holding a frosted sugar cookie. "Since you were MIA, I saved you guys one."

"Aw, thanks, Taylor." Blaze nabbed the cookie and held the treat up to Drake's mouth.

Drake bit into the sugary sweetness and chewed. He took the cookie from Blaze and fed him a bite.

Once Blaze swallowed, he kissed Drake gently on the mouth and then proclaimed, "It's not cake, but you should know we have the potential to be very happy together."

Taylor slapped them both on the back. "You two need to stop being so cute, or I'll have to think about finding Mrs. Right instead of Ms. Right Now."

Drake chuckled. "You're such an ass."

"Yeah, yeah. The reception is almost over. You guys going to see the fireworks afterward?"

"Fireworks?" Blaze asked as he guided Drake's hand to his mouth and took another bite of the sweet.

"Yeah, West Haven has the best Fourth of July weekend fireworks in the state. It's a huge celebration." Drake ate half of what remained, then held the last piece out for Blaze, who took the rest of the cookie with a grateful smile, and gently licked his fingers clean of crumbs.

After swallowing, Blaze commented, "But it's not July Fourth."

Drake nodded. "Happens on July third here, which is why Jasmine picked this venue."

"Easy access to the beach," Taylor finished the explanation. "And I remembered to bring shorts, T-shirts, and flip-flops."

"Really? Color me surprised." Drake teased because Taylor was notorious for forgetting the basics.

"You're welcome. Okay, it was your mom and mine who reminded me about six times, but it sounds better if I take the credit. I did remember to pack the shit into my trunk."

Blaze grinned. "You totally get credit, Taylor. Thank you. Though I still need to thank your mom and Drake's."

After a few more dances, the reception ended with the bride and groom kissing and hugging the guests, their parents, and siblings before fleeing to the beach in T-shirts with *Just Married* scrolled on the front and matching shorts.

Drake, Blaze, and Taylor changed, leaving their fancy clothes in Taylor's trunk.

"Blaze, enjoy the fireworks. D, I'll text you later." Taylor slapped them both on the back and meandered off, probably heading to find his latest conquest.

"We can cut back through the reception hall for the quickest way to the beach." Grabbing a blanket from the deck of the venue's patio, Drake led Blaze onto the sand to a place away from the crowd. With Blaze's help, they laid out the blanket, using their flip-flops in each corner to keep it spread open in spite of the breeze.

Blaze crashed down and leaned into Drake.

Drake could hear the wheels turning in Blaze's brain. "What?"

"Don't know whether it's the drink or you, but freedom and independence used to be really important to me. I didn't let anyone get close. And now, well, things have changed because of you."

The first fireworks streaked into the air and burst.

"What do you mean?" Drake had been almost afraid to ask.

"You fit me." The next explosion reflected in his eyes.

Drake combed his fingers through Blaze's hair. "I really do love you. I know you probably think it's too early to say that, but I do. This has been the best month and a half of my life."

Blaze took Drake's face in his hands and kissed him until he didn't know whether the fireworks were happening over the water or in his heart. When the kiss ended, Blaze said, "It's not too soon, because I love you too."

Chapter 15

BLAZE STUMBLED into their hotel room with his mouth attached to Drake's, needing a bed for their fireworks finale. His heart kept doing triple axels in time with the explosions outside their window.

"You want to?" Drake asked in between gasps and kisses.

He didn't have to ask what Drake meant. Somehow Blaze wanted the connection that being inside Drake would allow. Blaze couldn't give him words, so he nodded.

Drake separated his mouth from Blaze's. "Let me go grab a shower."

Reality started to seep in, but Blaze tried to sound normal. "Sure."

He fell onto the bed, back first, but bounced off, hurrying to sit in the chair across the room. The shower started.

He glared at the pristine all-white bed that mocked him. The turn-down service had tucked away the fussy decorative pillows, the white duvet had been folded down, and two bottles of water and a chocolate lay on each of the nightstands.

Was he one orgasm away from the end with Drake? That was insane, but old beliefs died hard. Their relationship didn't have to be at the end, right? Drake hadn't purposefully not been talking to him about the band; he hadn't known…. But he'd be going on tour.

This was actual boyfriend seal-the-deal intercourse. Shit! What was the agreement they were signing up for, and more to the point, what the hell did he even know about any of this?

He usually found a guy on a hookup app, met at their location, and screwed. Sometimes the random guy arranged for the door to be unlocked and the stranger was already bent over the couch or bed, waiting for a cock to arrive. No real names were ever exchanged, and sometimes there was no communication other than body language, a butt thrust toward him, or an escaped sigh. Then Blaze would walk away, sometimes without even talking.

The anonymity had been sexy in the beginning. A power trip for Blaze that someone he didn't know wanted to be fucked by him… but now?

That wouldn't be what this would be like. Right? Of course not. This was Drake.

But what if fucking ruined everything? He'd never gone beyond the fucking with the hookups, although emotionally he'd gone all the way with Drake and then some. He'd said he loved him, and screw everything if he didn't mean it with all his heart, but—

Drake stepped out of the bathroom in a towel.

Panic ripped through Blaze. "Um, I'm going to take a shower too. I got sweaty dancing, and well, I'll be right back."

He escaped into the bathroom. Dammit, why was this a big deal? It shouldn't be. They'd sucked each other off every day, sometimes three times a day. Also given each other slow, delicious hand jobs while they watched movies. So fucking him didn't have to be huge.

They loved each other. They were boyfriends... but for how long?

Trying not to hyperventilate, he turned on the water and stepped into the shower. Shit, he hadn't even been this nervous when he touched Olympic ice for the first time.

This was just sex….

His heart screamed this was so much more. Anything with Drake took on an importance he'd never experienced before.

Why had he confessed his love? He turned the pressure cooker of crazy to maximum.

He soaped, rinsed, and dried off.

After smelling the shorts and T-shirt he'd worn on the beach, he pulled the still clean clothing on. He needed the protection. Then he brushed his teeth and his hair.

Well, he couldn't stay in here all night.

A mostly naked Drake sat in the middle of the bed with his guitar. When he looked up, the smile he gave made Blaze feel like he could do twenty quads in a row, which was weird since he couldn't move.

Drake set his guitar aside and met him in front of the bed with a heart-stopping kiss.

Fear skittered through Blaze. He took control of the kiss and dragged his lips to Drake's ear. "Maybe we should wait."

"For?" Drake asked and started licking along Blaze's neck.

"I don't know. You must be tired." And he really didn't—

"Are you afraid to fuck me?" Drake guided him back toward the bed.

"Why would you think that? I've fucked tons of guys." That wasn't bragging, simply a fact, but still gross to say it like that. "I mean—"

"Then why haven't we screwed? We've done everything else. Blaze, talk to me." Drake's voice transformed from teasing to more understanding concern.

Blaze hated the sympathy and couldn't look at him for fear he'd see pity in Drake's eyes.

"What's going on?" Drake grabbed Blaze and ran his fingers through Blaze's hair.

Unfair! Drake had learned early on that playing with Blaze's hair sent shivers of pleasure through him, which turned off his resistance. Thankfully, there was only empathy and understanding in Drake's gaze.

Blaze sighed and confessed his stupidity. "What if we don't feel the same afterward?"

"Why would being together like this change our feelings?" Drake dropped his hands to his sides and gave him a bewildered look that made Blaze's heart ache.

God, was he this broken? Blaze moved to the window and stared out into the darkness. "I don't want you to be like all the others."

Drake opened the window, allowing the salty breeze in.

Blaze shivered at the chill, and Drake wrapped his arms around him, making him feel deceptively safe.

The firework finale began with colorful bursts lighting the sky.

"That's a peony in white, which is the most common firework." Drake identified the white stationary stars that had no tails filling the blackened sky. He gestured to the blue. "See the blue with the streaking tails? It's called a chrysanthemum."

Why hadn't Blaze wondered about the names of fireworks before now? "Cool. What's that one?"

Another white with a red center exploded. A blue with a white center took its place.

Drake kissed the side of Blaze's face. "That's almost a chrysanthemum, but because of the colored stars in the center, it's a diadem."

"Oh." Blaze resisted the need to "oh" and "ah" at each explosion, but that one slipped out.

Red, white, and blue burst, and each star broke off into smaller ones. "See the crisscross pattern? That's the crossette."

"How do you know—oh, that's my favorite." Blaze pointed to the dome-shaped, long-burning sparkles dripping down the sky.

"Mine too. It's the willow."

Blaze sighed. "You're truly amazing, and like no one else I've ever met."

"Is that why we haven't been together in this way, because you're worried this will turn out to be like one of your other hookups? Or I would?"

"When you say it like that…." Blaze pressed his lips together and found Drake's gaze reflected in the window. He hated to admit he was waiting for Drake to devastate him like Trent had done. Even though he knew it was insane, he shrugged.

"We definitely need to talk more, because I thought you just weren't ready. So I didn't push you." Drake gave him a small but sad smile and tucked behind his ear some of the hair that had allowed Blaze a place to hide. "It's okay if you want to wait."

Fireworks exploded in rapid sequence. The colors mixed as they raced to the ocean.

"I don't want to wait. I was ready the moment I saw you." That was the truth.

Drake tightened his arms around him. "I can still see a little doubt in your eyes. Let me explain something to you. You know what the difference between us and every other man you've ever been with is?"

Blaze stared at him. He opened his mouth—

"Love. We love each other. This one act isn't going to change that." Drake's steadiness was calming.

Though how could he make Drake comprehend the level of his dysfunction? "You know, that's why I blew you that first time. I wanted to put my emotions in order so I could file you away."

Blaze awaited indignation, hurt, and finally, dismissal. He got none of what he anticipated.

Straightening to his full height, Drake smirked and lifted his chin. "How did that work for you?"

The sky went dark, and the crowd applauded for the fireworks, not Drake's zinger.

Blaze glared at him through the window's reflection. He'd fallen in love with the bastard.

"Did you toss me away?" Drake asked, like that had ever been a question.

"No! Never!" Blaze didn't mean to sound so sharp, but no fucking way. Not even in his commitment-phobic mind would he allow Drake to think for a second that Blaze didn't want him.

"Then why would this change what we have?" Drake tilted his head and studied Blaze.

"I don't want to lose you, and that scares the fuck out of me." There was his truth.

"I hope not *all* the fuck, 'cause I'd still like your dick inside of me in this lifetime." Drake spun him away from the window and guided him to the bed.

Blaze snorted. "You're an idiot."

"I am. I'm an idiot for you. I don't give a shit if you blew me to reset your perspective and not because you couldn't resist the sexiness in front of you." Drake chuckled and pressed kisses on Blaze's cheeks and eyelids.

"The sexiness in front of me…." Blaze loved him so much, it was crazy.

"Blow me anytime you like to reset your priorities." Drake jerked his head in the general direction of a nightstand. "There's a bottle of lube in the drawer, on your side of the bed."

They had sides of the bed? Oh my God! He and Drake did have their own sides of the bed. He slept on the right side, and Drake curled up behind him on the left. When did that happen? Glancing at Drake, he realized it didn't matter, but he was elated it did.

"Unless you don't want to…."

Blaze clarified, "Oh, I want to fuck you until you see Jimi Hendrix."

Drake gave him another one of his sexy, infuriating, and completely calm grins. "Now that's tempting for *all* the reasons."

"Which are?" Blaze stepped away from the hug and put his hands on his hips.

"Well-fucked until I see the dead would be a pretty impressive altered state of reality." Drake's cheeks heated. "But just having you inside of me would be more than enough."

God, when Drake said things like that, everything Blaze had believed became twisted and got kicked to the curb. Drake's sincerity continued to touch places deep within his soul.

Systematically, Drake knocked down the walls of ice surrounding Blaze's heart, ice brick by ice brick. Now the final ice wall started to crumble, and instead of his fear trying to rebuild the barrier, something akin to relief and calm crept through him, revealing the rightness of them.

Hell, there were times Blaze even helped Drake to build a door when the wall had been too reinforced.

Skates on fire! He'd always wanted Drake to reach him. Blaze had been rooting for his own defeat so he could win.

Drake lay back on the bed. He toyed with the towel's end and then unwrapped the towel. Drake shifted on the bed, highlighting the fact his hard cock waited for Blaze. Drake once again magically yanked Blaze out of his spiraling crazy without much effort at all.

His long hair waved out over the pillow, and Drake tucked one hand under his head, reaching out with his other.

This was it. Did Blaze take the offer, or did he refuse?

Blaze grabbed his hand and allowed Drake to tug him onto the bed. He lay next to the delicious man-buffet ready for him. Out of everything he could have played with, he picked up a piece of Drake's hair, twirled the strands between his fingers. Feelings of affection grew so strong, they threatened to overwhelm him. His voice broke a little when he said, "You're beautiful."

"Thank you." Drake hauled him into a kiss.

The soft kiss was sweet and exactly like so many others they'd shared, but now Blaze had admitted he loved Drake. Shouldn't that change things?

He threw a leg over Drake with more possessiveness to get closer, pressing in as the kiss morphed into a toe-curling, blistering exchange of lips and tongue.

Drake turned toward him and rutted his hard-on against Blaze's thigh.

Pulling his mouth off Drake's, Blaze asked, "You really want to do this?"

Grinning, Drake rubbed his dick over Blaze's thigh again. "Yes, I really need you inside of me."

Blaze rolled him onto his stomach, exposing Drake.

Drake thrust back in invitation.

"Fucking hell," Blaze groaned and couldn't resist running his hands over Drake's asscheeks.

"I know I don't have a skater's ass, but I love your hands on me." Drake wiggled into Blaze's touch and arched his back.

"Your ass is a magnificent rock star's butt." Blaze polished his hands over Drake's butt like his cheeks were made of spun gold. Then he massaged Drake's rump, kneading the muscles, hoping to relax Drake—and himself.

Blaze pressed a gentle kiss on Drake's right cheek and another to his left, wet his lips, and traced his mouth over the curve of Drake's ass.

"Fuck," Drake groaned.

"Is this okay?" Blaze had never been so affectionate or careful when he was fucking, so was this weird? Maybe it wasn't what Drake wanted.

"Definitely." Drake ended in a gasp.

Blaze trailed his wet tongue along Drake's crease. Drake was warm and smelled of the hotel's sandalwood soap.

"No one… no one's ever done that." Drake's meaning fell out between heavy pants.

His breath caught. Blaze had never eaten anyone's ass before. It had always seemed way too intimate, but that was exactly why he wanted to share this with Drake. He loved how sexy, affectionate, and delectably filthy doing this to Drake made him feel.

Drake spread his knees, allowing Blaze deeper access.

Licking his tongue down his crack, Blaze adored how a simple well-placed swipe seemed to make Drake grind down into the bed.

Blaze parted Drake's asscheeks and ghosted warm breath over him, enjoying Drake's twists and hip swivels of anticipation, filled with what Blaze hoped was longing.

Drake pushed back onto Blaze's questing tongue, and Blaze rewarded him by separating his cheeks wider and dipping deeper along the crevice. Each time Blaze traveled the path, he burrowed his wet tongue closer to where Drake wanted him to be.

Drake glanced over his shoulder with a frown. "Do you regret telling me you loved me?"

"You really do talk a lot during sex." Blaze tried to make a joke, but Drake's frown intensified. "No, I don't regret it."

"Are you freaking out?" Drake studied Blaze way too closely.

"A little. But not like before." Until Drake brought it up. "Are you having second thoughts about telling me you love me?"

Drake scoffed as well as anyone could with his bare ass exposed. "Of course not. I just want you to know I want to make us work."

Blaze nodded. He wanted that too, much more than was comfortable. "I know. I do too."

Long licks should have made Drake want to focus on the sex.

Instead Drake promised, "Then we can."

"You're really a chatterbox. Let's try some dirty talk," Blaze begged, because this conversation reminded him of what was an impossible situation, and when had love ever really won anything?

Drake growled, "I want you to lick me out. Then I'm going to take you up my ass so far we won't know where you end and I begin."

"Mmmm, yes. Keep talking." Blaze drove tongue first into Drake's ass and made Drake's words a reality.

Drake's body welcoming him made Blaze crave even more of what would likely be out of his reach with their careers and their homes being thousands of miles apart. His heart rebelled now that he'd clarified they wanted the same things, and he couldn't help but hope they would figure out a way to make their relationship work somehow.

"Right there." Drake continued to shift and writhe, allowing Blaze access until his tongue was buried as deep as the length let him go. "More, Blaze. Please. More."

Blaze breathed heavily as he added his fingers and worked them in concert with his tongue. He relied on the expertise that only came with watching lots of rimming videos, and on Drake's sighs and whimpers.

Determined not to think about all the others, Blaze focused on Drake and how he melted into a squirming mess all for him.

Drake begged, "Blaze, come on. Give it to me."

He shouldn't have been worried; this time everything was different. This was Drake… and he didn't want to "give it" to him.

Blaze rolled him onto his back.

"Oh." Drake groaned, probably at his dick no longer getting friction from the bed. His glossy-tipped cock saluted and throbbed for attention. "Um, this way?"

"What?" Blaze froze. Had he done something wrong? He'd seen boyfriend videos where guys fucked like this so they could give googly eyes. Jesus, he'd never been this unsure of himself before, but he was pretty sure he wanted to make googly eyes at Drake.

"I've never done it this way."

Blaze stared down at him, feeling stupid and a bit exposed. "Me either, but if you'd rather we didn't do face-to-face, no worries."

"I want to be able to see you." Drake gave him a dreamy smile and definitely some googly eyes.

"I do too."

"This feels right, like this is the way it should be between us." Drake once again spoke his truth without worrying if he sounded like a sap or not.

The risk and trust Drake put in him made Blaze grin ear to ear. "Yeah."

No more backpedaling—this was the moment he'd been anticipating and avoiding.

Blaze's gaze zeroed in on Drake's erection, and then he gazed into Drake's eyes and licked his lips. His hair curtained his face as he leaned over and swiped his tongue to gather the precum Drake leaked, teasing them both.

"Oh God. Blaze," Drake begged.

Answering Drake's plea, Blaze finally took Drake into his mouth.

The hot, wet suction Blaze provided ripped another groan from Drake. He didn't even thrust his hips, because Blaze put forth all the effort. Working his O-shaped lips down to the root of Drake's dick, he swiped his tongue across his balls.

Drake's eyelids slid shut, but he kept blinking them open.

Show-off that he was, Blaze decided to impress Drake. He pressed his fingers back inside of Drake and then went down on him. He gagged a couple of times, which made Drake squeeze his soon-to-be-filled asscheeks.

"God, I love your mouth on me, but I need…." Drake's words came out sounding like a moan with syllables.

Blaze bobbed his head a few more times and pulled all the way off, smiling.

Drake tried to talk while Blaze pushed down his shorts and rolled a condom on. The words didn't turn into sentences. He added lube to his covered dick. This was no longer a concept. He'd be inside Drake soon.

Trembling, he couldn't ever remember wanting someone this bad, but even more than the physical, he longed for connection. Jesus! Who was he?

Drake didn't do much but lie there, though fuck, he looked incredibly sexy and willing. He reached out and clutched at Blaze with desperation, as if only Blaze could give him what he longed for.

Worry that Blaze would come immediately warred with excitement while he tried to make sense of his intense emotions.

He loved Drake, and regardless of what paths either of them took, Blaze wanted to make *this* work. Not just the sex, but them. Though the band wanted Drake back and there was the Olympics to consider. He needed to—

Close-clipped nails raked into Blaze's thigh, forcing him into the here and now. His beautiful rock-star boyfriend waited for him.

Blaze added some lube to his fingers and glided them into Drake. Tight and responsive, Drake's body squeezed around his fingers.

"Please. I'm ready." Drake panted.

Staring down into Drake's eyes, Blaze saw forever. He not only loved Drake, he wanted forever. *How in the fuck would that—*

Drake pulled back his knees, inviting Blaze to explore him further. Blaze's world shrank to this moment.

The position no longer represented submission in Blaze's head. It morphed into Drake offering more of himself to Blaze. More love burst through him.

Blaze twisted his fingers out, ran his erection over Drake's opening, and rested against him. "Do you want me to add more lube? I can—"

"No, I'm ready. I've never been face-to-face. I want to feel you in me."

Blaze nudged himself inside a bit.

Drake used one hand and pulled him down into a kiss, which made him sink farther into Drake's body.

Fuck, this felt so *personal, loving, good…* nothing like all the other times Blaze had screwed some nameless guy. He broke the kiss and could read every desire skittering across Drake's face. He wanted to fulfill all of them.

He put his hands on either side of Drake's head. Blaze surrounded him, but he was imprisoned by Drake's enthrallment, and he never wanted to be paroled.

"Ready?" The word had been sliced by the emotional razor blades in Blaze's throat, giving away much more than he'd ever wanted to willingly hand over in the past, but this was Drake. Not even everything was enough.

"Please." Drake begged for much more than the physical. Blaze heard, *"Please take what I offer. Please be who I think you are. Please love me back. Please, let's figure out forever."*

Blaze desperately wanted all those things too. He leaned down and pressed his mouth to Drake's at the moment he breached him farther with a slow, gentle push into the tight grip.

Drake inhaled sharply.

Freezing, Blaze gave him time to adjust. "A little more?"

Nodding, Drake moaned out, "Yeah."

Love flowed between them. Blaze imagined he could almost see the shared bond twining both of their hearts together like in one of the rom-coms he and Drake had watched on Netflix.

Drake let go of his knees and clasped Blaze's shoulders. "More. I want all of you."

And fuck if Blaze didn't want to give him that and more. Blaze sunk deeper and deeper still, until he was completely inside.

Drake clutched at Blaze's shoulders as his body clenched around the invading cock. Shifting back and forth, Drake demanded, "Come on."

Withdrawing on a gentle glide, Blaze closed his eyes to savor the tight grip of muscles. Drake's body pleaded with him to stay. Sliding in and out of Drake filled the empty parts of Blaze he hadn't even known were there.

He opened his eyes and brushed Drake's hair out of his face. He didn't bother to hide the love that threatened to overwhelm him.

Drake ran a finger over Blaze's lips and gave him a plucky grin.

Their rhythm faltered.

Drake surrendered to him, lying there naked and exposed.

Why did Blaze still have his T-shirt on? Shit, he should have undressed so they were skin on skin. He didn't want anything separating him from Drake.

Blaze threw off his T-shirt.

Ever since he'd known Drake, the man kept prying open the cracks in Blaze's protective walls, and now Drake helped him climb out from behind his self-made barricade.

Gasping, Drake closed his eyes. "Too much. Not enough."

Ah, there it was. Blaze's lips turned up in a smile laced with triumph at having found Drake's prostate, which Blaze zoned in on, trying to memorize the location.

He held out his hand to Drake. "Lick it. Use your tongue and get my palm wet."

Drake flicked his talented tongue over Blaze's palm.

Closing his fist around Drake's cock, Blaze gave him a long, slow stroke.

Drake twined his legs around Blaze's waist, whimpered, and pulled Blaze into him. He rocked into Blaze's thrust. "Want you in deep."

Blaze nailed Drake's prostate with precision again and again, impaling him with pleasure.

Gasping, Drake came all over his chest and Blaze's hand.

Blaze stroked him through his orgasm.

That was it. Blaze teetered on the precipice of need and just short of bliss.

Drake still moaned. Being with Drake was all too much.

His belly tensed. Sliding in deep, he threw back his head and groaned, "Drake."

Orgasm knocked through him with almost painful contractions. His body quivered on top of Drake. Endless waves coursed through him until he crashed down and held the man he loved. This was everything he'd never had.

Stupid happiness at having shared this with Drake knocked him sideways. Kissing the tip of Drake's nose, he pulled out and rolled off him. "Hate that."

Drake grimaced. "Yup."

Blaze stood and tossed the condom in the bathroom trash can. He gathered his shorts and threw them, along with his T-shirt, into his laundry bag.

"So, um, Blaze?"

"Yeah?" Blaze slipped the towel out from under Drake and wiped him down. After dropping the terry cloth to the floor, he tugged the bedding from under Drake and covered him. He slipped between the sheets himself.

"Um, Blaze, are we done with the bullshit? Or are you taking the train to Regretsville?" Drake's smile held worry, which drained the funny out of the attempted joke.

"I'm taking the express train to Sleepytown." Blaze read in Drake's expression that wasn't enough reassurance, or really any at all. "The only regret I have is not doing that with you sooner."

"Sooner?"

"Like the second I met you."

Drake snorted. "So you don't think it ruined everything?"

"No, but a lot has happened today. There's a bunch to figure out. We can start fresh tomorrow, right?"

"Yeah, I guess." Drake sighed and rolled into him.

"Oh, let me see if I can get us a late checkout." Blaze made the call and confirmed, "We have until tomorrow at two o'clock."

Drake wrapped him in a sleepy embrace, becoming the big spoon, and whispered, "Just so you know, I want to be your new safe haven. I know I'm tempting the fates by admitting that aloud again, but I want to make this work with you."

Blaze didn't respond—not because agreeing would tempt fate, but because he didn't see how this was going to work.

Chapter 16

THANK FUCK, Drake was glad when Blaze blinked his eyes open. Usually he rose before dawn, but today he had slept until 5:00 a.m. Finally, they could discuss the future… *their* future. "Good morning."

Blaze gave him a quick kiss, and then he must have caught sight of the clock. "Why are you up so early?"

Dare Drake admit he hadn't slept much? He'd showered, worked on the lyrics that seemed to flow, and tried not to obsess. He'd always give Blaze the truth. "I've been up since three."

"Aw, you only got like two hours of sleep." Blaze kissed his cheek.

That bit of affection gave him the courage he needed to spit out, "Well, we've got a lot to talk about."

He jumped to his feet, hit the prepped coffee maker, followed Blaze into the bathroom, and brushed his teeth.

Blaze used the toilet, washed his hands, and also brushed his teeth. Both of them returned to the bedroom, and as they started pulling out clothing to wear, Blaze began the conversation with "Okay, let's talk. I thought you knew about the band or I would have told you."

Drake shook his head. "I don't know how I avoided the information. Maybe I didn't want to know. I didn't want our magical bubble to burst."

"Ha, sweet talker. Though you must be excited about being back in the band," Blaze said over his shoulder as he grabbed a pair of sweatpants and slipped them on.

Drake enjoyed how the sweats did nothing to hide the perfection of Blaze's ass as he padded to the gray round leather couch and sat shirtless among all the decorative pillows.

He pulled on a pair of his own sweats. "Well, I haven't accepted the band's offer yet."

Blaze stared at him. "Oh? I thought you'd have done that immediately."

He handed Blaze the tea he'd made him. "I ran plain water through the machine so you won't have old coffee taste mixed with your tea."

"Thanks for doing that, and the tea. But you will tell the band yes, right?" Blaze asked as he finger combed his hair, like the answer was a foregone conclusion.

Drake hid his surprise by popping in the little pod of coffee and watching the hot ambrosia pour into his cup. "I don't know. It's one of the decisions we need to make."

"We?" Blaze choked on his tea.

Drake collapsed into the chair, and though he half expected to see the Blaze-relationship backpedal, it still frustrated him. "Yeah, *we*. Problem?"

Blaze shook his head. "Well, I mean… um, you know. You shouldn't make your career decisions based on me."

"I was under the impression you wanted to make us work. Aren't we going to try?" He'd feared this. Almost all previous interactions suggested Blaze would run.

"Yes. But you should make your decision on what *you* want. This is your second chance. Hell, you barely had your first chance. I don't want *us* to take that from you." Blaze pointed at him.

One of the things his father had drilled into Drake was that the most important decision a person makes is who to spend their life with. If you make the right choice, everything else falls into place from there. Drake expected he'd need to fight for what he desired and was ready to make compromises to follow through with what was happening between them.

Though Taylor's lesson in timing came to mind. At times, picking the right time made the difference between getting the answer you prayed for and getting a rejection. Right now, telling Blaze that Drake wanted him to be the center of his everything would be the worst timing ever.

Maybe for some people this would've been quick, but Drake knew what he wanted. He'd be patient. "Okay, changing gears. What do *you* want?"

Blaze's head dropped back against the sofa. He closed his eyes for a moment and sighed. "I don't know. But I do know I'm tired of missing out on life."

"Tell me what you mean?" Drake knew what he meant, but he wanted Blaze to talk his feelings and thoughts out to eliminate any confusion or assumptions.

"I've been skating seven days a week, training six out of the seven, since I was eight years old. I do weights, run, stretch, take ballet classes, my whole focus has been to be a better skater… and for what?"

Drake shrugged. "Gold medals, fame, and fortune."

Blaze snorted. "I don't know, maybe I want to try living my life for a little bit without a crazy training schedule."

"What?" Drake couldn't imagine Blaze not skating.

Blaze paced to the window and opened the heavy silverish gray drape, letting in the brightening sky. "In order to achieve what I have, I'd given up a lot."

"I know, your list has some really basic things on it." Drake would make sure they did everything on the list.

Blaze toyed with the drapery. "I'm embarrassed to say the actual list we've been working down is much longer than that. I don't know, maybe I want more of a real life. Do you know last night was the first fireworks show I've seen in person? I'm always asleep too early."

Drake wasn't surprised.

Blaze paced. "Even taking this driving trip with you has been astonishing and educational. I've seen so many things I never even knew existed."

"Yeah, that art fair in Chicago was pretty cool." Drake had made his mom and Blaze each a painted silk scarf.

Blaze sighed. "I've never taken the time to do an art fair or a farmers' market, even though Safe Haven has a bunch of them. There's so much more I haven't even experienced, because I've never been out of the rink for that long."

Drake rubbed his eyes as they adjusted to the brightness. "But what are you saying? I can't imagine you not skating."

"I'd still skate. I might not be training for the Olympics as hard. It's four years away. I could take some time off, and I'd have time to get back into competition form and qualify…."

Drake's gears turned quickly. Instead of thinking or biding his time, he spewed an idea, a fantasy really, that had been half-formed. "If I went on tour with the band, would you go with me?"

Blaze laughed but turned to stare at him. "What, as your personal groupie?"

"No, as my boyfriend." That could work. Why wouldn't it? Summer's fiancé joined them often enough.

Shaking his head, Blaze gasped. "I'd feel like—"

"That you'd be living your life and seeing the world with your boyfriend?" Drake finished quickly.

Blaze paced back to the sofa with his arms folded over his chest. "How would the band take that?"

Not a no. Fuck, yeah! That was not a no. "As long as being with you doesn't interfere with the band, why would they care?"

"Well, I think you need to find out." Blaze gave a dismissive gesture, like Drake wasn't serious.

Resisting the fist pump, Drake snatched his cell and typed out a text. *Any issue if Blaze Parker hangs out on the tour with me? I'll cover any additional expenses.* He hit Send.

Blaze stared at him with a tilted head. "Um, what did you do?"

"Asked." His phone started vibrating.

Swallowing hard, Blaze asked, "Don't you want to, you know, take some time and think about it?"

Drake chuckled. "I'm crystal clear on what I want."

His cell buzzed.

Heart pounding, Drake glanced at his screen.

"It's Summer." Her text didn't surprise him, considering she refused to let the tour bus stop at any anti-LGBTQIA fast-food chains. She claimed with pride her gold-star membership of never ever eating at chick-a-fuck was hers until death.

"What did she say?" Blaze sat on the bed next to Drake and bit his thumbnail.

Drake read the text out loud: "Does this mean you're in? If so, then I've got no issue. I'd appreciate having an ice skating diva who understands me."

His phone buzzed again and again.

"Amanda, she's the drummer, and her brother, Artano, who plays second guitar, texted, *Arty and I don't give a shit. You do you, man.* Jessie, the bass player, wrote, *As long as he's not terrible, I'm good.* I guess somebody named Sandy replaced Dixon the Dickhead, and they said they're good." Drake turned to Blaze.

Blaze wrung his hands.

Drake's phone buzzed again. He held up the phone and showed Blaze Summer's next text of *So, you in?*

He texted back, *I'll get back to you asap*, and turned the phone so Blaze could read it.

Blaze stared at him with his mouth open, but Drake gave him a go-ahead nod.

When Blaze didn't say anything, Drake clarified in case Blaze needed the summary, "I'd say the band has no issue with you joining us."

Blaze looked out of the window for a minute and then grabbed his cell phone. "Let me call Luke."

Maybe Drake should leave the room, but he wanted the information too desperately to make his feet move.

Drake stopped himself from rocking on the bed as descriptions of Ice's latest doggy adventure and the wedding were exchanged. Finally Blaze cleared his throat. "What would you think if I decided to ease up on my training for the next year or two?"

"Why?" Luke's shocked question could be heard throughout the room.

"Maybe I want a life. You know, sleep late, see the world, follow a band…. Yes, of course Midnight Shadow…. Ha! I doubt the federation would beg me for anything."

Holy shit, Blaze was really considering joining him.

Blaze wandered around the room without looking in Drake's direction. "Yeah, my fans would miss me, but I could do some exhibitions and make sure to post my adventures. It worked well on this road trip. Anna and her spies were all over my ass every time I was on the ice."

Nodding, he did a tight loop in front of the window. The sunlight made the lighter brown shades in his hair sparkle. Not for the first time, Drake's breath caught at how beautiful Blaze looked.

"I've been thinking about it since I stepped off the Olympic podium." Blaze continued pacing.

Finally Blaze glanced over his shoulder and grinned at Drake. "Luke, you're right. Thanks. Yeah, I know. I do too. A lot."

Drake's heart did a Bonaly. That had to be good news, right? Or was it bad? Did Luke convince him not to take time off?

Snorting, Blaze shook his head at whatever Luke said and responded, "I will." He ended the call.

Staring at Blaze, Drake tried to read his mind but failed. "What did he say?"

Blaze's lips twitched. "He still wants the first invite to the wedding. Idiot! But he thought taking a break might be good for me. Anna may have a different opinion, but… I want to take time off to live a little."

"Does that mean you'll tour with me?"

Blaze bit his lower lip and nodded.

"Whoop!" Drake picked him up in a twirling hug.

Laughing, Blaze wrapped his legs around Drake. "You're silly."

"I'm thrilled, excited, happy, and fine, so if you want to throw in silly that's good with me. I'll take care of everything. I've got some money saved—"

"You will not use your money on me. I've got investments, money in the bank, in my retirement account, and I've got several influencer deals happening. I've got plenty of money for day-to-day and long-term."

Drake stared at him. Wait, weren't skaters broke? "Money in your retirement?"

"Of course. Skaters don't make a ton of money, but if they're smart, they save and invest what they make, since our careers are relatively short. Also my parents had life insurance, so I have that as well as the influencer money—"

"What do you mean, 'influencer'?"

"Anna got me hooked into a social media influencer company. I already blog, do videos, post pictures, and have a brand. If there's a product I believe in, I let the company know I'm interested, or sometimes the social media company contacts me with things I might want to support and promote. My fans react and usually take my recommendations, purchasing the items I recommend."

"So you're paid for saying, 'Try this'?" Sounded too easy.

Blaze wrapped his arms around Drake's neck. "Yeah. It's a type of advertising, and it can pay reasonably well."

"Which is why you have a retirement account and I don't."

"Luke can help you set one up." Blaze licked his neck.

"I'd like that…. Mmmmm, what are you doing?"

"I thought we could enjoy our late checkout." Blaze stopped sucking on Drake's neck long enough to answer and then went right back to teasing Drake to distraction.

Drake glanced at the clock. They did have hours before they needed to leave. He pressed a kiss on Blaze's delicate wrist. "What do you have in mind?"

"I want you to fuck me," Blaze declared.

"I thought you didn't—"

"I don't bottom, but I want to try. Just like all the other things on my list…. I mean, unless you don't want to top." Blaze dropped backward, put his hands on the bed, and did a walkover, landing right in the middle of the bed, on his front.

"Um, no. I can. I want to if you want me to." It couldn't be much different than fucking a girl, right? He'd had ass sex with one of the girls

Brenda arranged. Same things applied—be careful, use lots of lube—though with Blaze, he'd want to find his prostate.

Drake could do this.

Blaze pulled off his sweats and reached toward the nightstand. His asscheeks were really…. Drake was positive they'd gotten even better than the vid clips Drake had enjoyed as a teen.

He accepted the bottle of lube and a condom. With this view, he had to ask, "Um, can I do something?"

Smirking over his shoulder while he wiggled his ass, Blaze purred, "I'm hoping you can."

Laughing released his tension. Drake shook his head. "No, I mean, I've always wanted to do something to your ass."

"Again, I'd hope so. That's the whole point." Blaze batted his eyelashes, flirting adorably, and shimmied his ass side to side.

Drake pushed off his sweats, and his dick was already erect and totally ready to participate in his all-time favorite fantasy. He gave his cock a slow stroke, trying to pacify it.

"Mmmmm, that looks good." Blaze stared over his shoulder.

"Want some?" Geez, that sounded stupid.

"Yeah, I think so. Though you're not going to be pissy if I don't like it, are you?" Blaze asked like he was concerned.

"Never. You tell me, and I'll stop immediately." Drake rolled on the condom and smothered slick all over his dick.

"How do you want me?" Blaze bit his bottom lip and glanced over his shoulder again, this time with more uncertainty than he usually showed.

"Just as you are." Drake couldn't imagine a better image, other than Blaze fucking him or sucking him or Drake sucking— *Calm the fuck down!*

Blaze sighed and rested his head on the pillow.

"Mmmm, so beautiful. No crash pads for you." Drake patted the ass of his teen fantasies. It wasn't the first time, but rubbing and touching his ass was always a cherished pleasure. Right under the skin were strong muscles, and to feel them under his hands was mind-blowing.

"Never in competition. Mmmm, practicing new moves, I have." Blaze's body went limp.

Drake kept massaging Blaze's asscheeks until his own cock begged for its wish. He knelt between Blaze's legs, dribbled some lube over Blaze's crack, and used his dick to part those two mounds of muscle.

"Eep!" Blaze shot up farther on the bed. "You can't. I've never—"

Drake shook his head, waving Blaze off. "No, no, I know. I'm rubbing you on the outside."

"Okay? But why?" Blaze moved back down to where he'd lain before, but grimaced with a look of bewilderment.

"Does it feel bad?"

"No, it's…. I don't know. I'd thought you wanted to fuck me." He repositioned himself so his ass once again invited Drake to do as he would.

Did he? He could and would give Blaze anything he wanted. "I do."

Blaze's eyes narrowed onto Drake. "Then why are you rubbing your dick between my asscheeks?"

"You'll think it's stupid." Drake sighed.

"I won't," Blaze promised.

How did he explain he'd never expected to be able to appreciate the spectacular view? "One of my favorite images to jerk off to was your ass—"

"Mine in particular, or asses in general?"

"Yours. I know it's kind of odd." Drake felt his face heat up. He wasn't embarrassed—well, okay, he totally was.

"You mean, kind of hot. Part my ass with your cock. Do it, Drake. Rub yourself between my cheeks." Blaze shifted, making his pert round ass surround Drake.

Drake groaned and separated Blaze's ass with his dick. God, he wanted to remember this moment, his dick sliding along Blaze's crack.

Blaze thrust back and shook his ass, making Drake shiver. "So was there a favorite picture?"

Drake spilled out the details Blaze seemed to crave. "If you must know, there was one picture of you. You were getting ready to do a triple axel, and my God, your ass is so perfect."

"Did you want to fuck it?"

"No, I wanted to do this." Again, Drake dragged his dick along Blaze's crease while Blaze's cheeks created a tight space. Dammit, the visual alone. Fucking amazing. If he wasn't careful, he'd come from rubbing.

"How do you want to fuck me?" Blaze asked. His voice wavered, and he frowned over his shoulder.

"Any way you want."

"Maybe I should turn over, like you were last night." Blaze did, and his foot nailed Drake's thigh… very close to his erection.

"Wow, that was close! Geez, you almost made me sing higher than Summer." Drake grabbed Blaze's battered foot, kissed the arch, and slid up Blaze's body to nibble on his earlobe.

"Mmmmm, get some more lube," Blaze muttered as he shifted around.

"Sure. You tell me if you don't like it."

Blaze nodded. He inhaled, then exhaled in an exaggerated way.

"What are you doing?" Drake asked as he used his lubed finger to breach Blaze.

"Trying to relax." Blaze's frown intensified as more lubed fingers joined the party.

Drake kissed Blaze's dragon tattoo. He ran his tongue over the outline and then over each color as he scissored his lubed fingers inside Blaze to open him.

"I must be ready," Blaze groaned.

"You sure?" Drake gave him a sheepish grin.

Blaze swallowed with a gulp. "Yeah. You'll stop if I don't like it, right?"

"We don't—"

"I want to try this with you. Go ahead." Blaze held his knees and presented Drake with an incredible target, but the look on Blaze's face screamed, *"Totally not into this!"*

Not wanting to annoy, Drake said one more time, "Tell me and I'll stop."

Blaze grabbed Drake's erection and aligned their bodies. "Do it."

Taking a deep breath, Drake pushed the head of his dick inside.

Blaze's face contorted into a frown. "Go ahead."

Drake thrust in a little more.

"Argh." Blaze writhed toward the top of the bed. He'd gone completely soft, which might not have been unusual, but his flaccid state wasn't because his sexual energy had been diverted to his ass.

"Blaze, do you like this at all?" Drake worried.

"Um… I like that I'm with you." A roundabout way of saying no.

"How about if you were with me a different way?"

"Like how? You want me to change positions?" Blaze's expression was a mix of concern and exasperation.

Drake chuckled. "Yeah, like how about you fuck my mouth."

"You don't want to be with me like this?" Blaze didn't bother keeping shock out of his tone.

"I can if you want me to." Drake needed to spell out the obvious. "Blaze, neither of us should force ourselves to do things we don't want for the other. That kind of self-sacrifice will lead to resentment."

Blaze shook his head. "But it's not fair that I'm not into being fucked."

Sliding out of a hissing Blaze, Drake changed tactics and fixated on the physical. That had worked in the past. Drake whispered, "I love you. Only thing that matters is getting you to make those good sounds."

Drake captured Blaze's flaccid dick and sucked.

"What sounds?" Blaze's words broke into moans filled with needy demands.

Pulling off for a moment, he grinned. "Those. Means I'm doing my job right."

"Oh. God, I love your mouth on me." Blaze wrapped his hands in Drake's hair and pulled him off. "But it's not fair."

"Why not?" Drake tried not to sound pissy, but being pulled away from Blaze's cock didn't please him. He'd really gotten good at sucking, and damned if he didn't love it.

"I can't bottom for you."

Drake almost accused Blaze of being too chatty during sex, but he managed to ask, "So? Do you think that's a deal breaker for me?"

"Is it?" Blaze pressed his lips together and held his breath.

"No, it's not. By the way, you prefer fucking, right?"

"Yeah, I guess." Blaze shrugged.

"Well, news flash, I'd rather be fucked. I get off on lying there with you fucking me. The orgasm is good and deep."

"Yeah, but before—"

"No longer matters. You topped before without feeling and wouldn't bottom because you didn't have someone you trusted. With me, you do trust me; it's simply a matter of you not liking getting fucked."

Blaze opened his mouth, then closed it.

Drake gave Blaze a slow stroke.

His mouth dropped open, and Blaze gasped.

"Not to point out the obvious, but I think there's a lot you and I both like," Drake clarified.

Nodding, Blaze exclaimed, "Definitely."

"So do you want me to suck you or let you suck me? Maybe I can slide between your perfect asscheeks again. Or do you want to fuck me. How about—"

"Yes."

"Yes, what?"

"All of that. Yes!"

Chapter 17

AFTER A quicker trip back to Colorado, Blaze slouched at Luke's kitchen table, propped his elbow on the table, and rested his chin on his hand. "Do you think I'm making a mistake?"

Luke slid hot tea in front of him. "Is that the right question?"

"What do you mean?" He was totally not in the mood to Sherlock Holmes his brother's question.

Sitting next to him, Luke took a sip of his coffee. "The question is, will you regret not taking this chance."

Blaze inhaled the spearmint fragrance of his tea and sipped, even though the heat would burn his tongue. *Ow!* "Yes, I would. I didn't realize how much I've missed."

"That's what I was always afraid of. I respected your drive and determination, but you sacrificed a normal life for skating."

"As did you. Don't think I haven't appreciated everything you've done for me. Without your support I wouldn't have gotten as far as I have." Words were inadequate and always had been when he tried to thank Luke.

Luke rolled his shoulders in a shrug.

Blaze sniffed. "And not once did you make me feel bad about all you gave up."

"Stop. You're my brother. We both support each other's dreams. Mine were simpler than yours."

Blaze sipped the tea.

Setting his coffee down, Luke leaned toward him. "Drake is a good man."

"Glad you approve." Blaze added snark to his tone to counterbalance the tears threatening to spill down his cheeks, but he meant it.

"Again, I want to be invited to the wedding so I can say I told you so!" Luke chuckled.

Blaze didn't even bother denying a wedding, because if he had his way— "I love him so much it scares me, you know? I mean, how crazy is it that I'm dropping everything and running off to be a groupie?"

"Maybe your ankles and body will appreciate the rest." Luke pointed out the obvious.

"Well, I guess, and it's not like I'm completely giving up skating or training, because it's easier to stay in shape than to get in shape." Drake had helped Blaze map out every venue the band would play and the closest ice rink.

Luke smirked. "You have ice time reserved already, don't you?"

"Only in some… okay, at most of the places on the tour, but it's still only a few times a week… and I know where my gyms are." Blaze shrugged, leaving out he'd be exercising daily regardless of gyms, though the look on Luke's face said the words weren't needed to confirm anything.

"You're still going for *it* in four years?" Luke asked the million-dollar question.

Blaze shrugged. "Honestly, I don't know, but I want to keep open the possibility of another shot at the Olympics. I do know I still want to do exhibitions."

Luke nodded. "Sounds good. So yeah, while you're gallivanting across the country, I'm doubling up on my classes. I'll be graduating next year."

"I'm proud of you." Blaze hugged his brother and buried his face in Luke's neck, trying to hide the sob.

"Hey, it's okay. With texting, Skype, Google Hangouts, and Discord, it'll be like you're just downstairs." Luke hugged him tighter and sniffed a bit.

The basement door cracked open. "Am I interrupting? I can come back—"

"Nah, you're fine." Luke shifted away from Blaze. "Coffee, Drake?"

"Um, no, but I'll take tea."

"Sticks and dirt, really?" Luke asked.

"Yeah, making Blaze's has given me an appreciation for the scent, and several types of tea taste pretty good too."

Luke was on his feet and pouring hot water into a cup. "Sit down and tell me about the tour. Where are you most excited to play?"

A couple of days before the tour starts….

BLAZE'S CELL phone buzzed, forcing him to stop trying to imagine getting everything on his bed into one big suitcase. He kept paring down, but argh! Glancing at the caller ID, panic raced through him. "Oh my God."

"What? Who is it?" Drake peered up from his guitar and lyric book. He'd been sitting in Blaze's bedroom corner chair.

Running away from reality had to be too good to be true. Whispering, Blaze said, "Summer Simpson. She's probably calling to tell me the band changed their mind. It's okay. I can—"

Drake gave him a *get-real* look and waved at him. "How about you answer the phone?"

Bracing himself, Blaze's voice trembled. "Hi, Summer. How are you doing?"

"Fine. I'm just packing for the tour. How about you?" Her words sounded more like a song than conversation.

"Same, as long as I'm still welcome."

"Of course you are. Don't be silly." She groaned. "However, from one diva to another, I realized I needed to tell you—you can take two big suitcases."

Blaze's heart leaped; he looked around at all the stuff he couldn't imagine living four months without, piled on his bed. "Two? Really?"

"Yes. I spaced on the fact that half of your suitcase will have your skates and skating stuff."

And costumes, his skating music, crash pads, a couple skating outfits in case something came up, among other things. "Thank you. The second bag will help."

"I actually purchased the trailer to go behind the tour bus this time, so I made sure we all have some extra room. Tell your man he can have all of his guitars with us instead of having them in the equipment truck. Musicians hate being separated from their instruments and can be such babies… especially guitarists."

Blaze snorted. "I will, and thank you again."

"I look forward to meeting you."

"Me too." Blaze breathed a sigh of relief and then fist-pumped. When did he pick up that habit?

Drake set his guitar aside. "Everything okay?"

"Yeah. Summer said you can put your guitars in the new trailer she bought and not in the equipment truck."

Drake scrunched his face. "That's funny. I guess she didn't know Jessie, Artano, and me have always kept them on the bus somewhere."

"Oh, I—"

Looking at his vibrating cell, Drake grinned. "It's Mom. If you're okay, I'll take this."

"Sure." Blaze went back to packing.

"Hey, Mom… um, yeah, he's here. Okay." Drake held out the phone. "Mom wants you."

What the hell? He took the phone and swallowed. Was she going to tell him it was a bad idea for him to follow Drake like a puppy? "Um, hi, Mrs.… I mean, Julia."

"Good save." She laughed and sounded a bit like Drake. "I know it's super early, but I wanted to invite you, your brother, anyone he's seeing, and your coach and her husband to Thanksgiving at our house."

Thanksgiving? That was months away. Would he and Drake even be together? He glanced over at his boyfriend, who made promises of love and sex with his eyes. Drake took his hand and kissed his knuckles. Doubts liquefied.

Blaze answered, "Luke and I would love to, Julia. And I'll check with Anna."

"Wonderful. Oh, and in the arenas near New Haven, Matthew and I will be attending the shows, but if during those days you find yourself at loose ends, let us know. We'd love to spend time with you."

Spend time with him? Instead of terror, happiness made him sniff and kiss Drake's cheek. "I'd enjoy that. I have early rink times at all the East Coast shows, so I'd be free around lunch."

"Terrific. We'll make plans."

"Sounds good."

"Oh, and if you don't mind, text me your number so Matthew and I can both have it."

"Of course. Here's Drake." Blaze handed the phone back to Drake and meandered back to stare at the piles of stuff.

This was real, and apparently he was all in. Drake's family not only accepted him, they welcomed him into the family. He checked for mental drama and found none, just the need to use Google to find activities near those shows that both Drake's parents might enjoy.

The Tour Begins….

DRAKE SCRATCHED Ice in the right place behind his ears. "Iceman. Dude, I'll bring your daddy back. And your uncle Luke says he'll bring you to some of the shows so we will see you soon."

Blaze tried not to cry. He'd see his dog about every three weeks, but argh. It was hard. "Ice, I love you, baby. Be good for Luke."

Luke patted him on the shoulder. "Ice will be fine. I installed a doggy door upstairs for him. I also got the same bed as you have downstairs and put it upstairs, and you've seen the fence extension to include my kitchen doorsteps with another doggy door. Plus, when you video chat with me, you'll talk to Ice like always too. He won't forget you while you go groupie."

Blaze swallowed and gave a jerky nod. It wasn't like he'd never gone away. He'd skated in a number of overseas competitions without Luke, but this seemed different… bigger.

Anna pulled into the driveway and got out of the car. "I saw the monstrosity of a bus a few blocks away. So here."

Blaze took the medicinal tea she shoved at him. "Thanks."

"For both of you. And Viktor and I are going to see you at a couple of shows too. You will send me clips of you on the ice. It will be just like the road trip. I can diagnose problems from cell phone…. Yes, you know I'm that good."

Drake snorted and gave her a hug.

"You take care of our boy, you hear me?" Anna waved her finger with less sternness.

"I'll do my best." Oh geez, Drake didn't know that was the worst thing to say to Anna.

She put up a hand to stop both Blaze and Luke jumping to Drake's defense. "There is no try. You will do or you will not do. Which is it?"

"I *will* take care of Blaze. You have my word," he told her with all of his sincerity.

"Good." She latched on to Blaze as she spoke to Drake. "Oh, and tell your mama my Viktor and I will join your family for Thanksgiving. Thank you and your family for the kind invitation."

"Great, I will." Drake grabbed two bags and followed Luke down the driveway.

"You have fun. Not too much. We have one thing yet to do in four years. Then you retire and teach young ones. Oh, and I've got some exhibition dates I want to run past—I'll email you."

The tour bus pulled to a stop in front of the house. The Midnight Shadow logo with a picture of the band beneath emblazoned one side of the huge bus.

Blaze hugged her. "I'll miss you, Anna."

"You won't. I'll be a bug in your ear, always buzzing." Anna smirked with too much wicked intention.

Blaze laughed, squeezed her tight, and followed after Luke and Drake, who had taken all the bags to the driver standing at the trailer.

The driver shook Blaze's hand. "I'm Joanna, and I'll give you the whole spiel when everyone else is onboard. You two were first on my schedule. But now, off we go to pick up the others."

Blaze nuzzled Ice one more time while Luke gave Drake a manly backslapping hug and said, "Wishing you and Midnight Shadow all the best. Make sure he has some fun."

Drake nodded. "Will do."

Launching himself at Luke one more time, Blaze whispered, "I love you, and I'll text you tonight."

Ice barked once as Drake and Blaze boarded the bus.

Blaze stared out the bus windows and had been determined he wouldn't cry, but fuck, a couple of tears slid down his face as he waved to Luke and Anna.

Drake put his hands onto Blaze's shoulders and squeezed. Tension started to slip away and everything got a little brighter. He wasn't giving up anything, and he'd be gaining everything.

The driver shut the doors, and they rumbled down the street Blaze had called home for years. Blaze and Drake stayed at the windows, waving until the bus turned the corner.

Drake pulled Blaze into the dark brown leather wraparound seating area that rimmed the first third of the bus. "You going to be okay?"

"Yeah, of course. It's hard." Blaze cuddled into Drake.

"I know. You saw when we left my parents' house after our visit. I get how tough leaving can be." Drake shook his head.

Blaze would never forget. Drake's dad came up with a thousand projects he needed help with, and his mom didn't release her son from her five-minute hug until her husband pried her fingers off, aiding in Drake's escape. "Yeah, I was surprised your mom didn't hide in the trunk."

"Shhh, don't give her any ideas. Let's look around. This is so much nicer than our last tour bus, which was probably a renovated dirty school bus."

Blaze couldn't imagine what the band traveled on during their last tour, even based on Drake's horrifying descriptions, but this brown-and-red décor seemed pretty nice. "The outside painting was impressive."

"Nah, that was a wrap. It'll be removed when we stop renting this bus."

"Hmmm," Blaze muttered as he followed Drake.

"Cool kitchen." The compact kitchenette had dark cherry cabinets, which Drake opened, revealing a microwave and an almost full-sized refrigerator filled with beer, soda, bottles of water, and microwavable food. The cabinets also held paper plates, cups, and utensils, probably because no one wanted to do dishes, even if the red ceramic sink made the matching interior and rugs pop.

Hidden on the opposite side were two burners, a toaster oven, a hot water kettle, and the trash can.

Drake chuckled. "I learned the hard way, don't use the microwave, kettle, hot pot, or toaster oven while the bus is parked. I tried to make soup in a hot pot and blew all the circuits. Luckily, no lasting harm occurred."

Blaze parted the brown-and-red curtains to stand in the bunk area, where full-sized beds with puffy red comforters and two pillows graced each.

"Whenever we can, we should take this one." Drake pointed to the lowest one.

"Why?" Why was crawling in and out the best option?

"I'm making this the junk bunk." Drake grabbed his guitar and their pilot bag and stuffed them to the far right. "It'll mean no one will be above us to hear anything."

"Ohhhh. Got it." Having intercourse would be impossible, but other things could be accomplished in the compressed space. "But what's a junk bunk?"

"Where everyone will stuff the things they want on the bus but there's no actual place for it. Everyone is allowed one pilot bag of their shit, consisting of chargers, medicines, laptops, tablets. Also, Amanda's candy stash with a case of drumsticks. The guitars, along with Jessie's bass, will all be here in case inspiration strikes."

Drake opened their carry-on and handed Blaze a baggie of items. "I want you to be prepared for life on tour. A bag like that and always taking a bottle of water into the bunk made the last tour survivable for me. And we'll get a bus key later."

"Thanks." He went through the essentials: earplugs, earbuds, eyeshades, warm socks, and a lanyard with his backstage pass. He stuffed the must-haves in his messenger bag.

They peeked in the red bathroom. There was a toilet, a mirror with plenty of lights over the sink, and a full-length mirror on the door. The brown marble vanity wrapped around until the glass shower stall took the rest of the space. Nice! "Ah, a place to fuck."

"Yeah, we just have to make sure no one needs the bathroom." Drake opened the cabinet drawers.

Blaze clarified, even though he didn't think that should be necessary, "I'm kidding."

"I'm not." Drake turned on the shower and put his hand under the water. "Pressure's not bad."

Blaze stared at him to see if he was kidding; he wasn't. Blaze still had to wrap his mind around the lack of privacy. "What's in there?" he asked, referring to a door to the back of the bus.

"That's where Summer sleeps. If she gets sick or hoarse, we're screwed, so we refused to let everyone take turns like she originally wanted."

Blaze understood their concerns but was sure over the course of four months he'd also regret their responsible decision.

"We stay in hotels a few times a week." Drake elbowed him.

"Are you reading my mind?"

"Always. Let me find out how long until the next pickup." Drake stalked off to the front of the bus and came back blushing.

"You look a bit red. What did Joanna say?"

"That we had two hours to fuck." Drake chuckled.

Blaze still wore his messenger bag, so he had everything they needed. He took Drake's hand and led him into the bathroom to spend one hour and forty-five minutes figuring out which positions made Drake the craziest. Five minutes of concentrated effort to make them come, and ten minutes to clean up.

Over the next couple of days, the bus picked up the entire band and headed toward their first show.

Everyone welcomed Blaze into life on the road and made him feel part of the group. They all fit comfortably on the wraparound couch, and easy conversation flowed around what they did on their time off.

"Summer, you're comfortable with the new agent?" Jessie asked. She'd been quiet and kept staring at Sandy.

"Dawn Diaz came highly recommended from our label. She'll share her strategy for Midnight Shadow when she meets with us."

Artano barked out a laugh. "That's a step up, an actual plan?"

Summer drank a sip of her tea. "Yup. She wants to build our careers slowly for the long term, which will include hiatuses to avoid burnout and band hate."

"Wow." Jessie added a whistle.

"I've only met her once, but she's nothing like Frank. I promise we'll never make a mistake based on desperation again. We almost lost Drake over his foolishness." Summer reached over Blaze and patted Drake's hand.

Amanda cleared her throat, then rapped Drake with her drumsticks. "Glad you came back to your musical family, D."

"Good to be back." Drake's words were thick with emotion.

"And you even brought a new fascinating person to get to know." Amanda tapped lightly on Blaze's thigh.

The gesture might have been a bit strange, but she seemed to tap on everyone, so he smiled at her.

Artano snorted and raised his bottle. "Well, you did pretty good with replacing Dixon. Sandy brought my favorite beer, so he's all right by me."

"Glad to share, dude." Sandy fist-bumped Artano.

At the first stop for gas, the bus driver stood in the front of the sitting area. "Now that you're all here, I want to introduce myself. I'm Joanna Heller. Most people just call me Hell. I'm an experienced driver and drove for a number of tours. I won't break the law, and I'll do my best to get you to the venues ahead of schedule. I'll announce the night before if I need to move the bus away from the venue for servicing or gas. I'll remind you the day before load-in starts so you can take all your stuff. I'm here to make your life easier; consider me part of your crew."

Everyone smiled and happily accepted the bus keys she passed out. "I'll be parked at the far end of the lot after I feed the beast."

Halfway through the tour….

BLAZE SETTLED into his seat next to Drake as the bus pulled out of the parking lot.

"Great concert everyone. Night." After everyone agreed, Summer and her fiancé headed to the private bedroom in the back of the bus.

Two months ago, when they first started, the band was thrilled with the luxury the bus offered. Drake had sighed in contentment about full-sized bunks with puffy comforters, but now the excitement had worn off. Touring and performing was fun but still took its toll.

"Amaretto, Blaze?" Jessie asked as she poured herself a drink.

"Yes. Thank you." Blaze still didn't drink much, but he found sipping a bit of amaretto helped him sleep through bumps in the road.

"Thanks, Sandy." Drake accepted the beer from their newest band member and pointed to the big-screen TV that was usually hidden by a screensaver of the band's logo. "You guys want to watch anything?"

"Nah, I'm going to finish this and head to bed." Jessie winked at Sandy.

"Hee-hee. To bed, but not to sleep." Sandy kissed her neck.

"Oh my God, Sandy. Shut up. Jesus, you talk more than your keyboard," Jessie growled as the tour bus picked up speed on the highway.

Rolling his eyes, Sandy shrugged at Blaze and Drake. "Most women like a man who talks."

"Humpf!" Jessie polished off her drink, tossed her cup in the trash, and hopped into a curtained bunk.

"Do they, though, Sandy?" Drake asked.

Blaze held in his snort. Traveling with the band was like hanging out with naughty sixth graders who loved to scuffle among themselves, but when push came to shove, they'd bloody anyone else for any trespass against a member. He'd learned to stay silent.

Jessie poked her head out. "I'm not most women. Sandy, are you coming?"

"Not yet, but we both will be soon." Sandy fist-bumped Blaze, jumped into the bunk, and velcroed the red curtains closed.

A giggle followed by a soft moan forced Blaze to put in his earbuds, which were connected to Drake's cell. They started watching myths debunked by science as they drank the last of their alcohol.

Drake yawned and leaned into him.

Blaze enjoyed the weight of his boyfriend pressing against him, letting him ease the stress he had to carry from the back-to-back shows. He pulled out Drake's earbud. "You look exhausted."

Taking out Blaze's earbud, Drake clarified, "I'm *exhaustipated.*"

"Exhaustipated?"

Drake smirked. "Yeah, when you're too tired to give a shit."

Blaze chortled with Drake, who scrunched his face behind his hand but didn't stop his belly laugh. "Hey, you wanna go rest? Our bunk is free."

Drake dropped his head onto Blaze's shoulder. "And by rest, you mean like last night?"

The bunks were too small to do much without contorting into a pretzel, and doing it on their sides didn't hit the spot for Drake. They saved intercourse for the hotels and usually went with blowjobs or hand jobs with a swallow ending because, really, there wasn't another way to avoid a mess.

"Sure." Blaze smiled, knowing Drake would be asleep before he even unzipped his pants. He hurried to the bathroom to do his nightly routine. It wasn't hard to find which was their bunk, because the bright bisexual flag socks his mom sent him identified the foot sticking out.

Drake's pants and T-shirt were in a ball at the end of the bed. However sexy his man in boxer briefs happened to be, he still snored softly.

Blaze grinned, slipped off his clothing, and carefully crawled into the tiny space.

Drake muttered, "I can suck ya."

"I know you can, but how about we sleep now and wake each other up with a blowjob. Whoever is up first swallows first."

"S'okay." Drake dropped an arm over Blaze and protectively spooned behind him.

Blaze could never have imagined he'd want this more than skating, but this was everything.

Epilogue

Five Years Later....

BLAZE HAD dusted his house twice already but gave the pictures on his nightstand a bit more attention.

He smiled at Flame and Smoke guarding the room, then studied the framed picture of him kissing Olympic ice for the third and final time. Another picture depicted him surrounded by Drake, Luke, and Anna as he held his last gold medal. The next one he cleaned was a silly snap, which still made him feel equal parts pleased and embarrassed. The picture had captured Drake dragging him onstage. Right after that picture was taken, the entire band and most of Midnight Shadow's audience sang "Happy Birthday" to him.

He dusted the last picture, taken the year before, from the engagement party. The picture had all the people Blaze cared about: the entire band, Julia and Matthew Keys, Luke with his new wife, Anna and her husband. Ice danced on his hind legs in front of everyone, and Blaze perched on Drake's back, kissing his cheek.

Drake slipped into the room and hugged him from behind. "You still going to marry me?"

Blaze grinned over his shoulder. "How could I accept a proposal from someone with such poor judgment and bad taste as to ask me?"

Snorting, Drake tossed him onto the bed. "Oh, I have a very *good* taste. You tell me that all the time."

Blaze pulled Drake into a kiss and murmured, "It's all the pineapple juice we drink that makes your cum taste like candy."

Smirking, Drake kissed Blaze's neck.

Blaze tilted his head so Drake could kiss that one special— "Mmmm, right there. You never had any doubts?"

"About us? Nope. You're it for me. However, you took a bit of convincing, but I enjoyed the work."

Blaze teased and pretended to try to get out of their bed. "I'm totally convinced, but I should finish dusting. I don't want my in-laws to think I'm a slob."

"Please stay. I've seen my dad use a hairdryer as a dust cloth. Our place is spotless, trust me." Drake pressed Blaze's shoulder to the bed and nuzzled his neck.

Blaze snorted and gasped at the same time.

Drake wiggled his fingers under Blaze's shirt and teased a finger under the waistband of his jeans. "Besides, they already love you more than me."

Shivering, Blaze tried to continue the conversation, even with lust bubbling through his body. "I doubt that, but just in case, I'll marry you so they don't have to make the choice."

"That's good, 'cause the wedding is tomorrow." Drake traced a finger over Blaze's lips. "And the living room is filled with things off of our wedding registry."

"Things that you and Luke picked out. Charger plates, ha." Blaze released Drake's hair from the thick elastic holding it back. Dark waves cascaded around him. Damn, his sexy rock star was hot and all his. Blaze was smart enough to put a ring on him.

"Only because you had no interest in housewares and wanted to go dress shopping with my mother." Drake kissed the pretend pout off Blaze's mouth.

Since Blaze couldn't uncurl his toes, he made a concession between kisses. "She needed help. Maybe I can finish dusting later. Marriage is about compromise, right?"

"Yes." Drake unzipped Blaze's pants, releasing his erection to the air. Blaze moaned his total agreement with Drake's wisdom.

Bending over Blaze's middle, scant inches from his cock, Drake asked, "You're sure you don't mind Summer using our wedding as a platform to tell everyone Midnight Shadow is coming out with new stuff?"

Blaze almost choked on his need, want, and laughter. "You're still a very chatty sucker, aren't you?"

Drake answered in between licking Blaze's cock, "I am."

"Hey, after Summer picked the perfect time to have a baby…. Mmmm, exactly when I needed to get back to serious training for the Olympics. Summer gets to do just about anything she wants." Her timing had allowed Blaze and Drake to stay together while he trained for the Olympics and Drake worked on the new songs.

"Talky talker, shhhhh, I'm sucking you off," Drake teased.

Blaze tried to roll his eyes, but a few sucks later, he lost it and came hard in Drake's mouth.

Still panting, a quick time check allowed Blaze to say, "Come on, get these pants off."

"You don't—"

Pretending to pout, Blaze was determined. "I want some of your candy."

"Oh, okay. As you said, marriage is about compromise." Drake unzipped and pushed off his pants.

In record time Blaze had him in his mouth, sucking for all he was worth, when a stray thought distracted him. "Do you really think Ice will be good being the ring bearer?"

"Iceman did fine at Luke's wedding." That much was true. Luke almost made him an honorary best man since Luke met his lovely wife at a doggy park while taking Ice out for a run.

Drake shifted on the bed. "Speaking of chatty—"

Blaze didn't let Drake finish his joke. He kept sucking until he swallowed for Drake and then licked him clean.

He collapsed next to Drake, still recovering from his own orgasm.

Just as he was drifting off, Drake's cell buzzed.

Since Blaze lay closer to Drake's discarded jeans, he handed the cell to Drake.

Drake grimaced at the screen and groaned.

"What?"

"Taylor texted that my ex-bandmate Dixon the Dick will be there tomorrow with a plus-one."

"Wow." Blaze wasn't sure why he'd felt the need to invite the jackass against Drake's pleas, but he had.

"Apparently he's working in my high school and will be bringing a teacher as his date."

"Well, glad to hear he's doing better."

Drake set his phone aside. "I love everything about you."

"Awwwww, I love everything about you. You've given me things I didn't even know I needed. Thank you." Blaze was feeling too many emotions.

"Welcome. So, do you think it was worth braving thin ice?" Drake asked with a confident smile.

"Absolutely. We didn't fall through, we simply rocked it." Blaze melted into Drake.

Z. ALLORA never expected to share her words with anyone, but things don't always work out as planned. Growing up in Upstate NY, she was a tomboy: playing basketball in the park, twirling a rifle in color guard, but composing stories filled with angst in secret.

Z. didn't always believe in romance, although before giving up on happily ever after completely, she took out a personal ad in a college newspaper. On October 20, 1987, at 5:08 PM, she found what she didn't think existed, and married her best friend five years later.

A bit of an overachiever, Z.'s earned three bachelor's degrees (Psychology, English, and Philosophy) and a master's degree in Psychology. She loved enhancing the quality of life of people in her residential and day programs, but her love's job swept Z. overseas to Singapore, Israel, and China.

While living in China, she discovered M/M romance. The magic of the genre gave her new insights about herself and those around her. When she saw protests in Malaysia by parents who genuinely believed watching a singer could make their children gay, the ignorance was too staggering to ignore. No longer content to keep her words to herself, she published her stories hoping to add another voice to foster understanding and to promote equality.

Z. believes each of us is wonderfully unique and deserving of a happily ever after. Regardless where we are in the infinite spectrum of gender identity, orientation, or sexuality, our differences and similarities should be both respected and celebrated.

Even though Z. identifies as nonbinary of the transmasculine variety, Z. has kept her original pronouns and presents as female (according to the current gender constructs).

One of the biggest goals of her writing is to validate everyone's individual uniqueness. There's an infinite spectrum within each stripe of the rainbow and Z. wants to explore them all.

However, Z. will never apologize for having too much yaoified smexy goodness in her books. She teases that plot is simply the words between the sex scenes (though that's a bit of an exaggeration). Sex is one of our most important and basic forms of communication, and she feels it's a vital part of understanding her characters.

Z. Allora truly believes this rainbow romance is changing hearts and minds, and will continue to speak out for love for all of us.

Email: Z.AlloraHappyEndings@gmail.com

Facebook: Z Allora Allora and join Z.'s Yaoified Love group (for fun, character chatters, giveaways, and silliness)
Website: www.zallorabooks.com
Blog: zallora.blogspot.com
Dreamspinner Press: www.dreamspinnerpress.com/books/z-allora-637-a

The
LIBRARIAN'S
RAKE

Z. ALLORA

Opposites might attract, but is acting on that attraction wise?

Librarian Tristan Cooper can't steer clear of sexy, motorcycle-riding bad boy Phillip—the man is hot—but Phillip is bound to find quiet, bookish Tristan boring, like all Tristan's boyfriends. Tristan yearns to explore his wild side, the part of himself he's only allowed into his fantasies, and maybe rakish Phillip is just what he needs to feel free.

Sexperienced hairdresser Phillip is more of a believer in happy endings than happily ever afters. Experience has taught him not to hope for more—until he meets sweet, vulnerable Tristan, who seems genuinely interested in his heart. But Phillip can't trust enough to see himself as a man Tristan might want for more than a night.

With the help of a pair of matchmaking grandfathers, Tristan and Phillip might find the courage to step beyond their comfort zones and discover what has been missing from their lives….

www.dreamspinnerpress.com

The Great Wall

Z. Allora

Made in China: Book One

Destiny will be decided by a battle between heart and mind….

Jun Tai "Styx" Wong loves two things: playing the drums, and his best friend, Jin. But being a good Chinese son means he can't have either—he'll have to marry a girl of his parents' choosing and settle into a traditional job. His move to the bigger city of Suzhou is both a blessing and curse, as living with Jin makes it harder for Styx to suppress his desires. Nearly dying while trying to eradicate his feelings serves as a wake-up call for Jin, who takes extreme measures to keep Styx safe from harm.

When given a second chance at life and happiness, will Styx be able to claim the future he wants with Jin, his bandmates, and his music? Can love and hope grow with the constantly looming threat of Styx's parents ordering him home? Great things await—if Styx finds the courage to break down the wall that stands between him and everything he wants.

www.dreamspinnerpress.com

The Temple of Heaven

Z. Allora

Made in China: Book Two

Music is Tian Di's life and his love, and he's made plenty of sacrifices. His career is finally taking off with his band, Made in China, and he'll continue to put music first… until he meets Jordon. Then insta-lust becomes insta-love and a commitment to the future—no matter how difficult it might be.

Jordon lives in a bubble constructed by his overprotective older brothers, who are so controlling that they've kept him from dating. A talented artist, Jordon managed to keep his success with a Japanese manga publisher a secret from his family, but now he fears discovery. It's easier to let his brothers handle everything, but Jordon has reached his limit. He's ready to draw some boundaries so he can be his own man and face all the challenges that come with that.

Their families and careers aren't the only obstacles. Jordon must accept his identity as a gay man who doesn't top or bottom. Fortunately, Tian Di—and his special talents—help Jordon open up to his sexuality in an erotic adventure that spans Japan and China, and with love, luck, hard work, and open minds, will end in a happily ever after.

www.dreamspinnerpress.com